The Game of Triumphs

The Game of Triumphs

LAURA POWELL

ALFRED A. KNOPF · NEW YORK

THIS IS A BORZOI BOOK PUBLISHED BY ALFRED A. KNOPF

Visit us on the Web! www.randomhouse.com/teens

Educators and librarians, for a variety of teaching tools, visit us at
www.randomhouse.com/teachers

Library of Congress Cataloging-in-Publication Data
Powell, Laura.
The game of triumphs/Laura Powell.—1st American ed.
p.   cm.
Summary: Fifteen-year-old Cat and three other London teens are drawn into a dangerous game in which Tarot cards open doorways into a different dimension, and while there is everything to win, losing can be fatal.
ISBN 978-0-375-86587-9 (trade) — ISBN 978-0-375-96587-6 (lib. bdg.) —
ISBN 978-0-375-89774-0 (ebook)
[1. Supernatural—Fiction. 2. Role playing—Fiction. 3. Games—Fiction.
4. Tarot—Fiction. 5. London (England)—Fiction. 6. England—Fiction.] I. Title.
PZ7.P87757Gam 2011
[Fic]—dc22
2010021813

The text of this book is set in 12-point Bembo.

Printed in the United States of America
August 2011
10 9 8 7 6 5 4 3 2 1

First American Edition

In memory of my grandfathers:

William Vaughan Wilkins (1890–1959)
Newby Odell Brantly (1905–1993)

The Wheel of Fortune turns,
I go down, demeaned;
Another is raised up;
Far too proud
Sits the king at the summit —
Let him fear ruin!
For under the axis we read
That Hecuba is queen.
From the Burana Codex, circa 1230

In every bet, there is a fool and a thief.
Chinese proverb

Cards played in the Game of Triumphs

The Greater Arcana
(Triumph Cards and Their Prizes)

ETERNITY

Victory

FAME

Fame

THE SUN

Beauty

THE MOON

Inspiration

THE STAR

Health

THE TOWER

Destruction

THE DEVIL

Hedonism

TEMPERANCE

Reconciliation

DEATH

Death

THE HANGED MAN

Sacrifice

STRENGTH

Strength

FORTUNE

*can be played to
win a new card*

Time   *Justice*   *Heroism*

Love   *Wisdom*

Leadership

Wealth

Prophecy

Charisma

*represents chancers
in the Game*

The Lesser Arcana
(Court Cards)

King/Queen of Cups
Knight of Cups
Knave of Cups
Ace of Cups   *Root of Water*
Two of Cups   *Reign of Love*
Three of Cups   *Reign of Abundance*
Four of Cups   *Reign of Blended Pleasure*
Five of Cups   *Reign of Lost Pleasure*
Six of Cups   *Reign of Past Pleasure*
Seven of Cups   *Reign of Illusionary Success*
Eight of Cups   *Reign of Abandoned Success*
Nine of Cups   *Reign of Material Happiness*
Ten of Cups   *Reign of Perfected Success*

King/Queen of Pentacles
Knight of Pentacles
Knave of Pentacles
Ace of Pentacles   *Root of Earth*
Two of Pentacles   *Reign of Change*
Three of Pentacles   *Reign of Material Works*
Four of Pentacles   *Reign of Possession*
Five of Pentacles   *Reign of Material Trouble*
Six of Pentacles   *Reign of Material Success*
Seven of Pentacles   *Reign of Success Unfulfilled*
Eight of Pentacles   *Reign of Prudence*
Nine of Pentacles   *Reign of Sheltered Luxury*
Ten of Pentacles   *Reign of Wealth*

King/Queen of Swords
Knight of Swords
Knave of Swords
Ace of Swords   *Root of Air*
Two of Swords   *Reign of Peace Restored*
Three of Swords   *Reign of Sorrow*
Four of Swords   *Reign of Rest from Strife*
Five of Swords   *Reign of Defeat*
Six of Swords   *Reign of Earned Success*
Seven of Swords   *Reign of Futility*
Eight of Swords   *Reign of Shortened Force*
Nine of Swords   *Reign of Despair*
Ten of Swords   *Reign of Ruin*

King/Queen of Wands
Knight of Wands
Knave of Wands
Ace of Wands   *Root of Fire*
Two of Wands   *Reign of Dominion*
Three of Wands   *Reign of Established Strength*
Four of Wands   *Reign of Perfected Work*
Five of Wands   *Reign of Strife*
Six of Wands   *Reign of Victory*
Seven of Wands   *Reign of Valor*
Eight of Wands   *Reign of Swiftness*
Nine of Wands   *Reign of Great Strength*
Ten of Wands   *Reign of Oppression*

CHAPTER ONE

IT WAS HIS BREATHING that she noticed first: the hoarse, ragged wheezing of someone who has been running hard. Which was odd, as the crowd hadn't moved more than five paces in the last ten minutes. Two escalators were down at the Piccadilly Circus Tube station, and at half past nine on a Friday night, the station was at a rowdy, jostling standstill.

"Oi, mate, shoving won't get you nowhere, all right?" said a woman ahead as they moved another inch toward the foot of the motionless escalator. The man slid his eyes toward Cat, as if in appeal, but she had her London face ready—blank and impenetrable. He was just a nondescript middle-aged guy in a suit, but that didn't mean anything. You met all sorts of nut jobs on the Tube. "Please," he wheezed to no one in particular. "Please." He closed his eyes and she caught the scent of his sweat. Must be claustrophobic, she decided.

At last they shuffled onto the escalator, their pace gaining momentum as people spilled off it toward the ticket barriers. With a whimper of relief, Heavy Breather pushed past her and was gone. She would have soon forgotten him if it hadn't been for a snatch of conversation she overheard a few minutes later. Two men and a woman, in dark clothes, lean and purposeful, had come out of the east exit. "He must have gone this way," said the woman. "It won't take long," said one of her companions. They set off up Regent Street, weaving through the crowds with practiced ease.

They're after that man, Cat thought, and though it was just a hunch, somehow she knew it was true. Perhaps he was a criminal, or perhaps his pursuers were.

It had nothing to do with her.

Cat went down Shaftesbury Avenue, turning left at Great Windmill Street and into Soho. Five minutes later she was letting herself into the flat. It was, as usual, dark and empty, although Bel had left a note on the kitchen table. Bel worked as a croupier at the local casino, which sounded a lot more glamorous than it was. From the kitchen window, Cat could look across the street to the windows of the gaming floor, blacked out so that gamblers would lose track of time. A neon sign fizzed below: Palais Luxe, it said, in acid pink. Palace de Crud, said Bel.

Bel was Cat's mum's sister, though she had never called her Auntie, and certainly not Aunt. She was always just Bel, like the owner of a saloon bar in some corny old Western. She looked the part, too, with her big red mouth and big red hair and a confident swagger. She'd only been nineteen when her elder sister and brother-in-law were killed in a car crash, leaving behind a child of three, but Bel hadn't hesitated. Cat was fifteen now and more Bel's than ever. Theirs was a partnership against the world.

"Mind—you'll always be an orphan," she'd say, squinting at Cat shrewdly, "and don't you forget it. People like a bit of tragedy. Adds color." When Cat was younger, Bel wasn't above improving on this "color." Her eyes would moisten, bosom heave, and she'd be off: "Struck dumb for a whole year afterward, poor mite. Even now, she'll wake screaming in the night—doctors say she'll never get over it. . . ." This was Cat's cue to look frail and interesting. All sorts of useful things followed, from hefty discounts to extra helpings.

Bel wasn't truly feckless, though, just footloose. They'd moved three times in the last five years, much more before that, keeping to small to middling-sized places, where it was possible for Bel to make the most of herself, and for Cat to stay in the background as she preferred. Then Bel met Greg. Greg, who told her he worked in a big London club and had a loft they could rent in the West End. "A third-rate casino, more like," she reported the night she got back from checking it out, "and a tiny Soho flat. But I tell you what, puss-cat, London's a town where anything could happen." Three weeks later they were there.

So perhaps Bel was a romantic; perhaps London was the destination she'd been rehearsing all those other arrivals for. Her big adventure. It might have been the same for Cat.

Her eyes were as cool and watchful as Bel's, her mouth just as stubborn. But in London, Cat's self-sufficiency had deserted her. There was just too much, of everything, always shifting and changing, everything for sale or rent or served hot. Even being invisible here was exhausting.

As autumn turned to winter, she headed for the Underground, where she sat tight on the Circle line, going round and round. There was no need to think or move in the endless looping tunnels. It felt like she was keeping the city at bay at last. Tonight it had taken three circuits before she changed lines for home, and that was only because she needed to pee.

Cat scowled at her reflection in the window above the sink. Thin, pale face; ragged black hair. "Nothing but a poor orphan child!" she mocked aloud, using Bel's voice. A poor, *starving* orphan, she amended. Overcome by a craving for comfort food—salty fish and chips, noodles swimming in soy sauce—she went out again.

It was still early in Soho terms: the Christmas lights sparkling, swarms of people cruising from pub to club— merry, mostly, not yet at the puking or brawling stage. Cat decided on noodles from the Vietnamese place she liked, and ducked down the little alley that led to Golden Square. She was just at the corner when she felt someone take hold of her arm. "Please," said a voice, very softly.

She tensed: ready to scream, to kick, to run. The place must be bristling with CCTV cameras—there were a couple of guys chatting only a few feet away—a girl on her cell at the corner—if she could just—"Please forgive the imposition," said her would-be assailant, his voice trembling as he withdrew his hand. "I didn't mean to alarm you." It was the heavy-breathing businessman from the Tube.

Cat relaxed slightly, although every nerve was on alert. "What d'you want?"

"I need help." His eyes were darting from side to side, his face clammy. "There—there are people after me."

It was as if she'd walked onto the set of some cheesy detective film, though she was finding it hard to cast this man as a fugitive criminal. He looked too ordinary for that: middle-aged, middle class, middle management. Still, she was wary. "You're being followed?" she asked, as noncommittally as possible.

"Yes, yes, that's right. Ten of Swords, you see. I think I gave them the slip at Argyll Street, but it won't be long now." He licked his lips nervously and gave her an odd sort of half smile.

"If you're in trouble, try the police."

"Oh no," he said, frowning slightly. "I couldn't possibly. It's against Game rules."

"*Game?*" God, there were some wackos around. Ten to one it was some kinky Soho sex thing. "Well, have fun then." She turned to go.

"No, wait. Please." He put out a hand to stop her, his expression crafty. "If you were to stay with me, Swords would have to back off. Bystanders can't engage in play, you see."

"I'm not going anywhere with you—"

"Just for a while," he wheedled, grabbing at her arm. "Just to give me some time—one last chance—" His whole body was shaking, but there was a spark of something in his eyes. Fear, yes, but also excitement, and a kind of greed. She swore, and shook him off.

His face hardened into a snarl; then he turned and disappeared up the alley. And good riddance, thought Cat. But as she turned to go, three people appeared at the top of the street. Two men and a woman, dark and purposeful. They moved swiftly, and would have gone past the alley if Cat hadn't caught the woman's eye. "If you're looking for a running man," she said, "he went up that way." Serve him right for creeping her out.

The three of them stopped dead in their tracks and turned their gaze on her. Under their cold scrutiny Cat felt sudden misgivings. But it was too late now. The woman gave a terse nod, and before Cat knew what was happening, they swept past her up the alley.

Crazy way to spend a Friday night, she thought, looking after them. Something on the pavement drew her eye—a postcard or flyer that the man must have dropped. It appeared to be a playing card, though not from any game Cat was familiar with. One side was patterned with interlocking circles or wheels; on the other was a picture of a fallen figure in a barren landscape, a cluster of swords stuck in his back. There was red blood and black clouds, and the top of the card was marked with an *X*.

A game, the man had said, just a game. . . . But Cat's misgivings increased. Not quite knowing what she was doing or why, she doubled back up the alley. She didn't really believe she would find them in the Friday-night bustle, but then she saw one of the men whisk around a corner and found herself jogging to catch up.

They were in the heart of Soho now, a maze of narrow streets heaving with people, and the hunt—if a hunt it was—was zigzagging through the crowds. At one point Cat thought she had lost them, but then she saw the woman's head in profile, eyes scanning the street, before she turned right and disappeared.

When Cat reached the turning point, she found herself at a dead end, a little courtyard crowded with trash bags and empty beer crates. It was the back entrance to a pub. The others would have gone straight through and out onto the street again. Or maybe this was home base and they were downing pints at the bar by now, adding up their points and penalties or whatever it was.

Yet this cozy vision didn't quite convince. A creepy playing card was one thing, but there was something about the way those three people had looked at her—so cold and resolute—that felt wrong. As Bel always said, *Don't go looking for trouble, else trouble comes looking for you.* But perhaps because Cat was tired of these empty weeks, of feeling so damn *lost,* she decided that now was the moment to get a grip and make a move. She walked past the trash bags and through the door.

Inside, there was a dark passageway ending in a door to the bar, and a narrow set of stairs to the right. Although she could hear the bar crowd through the frosted glass of the door, the handle wouldn't open. Locked. But those people must have come in here. Her stomach let out a growl of hunger, or it might have been nerves. She gave herself a shake, then turned and began to climb the stairs. At the top was another door, with a ragged sort of circle scratched into the wood. Cat hung back for a moment, then opened it and walked in.

She was in a room that looked halfway between some sort of fancy, members-only club and a caretaker's closet. There was a stack of paint cans and a battered filing cabinet in one corner, with a small TV on top showing nothing but static. The walls were paneled with wood, badly scuffed, but an old-fashioned oil lamp was glowing on the windowsill, and the carpet beneath her feet felt thick and rich. In the center of the room, four people were seated around a table covered in green felt, playing a game of cards. They all looked up at her entrance, but not in an outraged sort of way. They didn't even seem that surprised. "Ah," said one of the ladies, arching her brow. There was an expectant silence.

Cat knew that she should begin with an apology or excuse of some sort: "I don't mean to interrupt but . . ." or "I'm sorry to intrude . . ." Instead, she stepped forward holding out the crumpled card. "There was a man," she said, "a man I followed here. I think he's in some sort of trouble. Do you—have you—" She ground to a halt.

The man sitting nearest to her got up in one graceful movement, came across and took the card. Glancing at it— the blood, the swords, the lowering storm—he gave her a quizzical smile. "Trouble? Yes, I should think he is." He looked to be in his late twenties, tousle-haired, with a boyishly sophisticated face and sleepy eyes.

Cat tried again. "He asked for help. Some people were

after him. I . . . I followed them here." She found she didn't want to admit that it was *she* who had set them on his trail. And even as she spoke, she felt the absurdity of her words—the only intruder in the room was her.

"The player was attempting to cheat. Involving a bystander is an invalid move," said one of the two women. She turned to gesture at the TV screen and its impenetrable flicker. "Wands should pay the forfeit." She was in early middle age and darkly glamorous, wearing an evening dress of burgundy velvet. Her companions were a stern-faced black man, his hair just beginning to gray, and a blonde in a white pantsuit and dark glasses. Cat thought she looked stupid, wearing sunglasses in a lamp-lit room.

"I disagree with Lucrezia," said the black man heavily. "The bystander intervened of her own accord. And since her actions were to the disadvantage of Wands, my player has already paid for his error."

"Come now, Ahab!" chided the younger man. "It's clear the intervention would never have occurred if Wands hadn't broken the rules in the first place."

The dark-haired woman turned to the blonde. "Odile? What's your call?"

"There is only one rule of significance here," she replied, sipping daintily from a cup of pale tea. "And that is, a bystander whose intervention has changed the course of the Game is no longer a bystander. We must issue the usual invitation and await further play."

"What is this *about*?" Frustration and nervousness combined to make Cat aggressive. She took another step toward the table and saw that the cards they were playing with were not from a normal deck, but in the same style as the one she had found in the street. Strange images and symbols in rich, harsh colors. Tarot cards, maybe. So what were they doing—fortune-telling? Or had she stumbled into some creepy occult society? She shivered, and looked to the door. The room must be soundproofed, she decided, because there was no sound from the street or the bar below.

"Please don't be alarmed," said the young man charmingly. "It's only a game."

The older woman, Lucrezia, flashed Cat a roguish smile. "We are perfectly in order, I assure you!"

"I don't understand," she said. "Who are you people?"

"Me? I'm Alastor, King of Swords," said the young man, cocking his eyebrow at her and laughing. "And these are my companions: Ahab, King of Wands; Odile, Queen of Cups; and Lucrezia, Queen of Pentacles."

Kings and queens and mystic cards—they *were* one of those dorky role-playing groups! For all their glamorous clothes and enigmatic airs, they were really just a bunch of nerds huddled above a pub to act out some fantasy quest.

Cat suppressed a smirk. "I s'pose the royal titles mean you're team leaders in this game of yours."

"We rule the players in our court," the black man, Ahab, replied seriously. "The man you met is one of the knights of the Court of Wands. I am his king, and he plays for me."

"Right . . . so chasing after him is part of a competition you've set up? With rules and prizes and stuff?"

"There are rules, and also principles." The blonde took another sip of tea, its steam perfuming the air with the scent of jasmine. "The knight in question has flouted both."

"Admittedly, he was dealt a difficult card. The Ten of Swords' formal title is Reign of Ruin," Lucrezia explained in a conversational tone, lighting a cigarette. "It is a card that traditionally pits a knight against knaves. Alastor gave it in challenge to Ahab's knight."

"Knaves? Are they your henchmen, or something?"

"A king must have his servants," Alastor said smoothly. "These do our bidding, both in and out of the Arcanum."

"Arc-what?"

"It is the board on which our Game is played. However, this Knight of Wands fled his move without even attempting to engage in play." He looked slyly at Ahab. "All things considered, I can't imagine his failure would be much of a loss for your court, Ahab. Hardly champion material, is he?"

Ahab frowned.

"Of course, we could have imposed a forfeit on him as punishment," Alastor continued. "Or even canceled his round. But I was merciful. I gave the knight the chance to complete his move outside of the Arcanum, and ordered my knaves to go after him."

Cat was getting interested in spite of herself. "So what's the knight have to do to win?"

"Oh, merely escape his pursuers in the time period set." He gave a sigh of mock regret. "Alas for Wands, though, his rule breaking has come to no good, and now my knaves have the advantage. . . . Furthermore, another card has entered the Game."

The King of Swords slid a card over to her. It showed a figure dressed in patchwork rags, poised at the brink of a precipice.

"And what's that one called?" Cat asked.

"The Fool," said Ahab impassively. The blonde waited, motionless as a mannequin. In the sudden silence, Cat noticed the other two staring at her intently, eagerly even, and her misgivings returned. It was just so odd. They were odd, all of them.

"I'd best be off," she said abruptly. "Goodbye."

Alastor moved ahead to open the door for her. "I do hope you won't intervene in play again. Second time round, we'd have to impose a forfeit. And then where would you be?" He winked conspiratorially as she brushed past, her heart jumping, anxious for fresh air, for crowds and noise again.

Once she was out in the street, however, her nerves seemed ridiculous. Those people were strange, sure, but it was nothing to her how they chose to spend their time. King of Swords! Mr. Boring Banker, more like. Or one of those super-smooth lawyer types, playing at world domination on his days off.

FORTUNE

ℭHAPTER 𝔍WO

ON SATURDAY, CAT WOKE to find Bel cooking breakfast. Greg was there too, and the flat was filled with an eye-watering smell of burned toast and cigarettes and bacon frying. Bel's shift usually ended at four, and it didn't look like she'd been to bed in the meantime—her makeup had that lopsided, end-of-the-night look, and she was still wearing stockings under her bathrobe. Her throaty laughter raised itself above the radio to rattle the windowpanes.

"Check it out, puss-cat!" she called. "You're looking at the Palais Luxe's new senior croupier! Bacon sandwiches and bubbles to celebrate!" She was flourishing a bottle of cava, courtesy of Greg, presumably, who had gone a bashful pink around the ears. Greg had a long, rather drooping face and small delicate hands, like a girl's. Cat had always thought he looked more like a small-town librarian than the pit boss at a seedy casino.

She eyed Bel thoughtfully over a juice glass of slightly warm fizz. London had gone to Bel's head like the bubbles in her wine. "Told you this city was going to work for me!" she exclaimed as she sashayed off to the bathroom.

"Bumped into some real weirdos last night," Cat said casually.

"Weirdos like what? Perverts?" Greg lowered his voice, with an anxious glance at the bathroom door.

"Nah, these weren't the kinky kind. Bunch of bankers playing this card game where you had to run around acting things out. Quests and chases and stuff."

"Sounds like those Dungeons and Dragons fans."

"Dungeons! Now *that* sounds kinky."

"Ah, but these are the imaginary kind." Greg looked knowledgeable. "For imaginary adventures. You're given tasks or puzzles, and you build a story round them. Some people really get into it: write scripts, make costumes. . . . Though I've heard it can turn nasty, mind."

"Nasty?"

"Ooh yes. There was a murder. Some kid killed another one, or got his friend to kill somebody else—I can't remember which—and they said it was all part of this fantasy role-play business. It was in the papers a while back, and I don't reckon it was a one-off, neither. . . . I'd steer well clear, dungeons or no."

"Fine by me," said Cat, reaching for another slice of bacon.

❧

The day was cold but clear, and after breakfast Cat went out to mingle with the Christmas shoppers and sightseers. After her days of drifting, it was almost disconcerting to have a destination in mind. Her route crossed paths with the one she'd taken last night, the scene of the chase, or game, or whatever it was, but the streets were bright and the crowds unthreatening.

Dark Portal was a sci-fi and fantasy shop on the Charing Cross Road that sold an assortment of books, DVDs and comics, together with film and TV memorabilia. The window display had a signed poster of Buffy the Vampire Slayer, a collection of model dragons holding crystals in their claws and a "limited edition" Luke Skywalker doll. Cat went inside with the same furtive air as customers at the local porno store.

Inside, the shop was orderly and well lit, and she was relieved to see her fellow browsers didn't look too odd— only a couple of beards between them. She went up to the register, where a bored-looking student type was reading Sartre.

"Excuse me?"

"Yeah?"

"Do you deal in, er, role-playing games?"

He heaved a long-suffering sigh. "What're you into?"

"I'm not sure. . . ."

"Space opera, Western, Wicca, detective . . . or maybe you're more the post-Apocalyptic type?"

"I don't th—"

"Of course, sword 'n' sorcery is always popular." He waved his hand toward a display cabinet full of little figurines. "I'm told we have a particularly fine selection of hobbits." Now he was smirking and she stared at him coldly. Weren't these places supposed to be run by geeky enthusiasts?

"Can I help you?" A little man came bustling over.

"I was asking about role-playing games," she said, turning her back firmly on Mr. Too Cool for Tolkien.

The man beamed, practically twitching with enthusiasm. This was more like it. "Do you know what you're looking for?"

"Not exactly. I wondered . . . do you know of any role-play games based on, like, Tarot cards?" she asked.

"Well, some game masters use them, but usually as a basis for building up a wider fantasy scenario. People either create their own game from scratch, you see, or else they buy ready-made packs and plot guides to get them going. If you're interested, I could get you our catalogue."

Was this how those people on Friday night had got started: chatting over the miniature hobbits? Cat was suddenly embarrassed by her questions. She didn't belong in a place like this. "Uh, thanks—maybe I'll look into it." She was already backing out the door.

Over the next week, Cat stopped riding the Tube and spent her after-school hours walking around instead. For the most part, the West End had a holiday feel, its lights garish but cheerful. Cat wasn't stupid, though; she never loitered in the dead hours after the pubs and coffee shops had emptied, the office workers and tourists had melted away, and the older, darker city came to claim its own. Besides, at ten-thirty sharp, Bel would telephone the flat, and all hell would break loose if Cat wasn't there to answer.

Sometimes Cat would pass a group of girls giggling in the window of a café, or a couple entwined outside a bar, and feel a fleeting restlessness. Once, when Cat was about eight, she'd had a friend at school, a *best* friend, Tara, and when she'd heard they were moving again, she'd cried for a day. Bel had been kind but tough. "You meet the same people wherever you go and whatever you do. Truth is, most people are replaceable, if you look hard enough." As she got older, Cat decided Bel was right. The Taras and Gregs of the world were nice enough, useful even, but they didn't last. Whereas Bel and Cat were forever. That was their pact.

Meanwhile, all schools had become alike to Cat—even if this latest one was more chaotic than most—and by now she was adept at putting in just the right amount of effort not to draw attention to herself. It was the same with the in-groups and alliances outside of class.

On the last Friday before Christmas break, she went to hang out in a coffee shop with a bunch of girls from her class; they were going on to a party afterward, but by then she'd had enough. Once she got back to the flat, however, she had time to regret it. After half an hour listening to the thump of drum 'n' bass from the place next door, Cat gave in. Just because she'd missed her chance with the party didn't mean she had to be stuck at home all night.

Almost without noticing it, she had begun to form an internal map of the neighborhood, the ebb and flow of its streets. As Cat neared the entrance to the strip joint at the end of her road, she automatically noted that it was the Saturday blonde at the door, not the black girl who usually took the Friday-night shift. The girl gave a brief nod of greeting as Cat walked past, the fan heater by her bare legs blowing sudden warmth across the pavement. Cat shivered, and hunched farther into her coat.

Thrusting her hands deep into the pockets, she felt something poking out of the inner lining of the left one. It was a card: thick, gilt-edged, and with a familiar illustration. No swords or blood at least, but the happy Fool, poised between the light and the dark, the open sky and the abyss.

What the . . . ? Cat stared at it for a moment, before re-membering that this was the coat she'd been wearing a week ago, the night of her encounter with the cardplayers above the pub. The King of Whatsit must have slipped it into her pocket on her way out, and it had somehow worked its way into the torn lining.

Cat walked over to a brightly lit shop window to take a closer look. The reverse of the card was printed with a curly black script.

The Arcanum
Temple House, Mercury Square

Admits One

Throw the coin, turn the card.
What will you play for?

There was a little icon of a four-spoked wheel, but no date or RSVP, no real information about what it was inviting her to. Hadn't the cardplayers said the Arcanum was a kind of board game? But what did it mean about throwing coins?

"Got a light, miss?"

Cat started: she had been too absorbed in her discovery to pay attention to what was going on around her. An older Asian boy, face half-hidden by a baseball cap, was leaning toward her expectantly.

"Sorry," she said, moving off. The area always had an assortment of young men with pinched, unhealthy faces loitering on corners and outside doorways, doing furtive business of one sort or another. Up till now, she had managed to steer clear of them.

"Spare some change for the bus, then?"

"No."

Cat moved more quickly into the crowds, and he began to follow her. She remembered the businessman fleeing down the alley, the set faces of those in pursuit, though she immediately shook the thought off. That whole thing had been a misunderstanding. She was perfectly safe. There were people everywhere. . . . Even so, she walked briskly, away from her original direction. She glanced back to see if he was still following her. Yes. She turned another corner and looked back again.

He had stopped, was standing, staring, on the curb. The light of a taxi swung round, and for a moment he was illuminated in its beam: a dark face and glittering eyes. Then he tugged his cap down low again, turned his back on her and melted away.

Cat was embarrassed to find she was breathing hard, her palms clammy. She must have come farther than she had realized; she was out of the warren of streets around Soho and in one of the grand old squares that lie in the heart of the city. At this time of year, many squares had trees decked in ropes of lights, but not here. Shadows rustled behind the park railings. It looked as if most of the houses around the square had been converted into offices, since the buildings were dark and silent. Except for one, that is, where the windows glowed richly and the faint hum of talk and laughter spilled into the air.

Cat drew nearer to the pools of light, as if standing in them could make her warmer. The front door was invitingly ajar, and a discreet bronze plaque to one side of it said:

TEMPLE HOUSE

She half laughed and felt for the card in her pocket. *The Arcanum, Temple House, Mercury Square.* A sudden wind gusted; the drizzle had turned to sleet and stung her face. Talk about good timing! From the sound of it, there was some sort of party going on. Cat didn't mind large, anonymous crowds; slipping around the edge of things was her specialty. She might as well give it a go: maybe get something to eat, wait until the sleet had eased. . . .

The door opened onto a hallway with a marble floor checkered in black and white. A man was seated at a desk immediately inside the door, while the rest of the hall behind him was shut off by a heavy curtain of gold brocade. The sounds that came from the other side were oddly muffled, though Cat could hear laughter and the chink of glasses.

The doorkeeper was dressed in black-and-gold livery, the kind that concierges wear at expensive hotels. He had a withered face and clouded eyes. "You're just in time," he said. "May I see your card?"

Cat produced the invitation, half expecting to be turned away. It was possible she'd got things wrong, and she didn't exactly blend in with the fittings. Her damp hair straggled around her face and she was wearing an old blue V-neck and jeans under her coat. If there was a dress code, she was screwed.

She waited as the doorkeeper studied the card and then

her face. Finally, he took out a dark coin from his pocket, and laid it on the table. "Do you choose to enter the Arcanum and play the Game?" he asked.

"There's no membership fee, is there?"

"Anyone can join," he said gravely, "who accepts the invitation."

"OK, then."

"Catch."

In a sudden movement, the man threw her the coin. Startled, she put her hand up. She could have sworn she'd caught it—she felt the cool hardness of metal in her fist—but when she opened her hand, it was empty.

She looked around the floor. "Where'd it go?"

"You will find it later," the doorkeeper replied. Then he reached for the stamp and ink pad beside him. "If I may?"

Cat proffered her right hand, and he turned it over, pressing the stamp onto her palm. The ink burned on contact, but the sensation was so brief she thought she must have imagined it. All that showed on her skin was the smudgy black outline of a wheel.

"Cool. Do I get a plastic wristband as well?"

He stared back at her, unsmiling.

"Welcome to the Game."

Before she could change her mind, Cat went past the desk, drew back the heavy brocade drapes and stepped through. The building was even larger and grander than it appeared from the outside; the entrance hall was enormous and swarming with people. It was lit by an elaborate chandelier.

At the back of the hall, a flight of stairs swept up to a second-floor gallery. There were rooms that opened on either side of the hall, and somewhere a piano was being played—a complicated modern piece with little obvious melody.

If Bel had been at this party, she would have lifted her chin, pulled down her neckline, sauntered over to the largest and liveliest group—glass in hand—and just stood there, waiting for their attention to turn. Cat, however, was equally accomplished at keeping a distance. It wasn't simply a matter of skulking in corners; instead, she had learned to hold herself aloof, to stay watchful but relaxed. That way, she could be left to her own devices.

She accepted a drink from a passing waiter, and wandered to the entrance of the room on her right. Inside, a group was clustered around a green felt table, but as far as she could see it was just an ordinary card game—poker, maybe. The guests were a range of ages, and most had dressed up for the occasion in cocktail dresses or suits. A few people looked as if they'd come straight from the office. Nobody gave her a second glance. Cat found a chair in a quiet corner, and allowed herself to relax.

In some ways, her senses were heightened by her surroundings. The prickle of champagne in her mouth, the scent of the women's perfume rising in the warmth, the click of heels on wood and the chiming of glass—all these things were sharp and clear. And yet there was a drowsy, muddled feeling that she couldn't quite shake off. When she tried to pick up what people were talking about, she found she couldn't concentrate, kept losing the thread. She thought she saw a well-known actress languishing against the wall, and didn't she recognize that jowly, gray-faced man? A politician or anchorman, perhaps. But when she looked again, she couldn't be sure. It was as if her focus had gone. Champagne on an empty stomach, she supposed, though it wasn't as if she had much experience of the stuff.

She put her glass down and wandered through to another crowded room on the other side of the entrance hall, with the vague idea of trying to find the piano. This room had an immense, gilt-framed mirror above the mantelpiece, and Cat saw a new glow and softness in her reflection, as if the luster of the place was rubbing off on her.

The light-headed feeling was definitely getting stronger. She found a seat, sat down and closed her eyes, trying to trace a thread of melody in the distant music. Every time she thought she caught the tune, it slipped away or subtly altered, so that she was unsure if sweetness or melancholy had been the dominant key. Somewhere a clock chimed; she tried and failed to count the hour. Her watch showed the second hand twitching on the spot like something trapped behind glass.

Cat decided she needed to find somewhere quiet and cool where she could clear her head. She went back into the entrance hall and, on a whim, climbed the stairs to the gallery above. She tried the doors along the corridor at random, hoping to find a restroom.

Through the first door, she glimpsed a room with walls lined in crimson silk, unfurnished except for a piano. A blonde in dark glasses and a white ball gown was sitting with her back to the door and playing an old-fashioned waltz. The room next to it was a book-lined study where a group of people were exclaiming over a game of dice. Surveying them from a sofa was the older woman from the night of the Tarot cards. Beside Cat lounged the guy who'd followed her in Soho; his cap was gone and his face was blank and glassy-eyed. As she paused on the threshold, Lucrezia smiled at her, then, holding her gaze, ran her hand through the boy's black hair.

The doors on the front side of the house opened into a long, bare room that ran the length of the building. Tall windows lined the wall overlooking the square; they had no curtains or shutters and the panes were shining black. The other side of the room was hung with pictures. It was like being in a museum, Cat thought, her steps creaking on the polished wooden floor. Cat didn't know anything about art, but these pictures looked old, centuries old maybe, for the colors were rich but faded, and patches of paint were nothing but a cracked blur.

The painting on the left was of a man and a woman standing naked among rainbows and flowers, with an angel holding a flaming sword behind them. The next depicted an armored knight on a white horse, but where his face should have been was a gleaming skull. Both these paintings, and the two at the far end of the room, were about four feet by five. The central painting, however, was much bigger. It depicted a vast four-spoked wheel with fantastical figures climbing or tumbling on its rim and a woman in the center. After that came a painting featuring an angel with a trumpet and, finally, a desert landscape with a robed figure bearing an hourglass.

She turned back to the picture of the wheel. Close up, she saw the woman in the middle was blindfolded and carried a banner bearing an inscription in a foreign script. Latin, perhaps. Her smile was shadowy, knowing. And now Cat saw that the wheel itself was inlaid with many smaller images: a chariot, drawn by sphinxes; a flaming tower; a woman wrestling a lion . . .

A soft noise at the other end of the room made her turn round, and she saw she was no longer alone. The young man who had called himself the King of Swords was lounging against the door, a cigarette in one hand. "Hello again," he said.

She nodded briefly and turned back to the painting, feeling self-conscious. Her head had begun to ache, and she hoped he'd leave her alone, but he was already moving to join her. He was dressed more casually than before, scruffy almost, in a faded gray T-shirt and with bare feet. Pad, pad, pad along the floor. He looked younger than she remembered. "So you found us all right."

"Yeah." This was her prompt to say what a nice party it was, how kind of you, blah blah blah. Instead, she frowned, trying to think past the fuzziness. "Why'd you invite me?" It came out more abruptly than she'd intended, but he didn't seem to mind, just smiled and took another drag of his cigarette.

"Why did you come?" he countered, watching her

through the smoke with sleepy eyes. There was a pause. "I'm Alastor, as you may remember."

"The King of Swords."

"And you are the Cat Who Walks by Herself."

That rattled her. It was what Bel used to call her, quoting from some old kid's book, she said, though she'd never remembered the title. Had Cat even told him her name, or was it just an uncanny coincidence? She hunched her shoulders defensively and moved away a little, until she was standing beneath the painting of the knight with the bone face.

"The Triumph of Death," he told her, and gestured toward the painting to its right, the one of the man and the woman in the garden. "Over the Triumph of Love."

"Not very romantic."

"No."

Cat could feel him watching her, not in a sleazy way, but thoughtfully, as if she was being measured for something.

"The pictures tell a story?" she prompted.

"An allegory. It begins with Love or, in a more general sense, humanity," he explained, sounding relaxed and perhaps a little bored. "Love is overpowered by Death, who prevails over mortal passions and endeavors. Next comes Fame, the golden messenger who survives Death, and so defeats him. But even Fame, like memory, must fall to Time. Our friend with the hourglass."

Cat digested this. "So where does the wheel fit in?"

"The Triumph of Fortune. *Regnabo, regno, regnavi, sum sine regno.*" Now his voice was mocking, though of whom or what she wasn't sure. "One could say that Fortune prevails over every other triumph, determining the nature of our loves, deaths, legacies. . . . Perhaps even Time's victory is not so absolute. The Wheel turns, life begins again."

"And . . . and the woman at the center?"

"Take your pick. Tuche. Domina Casus. Queen Hecate. Fors Fortuna, goddess of fate and luck."

Cat frowned. "Fate and luck aren't the same thing."

"No." He was playing with his lighter: flicking the flame up and off again. The spark of it danced in his eyes. "But who's to say what's behind the throw of a die, the turn of a card? However skilled the player, whatever the stake, those who win their triumph have Fortune on their side."

"The Game of Triumphs," she whispered, as if she'd known it all along. She thought back to their first meeting, the Knight of Wands and a card called the Ten of Swords. What had the dark-haired woman said? *He was dealt a difficult card . . . it pits a knight against knaves.* "You deal the cards and the other players act out whatever's on them. Why?"

"For the prizes you see here and more—Love, Death, Fame . . . and all the other delights our cards bestow. Believe me, Cat, there's *everything* to play for."

How was a card a prize? And how could you win something as abstract as love, anyway? But Cat sensed he was laughing at her. She didn't want to give him the satisfaction of her curiosity.

Alastor moved toward the door. "I believe the evening's

Lottery is about to begin," he said, looking back over his shoulder. "That should answer your questions, if you care to join us."

She shrugged. "Depends on the jackpot."

"Ah, but our Lottery offers a different reward: the chance for our players to pick a new card and find a new fate. Who could resist?"

Left alone in the gallery, Cat spent the next few minutes listing all the reasons it was time to go home. The longer she stayed, the more confusing the whole setup became. But in spite of her best intentions, when she left the room she let herself be caught up in a crowd of guests who were surging along the hallway; it seemed easier to go with the flow and be jostled toward the stairs, up to the third and final floor of the house. The black-and-gold-patterned doors at the head of the stairs had been flung open, and Cat saw that the entire floor was one vast mirrored ballroom.

Soon the room was thronged with people. It was difficult to judge the space, since the mirrors around the walls reflected the scene back and forth and around in a kaleidoscopic whirl of people and lights and sparkling glass. For a moment, it was as if Cat was looking through the mirrors into myriad other crowds in myriad other rooms, but then she blinked, and the impression was gone. A hush descended.

At the far end of the room, the kings and queens were seated in a row behind a long narrow table, like members of a board. Behind them, suspended from the ceiling, was a TV monitor showing a silent blizzard of static. In front of them was a wheel. Cat edged her way forward to get a better look.

After the buildup, she was expecting something spectacular, studded with gems, perhaps, and a flaming cresset at the center, but in fact the wheel looked very similar to what any ordinary casino would use for roulette: about three feet in diameter and made of dark polished wood, with numbered slots in alternating checks of black, white, silver and gold. The doorkeeper stood next to it, one hand resting gently on the side.

"The players are assembled," he announced. "Who is presented for the Lottery?"

"The Queen of Cups calls upon a Knight of Cups," said Odile, blank-faced behind her dark glasses.

A woman stepped forward from within the crowd. The doorkeeper turned to face her. "Speak, Knight, and name the prize that you play for."

The knight was lanky and dark, and her voice shook slightly as she spoke. "I—I'm playing for the Triumph of the Moon."

Cat gave a snort of disbelief. What could this woman have to gain from the moon? Space travel? A hot date with an astronaut?

The man standing next to her gave her a disapproving look. But someone else—a freckle-faced boy of about her own age—leaned to whisper in her ear. "It represents artistic inspiration," he explained, as if he'd guessed her question.

The King of Swords looked unimpressed. "Question is," he drawled, tipping back in his chair, "will a cure for writer's block do our friend any good, without the Triumph of Fame to enjoy it?"

The crowd laughed, and the knight licked her lips uneasily.

"Which court holds the Triumph of the Moon?" asked the doorkeeper in ritual tones.

"The Court of Wands," replied Ahab—who, dressed in a pinstripe suit, really did look as if he was attending a business meeting.

The doorkeeper nodded. "Let the courts name the cards they have dealt, and the knight's progress through them."

"Nine of Cups, Reign of Material Happiness," said Odile, sounding a little bored. "Played, and won."

"Seven of Pentacles, Reign of Success Unfulfilled," said Lucrezia. "Also played and won."

"Ten of Wands, Reign of Oppression," said Ahab. "Not yet played."

"Eight of Swords, Reign of Shortened Force," yawned Alastor. "Not yet played."

The audience murmured. Several people could be heard observing it was a hard round.

So a knight had four cards to play, one from each court. Cat thought the Reign of Material Happiness sounded OK. If the knight belonged to the Court of Cups, then it made sense for the Queen of Cups to give her an easy ride. But Cat didn't like the sound of any of the other moves.

"Which is the card the Knight of Cups wishes to exchange?" the doorkeeper asked.

"The Ten of Wands," Odile replied.

31

"A Lottery may only be held when the Triumph of Fortune has entered play," the old man said gravely.

"But of course." Odile waved toward the knight, who brought out a card from her pocket. In her excitement or nervousness she nearly dropped it as she handed it to the doorkeeper. Cat couldn't see the illustration, but she guessed it must resemble the picture of the woman and wheel that she'd seen in the gallery.

"Fortune's card is hidden in different moves throughout the Arcanum," the boy at her shoulder said in an undertone. "Players aren't dealt it; they have to find it for themselves. It means they can swap one of their cards for another, picked at random by the wheel."

Cat nodded to show her appreciation, but at the same time wished he'd shut up. They were getting black looks from their neighbors.

"The Triumph of Fortune has been accepted," said the doorkeeper, "and the Lottery may proceed."

The Queen of Cups inclined her head toward the King of Wands, who bowed slightly in return. Then she rose to stand before the wheel. The King of Swords stopped swinging on his chair and leaned forward with narrowed eyes. Even the Queen of Pentacles, who had been toying with the rope of jet around her neck, became still and watchful. Meanwhile, the knight waited to one side. She was visibly sweating.

Odile produced a silk pouch, from which she took out a small gleaming ball that she held up before the crowd. "A crystal die for Cups, ebony for Wands," whispered Cat's informant. "Gold for Pentacles and silver for Swords. The numbers and colors in the wheel's slots refer to the sequence of cards in the deck." After a brief pause, the doorman spun the wheel and, with a graceful flick of her wrist, the queen launched the circular die. There was absolute silence as the wheel whirled and the ball rattled. The whole room seemed to be holding its breath.

At last, the spinning stopped and the ball dropped into its slot. The doorkeeper bent to inspect it. The wait seemed to stretch on forever.

"Four of Pentacles!" he called.

At once, the place erupted into a tumult of exclamations and acclaim. It appeared that the Four of Pentacles meant something good, for the knight was grinning dazedly, her face foolish with relief. Even though Cat barely understood what had gone on, she found herself joining the applause.

The doorkeeper raised a hand for quiet. "The wheel has turned. The Knight of Cups exchanges the Ten of Wands for the Four of Pentacles, Reign of Possession."

The knight handed over a card to the doorkeeper and accepted another from the Queen of Pentacles.

"A fine gamble," Lucrezia said appreciatively. "And now I have news of a winning one."

Buzzing and rustling from the floor.

"Yes," the dark-haired queen continued, voice raised, "it is my pleasure and privilege to announce that the Court of

Pentacles has won another triumph. After completing a successful round, a Knight of Pentacles has taken the Triumph of the Devil from the Court of Swords."

Her announcement was greeted with gasps and applause. Meanwhile, Cat shifted uncomfortably. Talk of the moon and fame was one thing, but the devil. . . . Once again, the freckle-faced boy leaned in to explain. "It's the hedonist's card. Sex, drugs and rock 'n' roll!" he said, eyes shining. This didn't leave Cat much the wiser.

The doorkeeper rapped on the edge of the wheel for silence. "Does the Court of Swords accept the loss of the Triumph of the Devil?"

Alastor's jaw tightened but his expression stayed carefully neutral. "Naturally," he said, as he took out a card from his pocket and slid it across the table to Lucrezia with an ironic little half bow. "Though I'm sure it won't be long before we win it back again."

"I call upon the Knight of Pentacles to come forward and receive her prize."

A young woman pushed her way out from the center of the throng: a tall angular girl, her mouth a slash of scarlet and her eyes outlined in startlingly thick swoops of kohl.

"Pass it over, then," she said.

The doorkeeper looked offended. Clearly, this wasn't part of the script. But the King of Swords didn't take offence. In fact, he was looking the knight up and down approvingly. "I hope you'll make the most of your reward."

"Oh, you can count on it." She held out her hand.

As the other king and queens looked on, smiling indulgently, Alastor handed her a small metal object—a ball like the one Odile had spun into the wheel, but made of silver for the Court of Swords.

"After you leave Temple House, cast the die back over its threshold, and the powers of the Devil will be yours. You have played a fine Game and earned your triumph."

Cat was disappointed. Alastor had told her that the Lottery would explain things, but it had only left her more confused. She still didn't see how playing cards and metal balls worked as prizes. These people didn't *really* believe such things could give them supernatural powers . . . did they?

Yet all around her, the faces of the other players were suffused with a mixture of yearning and envy. A kind of reverence, too, as if this moment of victory was a sacred thing. And as the winning knight turned to leave, her hand clenched over her prize, the crowd parted to form an aisle of honor for her to walk out of the room. There was no more applause, just a long, soft sighing sound as the doors closed behind her.

Further speeches followed, but Cat barely heard them. She was still trying to process all the things she had witnessed. Finally, she became aware that the doorkeeper was bringing events to an end: ". . . for the night is young," he was saying, "and the Game is long. May Lady Luck favor you all." He stepped toward the wheel. "Let play begin."

As he set the wheel spinning round, for a confused second the mirrored walls seemed to be whirling, too.

There was a final cheer, and everyone began swarming

35

out of the room. As Cat was borne along by the rush, she heard snatches of commentary. "The Devil hasn't been attempted for a while"—"Or won, either"—"Yes, but if Cups take the Moon, they may draw level with Pentacles"—"Wands are pressing hard, but they lost another knight last week . . ." Meanwhile, the doors swung shut on the kings and queens. They were turning round to face the TV monitor, in which shapes and movement had begun to swim through the static.

Back in the hallway, Cat stood aside to let the other guests stream past her. The party was resuming with new vigor—shouts and raucous laughter filled the house. The questions massing in her head were like a hundred spinning wheels, but she couldn't think past them. All she wanted was to go home.

She'd made it to the bottom of the stairs and was heading for the door when someone caught her arm. It was the boy who had whispered to her in the ballroom. "You can't leave now!" he said, frowning. Her head ached and throbbed. She shook him off and stumbled across the black-and-white-checkered floor that seemed to sway beneath her feet, clawed her way past the muffling brocade and spun—at last—into the damp night air.

Cat didn't remember much of the walk home or what time it was when she tumbled, fully clothed, into bed. Sleep came instantly, her dreams crowded with feverish images. There was the knight on his horse, but instead of a skull he had the face of the King of Swords. She saw the wheel in the painting again, spinning, and sometimes the figure in the center was Bel, and sometimes her mother, and once it was the businessman from the Tube. One last chance, he told her. But I couldn't possibly, she replied. It's all for the Game. At one point she dreamed she woke up and saw the print of the wheel on her right palm glow silver-bright as it burned, burned into her skin like ice. And then she was falling among images that cascaded like a stack of cards: a floor like a chessboard, a ruined tower, a garden full of roses and a flaming sword behind. . . .

CHAPTER THREE

"LOOK WHAT THE CAT drags in," said Bel sardonically. It was past noon, and the winter sunlight coming into the kitchen made Cat groan and screw up her eyes. Bel didn't have many rules, but those she did weren't open to negotiation. Curfew was one of them.

"Still," her aunt continued, "you sounded perkier on the phone last night than I've heard you for a while. I'm guessing your end-of-term bash was a good one."

So she hadn't stayed that late at the party after all—not if she'd been home in time to answer Bel's ten-thirty checkup and make up some story to account for her evening. She didn't have any memory of it. Cat wondered if she'd drunk more than she realized, even though she wasn't actually hungover: just tired and rumpled and out of sorts.

Bel started crashing the kettle and mugs around. "At someone's house, you said. Any gossip, then?"

"Not likely. Bad music and a load of geeks talking fantasy games."

"Ouch. Still, always good to put in an appearance."

Cat grunted noncommittally. She knew Bel would have enjoyed hearing about the real party: the swanky guests, the mansion, the champagne. Like something out of one of those glossy lifestyle magazines. The weirdo stuff with the wheel and the triumph cards would have made a good story, too; there wasn't any reason she needed to lie about it. But as she squinted round the frowsty kitchen, with its clutter of unwashed dishes and Bel's underwear soaking in detergent in the sink, the evening before seemed very far away. Unreal, almost . . . like the images from the picture gallery that had followed her into her dreams. Glancing down at her right palm, she was disproportionately relieved to see nothing but a faint, graying circle where the wheel had been.

"Right," she said. "I'm going to grab a shower. See you in a bit."

Bel looked disappointed, but she let her go.

There wasn't enough hot water for a proper shower, but Cat still took her time over it, standing under the tepid sprinkle until the last trace of fuzziness was washed from her brain.

Once she got out of the bathroom, she found a note from Bel to say she was out shopping. Underwear still dripped in the sink; Friday's evening paper was still strewn under the greasy remains of Saturday's lunch. Cat stomped around tidying things away. She was annoyed with herself for getting spooked, for allowing herself—nearly—to be drawn in. Irritably, she grabbed the last of the newspaper and started stuffing it into the bin. Then her eye was caught by the headline: "Businessman's Body Recovered from Thames." And next to it, a photograph that seemed vaguely familiar.

Police have confirmed that the body pulled out of the Thames on Thursday morning is that of London businessman Anthony Linebeg, 47. The body was found with multiple stab wounds in the back and had been in the water for approximately a week. Investigators do not believe robbery to be a motive for the murder, since the victim's wallet and watch had not been taken. Linebeg, a freelance IT consultant, who lived alone, was reported missing after he failed to appear at a seminar last Monday.

Anyone with information relating to the crime was urged to contact the police. A telephone number was provided.

Cat didn't know how long she sat there staring at the page, smoothing out the creases in the paper over and over. The photograph of the victim could have been of any middle-aged, balding guy in a suit; she couldn't be sure it was the man she'd met. But all the same . . . Dead a week, they thought. She closed her eyes and once more saw that card—the blood, the black clouds, the cluster of blades: the Ten of Swords. How many stab wounds were "multiple"?

Cat's hand hovered over her phone, then returned to fidget on the page again. She both wished Bel was here and felt relieved she wasn't. Bel had no patience with uncertainty: her decisions were instinctive and absolute. Yet Cat could find no certainties here.

For the first time in a long while, she thought of her parents, and whether this was something she could have brought to them. Would they have believed her? What might they have done?

Bel's stories about her sister were nearly always taken from their childhood, not from Caroline's life as a wife and mother. Cat could see from photographs that she had her father's black hair and her mother's gray eyes. But more often than not she thought of her own eyes as being like her aunt's. Though Bel had always told Cat that her parents were good and loving people, and their life had been a happy one, this wasn't enough to make their memory real.

Sometimes she had dreams of being very small and held close by some unseen presence. When she woke up, a sadness would be within her all day, and also the sense that, if she screwed herself up to do it, certain memories could be brought to the surface again, where they would have shape and weight and warmth.

However, that kind of thinking was morbid, and best

left alone; that's what Bel always said. It was certainly of no use to her now.

In the end, Cat folded the article into her pocket and went outside, back to Dark Portal, where she found Too Cool for Tolkien enthroned at the information desk.

"D'you have any books on Tarot?"

"This isn't a *New Age* store." If possible, his expression was even more contemptuous than when she'd inquired about role-playing games. Then, just as she was about to turn away, he cleared his throat in a grudging sort of way. "Though I s'pose you could try Reference."

The book section turned out to be in the basement, and was deserted. It was mostly sci-fi and fantasy fiction—everything from Arthur C. Clarke to the soft-porn exploits of space babes with laser guns. There was no reference section. However, the bottom shelf of the last bookcase was labeled MISC., and contained a step-by-step guide to building a model starship *Enterprise,* a book on the history of vampires and, stuffed wrong-side up next to an encyclopedia of Middle Earth, *The Wondrous World of Tarot.* Bingo.

The book was not particularly wondrous in its appearance. Its pages were grubby; the jacket—a riot of lurid psychedelic swirls—was torn. If the overexcited introduction was to be believed, Tarot cards incorporated myths and symbols from prehistoric Norse tribes to the classical world, the ancient religions of China, India and Egypt, and the medieval courts of Italy and France. One theory was that the first cards were made by the deity known as Thoth to the Egyptians, Hermes to the Greeks, and Mercury to the

Romans. As the scribe and magician of the gods, he created The Tarot deck from The Book of the Dead, imbuing the cards with the lost magic of antiquity. Cat wondered if the location of Temple House in Mercury Square was a coincidence, or if those people took all this stuff seriously.

In any case, a lot of the references from last night were beginning to fall into place. The Arcanum, she now realized, must be some kind of allusion to the division of the Tarot deck into two sections: the Greater Arcana and the Lesser Arcana. The Lesser Arcana was fifty-six cards divided into four courts or suits, which corresponded to an ordinary card deck: Wands (Clubs), Cups (Hearts), Pentacles (Diamonds) and Swords (Spades). Each court or suit had its own Queen, King, Knight and Knave.

The twenty-two trump cards (or "triumphs") in the Greater Arcana were supposed to depict a journey through one's life, starting with the Fool, designated as zero, and ending with number twenty-one, the World. The Fool was apparently the ancestor of the modern joker in the pack.

The rest was mostly teach-yourself fortune-telling, or "divination" as the author preferred it. Cat wasn't much interested in fortunes, but she did spend a while looking at the illustrated section in the middle, which showed pictures of all the cards, as well as a selection of Tarot decks through the ages. She was surprised to find that there were a range of different designs and even names for the cards. In some decks the High Priestess was depicted as a female pope, the World was called Eternity, Time was transformed into the Hermit and Fame into Judgment. However, the basic symbols and their interpretations seemed fairly consistent. She even found images similar to the paintings she'd seen in the gallery at Temple House.

Cat flicked through the last few pages of the book with mixed feelings. In some ways, what had seemed strange and possibly threatening a short while ago was easy to dismiss once she saw its sources laid out in a tacky little book. All that hocus-pocus about ancient gods and Kabbalistic cults was the kind of thing she associated with your stereotypical Tarot fans: droopy girls with unwashed hair and too much eyeliner, burning incense in dark rooms. But then she'd always thought role-play games were for pimple-faced nerds living in basements. . . .

Trouble was, she was no closer to understanding how the Game of Triumphs worked, or if it was connected to the newspaper article in her pocket. There certainly weren't any guides to divination that could tell her what exactly she had seen, or not seen, that Friday night. She remembered the hunted man's fear, but also his air of suppressed excitement, how he had clutched at her arm with greed in his eyes. And what was her real motivation here—her pricking conscience or curiosity?

Lost in thought, she turned to place the book back on the shelf—and only then realized someone else had come into the basement and was leaning against the other end of the bookcase, openly staring at her. He was a boy of her own age, or maybe a year younger, with a clever, freckled face and an unruly mop of sandy hair.

"I remember you. You were at the party yesterday."

She must have heard him wrong, or else it was a case of mistaken identity. "I don't think—"

"You know, the Lottery. I was explaining about the triumphs. The Moon and Devil."

The shock of his words brought home to her that she hadn't yet reconciled last night with the ordinary world. She opened her mouth, but no words came.

"Pretty wild, huh?" The boy gave an odd little giggle. "I'm Toby, by the way."

"Cat," she said reluctantly.

Close up, Toby didn't look much like the poised, glossy guests that she remembered. He was wearing a battered tweed hunting jacket over a Godzilla T-shirt and baggy cords. The outfit was hardly radical in this neighborhood, but there was something a little bit staged, a little bit self-conscious about the way he wore it. He didn't look entirely comfortable anyway, hunched into his jacket, one foot tapping agitatedly on the floor. "So, how did you first enter play?"

"I'm not playing anything."

"You were there last night, weren't you?" He gestured toward her right hand and she felt a brief twinge where the stamp of the wheel had been. Or rather, where it still was. She could have sworn the last of the ink had washed off in the shower, but now she saw that a smudgy gray circle still lingered. Reflexively, she put her hand behind her back.

"Look, the only reason I was at that party was for the free booze. Sorry to be rude, but I think your gang's little fantasy world is a load of crap."

Toby didn't look offended. "Aw, don't tell me you aren't curious. Why else are you here?"

Cat realized she'd left *The Wondrous World of Tarot* face out. And of course he was right. "Maybe I do have some questions."

"And maybe I have some answers." He smirked. "Come here often, do you?"

"No."

"But you live nearby? You're a local?"

"I guess."

"A Soho girl! Cool," he said, a bit too eagerly, like he meant it.

"All right then," she said brusquely. "Tell me about this game of yours."

"I knew it. You're hooked." He leaned toward her, sandy hair falling into his eyes, and lowered his voice to a dark whisper. "It's not just a game, you see; it's a way of life—the gateway to another dimension!"

An older man had come into the basement and was looking at the fiction shelves, but he gave them no more than a passing glance. Cat supposed this kind of conversation was standard-issue for Dark Portal customers. "Let's stick with this dimension for now."

Toby took this as an invitation to begin. "As you know, the kings and queens are in charge of four courts: Wands, Swords, Cups and Pentacles," he began importantly. "Each of the courts possesses a number of different triumphs. They're the prizes. A knight has to play a round of cards to win them. Then, if he's successful, he'll win the triumph both for himself and his court."

"So it's just a competition to see who can collect the most triumph thingies."

"Well, the knights are trying to win the power a triumph represents, but the kings and queens hold the cards. You see?"

"Er . . . kind of," she said dubiously.

"Now, each card represents a test of some kind. Either you have to complete a task or escape a danger. Some cards are easy, and some are really nasty."

Cat nodded to show she was listening, a fixed smile on her face, as her fingers brushed the crumpled newsprint in her pocket.

"Is that what last night's Lottery was about? Swapping a nasty card for a nicer one?"

"That's the idea. Of course, knights hope the wheel will give them a better card than the one they've been dealt, but there's always the risk it could be worse."

"And what kind of, er, knight are you—I mean, which court do you belong to?"

"Ah, but I'm not a knight. I don't play for any court, either. No . . . I'm a chancer—a joker in the pack!" He gave a nervous giggle. "And you too, I think. That's why I made contact outside the Arcanum." He leaned toward her in a conspiratorial manner. "You see, now that the two of us are together, our alliance could have untold consequences for the State of Play."

Okaaay. Cat had had enough. She started edging toward the stairs. "Right, thanks for the explanation, then. It's been . . . interesting."

"You're not going already?" Toby's face crumpled with disappointment. "But we've got so much to talk about!"

"Sorry, but I really have to go."

"Oh. Well, maybe we should swap numbers, then."

She pretended she hadn't heard him. After all, she was already halfway up the stairs. "I'll leave my details by the Tarot book," he called plaintively as she reached the top. "And I guess I'll be seeing you around. . . ."

Not if I see you first, thought Cat.

But whether she liked it or not, Toby and his stories had got under her skin. His explanations only raised more doubts. And so, after leaving Dark Portal, she found herself heading for Temple House.

It took a while for her to find it again. The square wasn't off the street she thought it was, and she spent a frustrating half hour wandering around, trying to trace her route from the night before. And when she finally found it, the square was considerably less impressive than she remembered. The buildings looked shabbier in the cold light of day, their grandeur let down by ugly office conversions and dingy brickwork. The garden in the middle, which had seemed so abundant and mysterious in the dark, was just a scruffy grass space fringed by droopy-looking trees and a few shrubs.

Temple House wasn't as she remembered it, either. The paint on the door was peeling, the plasterwork cracked and stained. On a whim, she pushed the bell, but no signs of life came from behind the shuttered windows. A burger wrapper was half stuffed into the letter box. If she hadn't known better, she would have thought the place was derelict.

Cat slumped down on the steps, swearing under her breath. Her right hand had pins and needles, and she absently rubbed it against her jeans. What had she been expecting to find today, anyway? All this time wasted on tacky books and the ramblings of random nutcases. She didn't even know what she was looking for, she thought, as she stared into the garden. A gaggle of young guys in hooded sweatshirts were kicking a beer can around in a desultory sort of way. A tramp snored on a bench beneath a lopsided apple tree.

She took the newspaper page from her pocket and stared at the dead man's face, trying to imagine what she would say to a police officer. A man she couldn't positively identify, a hunt that had vanished into thin air, a game that might have turned murderous . . . It was all so far-fetched, and that was before she got to the bit about Temple House and *The Wondrous World of Tarot*. But if she was right, and the murder victim *was* the man she'd met, other people might have seen something that night. And even if she didn't understand what she'd stumbled into, the police might. . . .

Still, knowing what she should do didn't make it any easier to leap into action. Cat idled on the steps, fiddling with her hair and looking out over the square.

Some sort of confrontation had started between the tramp and the boys in hoods. She wasn't sure what was going on at first, because her vision was oddly unfocused, as if her eyes were out of sync. Then she blinked, and the unsteadiness cleared. She saw that the tramp had got up from his bench and was flailing his arms about and shouting, his ragged coattails flapping in the wind. His adversaries' goading laughter increased. One of them kicked the can they'd been playing ball with so that it clattered against the man's leg. It was the kind of scene you saw all the time. A young mother, wearily pushing a stroller along the pavement close to Cat, didn't even give it a second's glance. Nor did the couple climbing out of a taxi. Not even the boy at the other end of the square chucking pebbles at a tree-bound cat seemed to notice.

Then something changed. The tramp's voice rose again—harsh squawking, spat like a curse. The youths weren't laughing anymore; they stood together, hoods down, and there was something predatory about their stillness. One of them raised his arm. It was a strangely formal gesture, half command, half salute, and it was only then that Cat saw each of the four was grasping something in his right hand. Not knives: short wooden bats, like truncheons. She scrambled to her feet, adrenaline surging in her blood, her vision blurry with shock. Time seemed to slow. The scene before her had the private leisureliness of a nightmare.

And then the tramp took a card from his pocket and tore it in half. At once, the ground in front of him burst into flame.

It combusted with a soft *whump!* and spread into a ring of fire that lit the entire square. The gray air above it shimmered with heat; the apple tree was showered in sparks of gold. Cat opened her mouth to scream but no sound came. It was as if her breath was frozen in her throat. She spun around, gesturing in incoherent appeal to the woman with the baby, who was just five feet or so away. The woman looked up at her strangled half cry, then immediately hunched back over the stroller, paying no attention to the conflagration or the circling youths.

"Wait," Cat croaked. "We have to—someone—we must—someone must stop—"

But the woman was already hurrying away. Cat stumbled toward the railings, began to shout out something indistinguishable. The grass must have been soaked in gasoline and he'd thrown a match, that must be it. . . . It seemed impossible that the whole garden was not alight, yet both the tramp and his surroundings seemed immune to the flames. Meanwhile, the youths prowled, still tensed for action, occasionally jumping back as the breeze sent the fire licking toward them.

"Help! Please!" Cat begged, although she knew it was futile. A spark blew onto her cheek, and she slapped at it frantically. At the far end of the garden, the other boy loitered, his baiting of the cat abandoned. He, too, was staring— but not at the blaze. He was staring at her. So were the couple standing on the opposite side of the garden. Their faces were wrinkled with distaste. A car turned into the square, purred smoothly past and then out again.

It was then that the true horror of the situation took hold. Nobody else could see what was happening. As far as these others were concerned, the only strangeness in their afternoon was the crazy girl, babbling to herself and gesturing wildly at things that weren't there.

Cat clutched the iron railings so that the cold metal bit into her flesh. As she did so, she felt a twinge on her right palm. The mark of the wheel throbbed as it had in her dream; she could see the trace of it like a silvery, glowing scar. She cried out and closed her eyes and put her hands over her ears as if she could blot everything out, as if she could start over. And when she opened her eyes again, she was looking into a quiet London square. Not so much as a speck of ash remained; the empty beer can had vanished along with the tramp and his adversaries. Cat fell down on all fours and retched.

For what felt like a long time she squatted by the railings, sick to the pit of her stomach. After the heaving subsided, she found she couldn't stop shaking.

"Uh, are you OK?"

Somebody was crouched beside her. She nearly screamed before she realized that he wasn't one of the hooded youths with the bats, that he must be the boy who'd been throwing pebbles. He had a blunt, tough face and his bitten fingernails were grimy, but his expression was concerned. Or maybe just curious.

She licked her dry lips. "I felt a bit ill, that's all. I'm all right now." Get a grip, she had to get a grip. . . .

"You should go home."

His eyes fixed on hers. They were very dark, and ringed with the bruising of fatigue. He looked like a street kid, with his grubby hands and shapeless clothes, but he wasn't threatening. He was of her world. She felt an impossible urge to clutch hold of him as hard as those iron railings.

But whatever impulse had brought him over was already fading, for he had got to his feet and was slouching away.

The shaking and queasiness passed. Of course it did: Cat was tough, Cat wasn't the type to fuss. She wasn't crazy, either. Or dreaming. Or high. That's what was so terrifying. Her cheek still stung from the stray ember; she could smell smoke in her hair. The roar of the flames and the tramp's hoarse cries had been as clear and present as the uninterrupted grind of city traffic or the crying of the child in the stroller.

Toby's excitable voice echoed in her head. What had he called it? *Not just a game: a gateway to another dimension.* Cat gave a half laugh, half sob. Loneliness had become her natural state, but now she was a true exile. All thoughts of going to the police dissolved. No one would believe her, no one could help her.

Except one, she thought grimly. Toby.

KNIGHT OF WANDS

CHAPTER FOUR

WHEN CAT GOT BACK to the basement of Dark Portal, the book on Tarot had gone. There was, however, a folded-up piece of paper with her name on it tucked alongside the encyclopedia of Middle Earth. It contained a phone number and a hastily scrawled line:

> Hey Cat, hope you'll get in touch
> sometime (?) Toby.

Dizzy with relief, she found a bench not far from the shop and called the number, trying not to wonder what she'd do if he didn't pick up. When he finally answered, she clenched her fist, hard. "It's Cat. I need to see you."

"Hi, Cat! This is so great. I mean, it's great you got in touch. OK, so what do you—"

"I'm outside Dark Portal. Come now." Then she hit the off button, not trusting herself to speak any more.

They went to a run-down café around the corner. Toby was oddly proud of the place, glancing round with an almost proprietary air at the smoke-stained walls and grubby Formica. "This is the authentic Soho," he told her. "It's got real character, not like most of the neighborhood tourist traps."

Cat looked into her cup of overboiled coffee. What did this boy, with his cultured accent and ironically retro clothes, know about Soho's "character"? She'd bet *he* didn't live on the same street as a crappy casino and a strip joint.

Toby didn't seem to mind her continued silençe. His foot tapped nervously under the table, but away from the shop he seemed more relaxed. Pleased with himself. Cat noticed there was a fleck of milk froth on his upper lip. It was impossible that she could sit here in a normal café, surrounded by normal people, while the world as she knew it had just been wrenched into some parallel reality. Or Dark Portal. If it wasn't so terrifying, it would be ridiculous.

"Aren't you going to ask why I called you?" she said at last.

He glanced at her sidelong, his expression both sly and hopeful. "Well, I'm guessing it's to do with the Arcanum."

"I don't know what that means," she said. Deep breath. "All I know . . . is that I, uh, saw something that wasn't there. In the square by Temple House."

"Mercury Square."

"OK. Mercury Square. There was a tramp in the garden, see, and he got into an argument with some guys. They had these wooden . . . truncheon things and I thought there was going to be a fight." She took a sip of coffee to steady her, feeling the hot liquid scald her throat. "But then the tramp pulled out a card from his pocket and tore it in half. And suddenly the ground around him burst into flame. A whole wall of it, just like that. The fire was protecting him, keeping the others back. The thing was . . . the thing is, nobody else—the other passersby—could see what was happening. They thought I was out of my mind." She looked into her cup. "But I'm not, am I?"

"I doubt it," said Toby cheerfully. "What happened next?"

"I'm not sure. I closed my eyes. I felt like I was going to faint. Then when I opened them again, everything was back to normal and the people in the garden had . . . vanished."

Toby linked his hands round the back of his head and leaned back in his chair. "Interesting. Your tramp must've been using the Ace of Wands to defend himself. It's known as the Root of Fire."

"What the hell's that supposed to mean?"

"Have a look." He turned to rummage in his bag. "I bought this for you, just in case."

It was *The Wondrous World of Tarot*. Dumbly, Cat flicked through until she found an illustrated layout of the suit of Wands. The Ace was a disembodied hand grasping a flowering branch from which sparks flew.

"Fire, see? Each ace represents one of the four elements.

Like the Triumph of Fortune, they aren't dealt by the kings and queens, but pop up in the Arcanum for the knights to find. As a kind of lucky bonus. They even have a limited power in our own world, though using them here isn't as effective."

Cat could only stare back at him in incomprehension.

"This should also look familiar." Toby tapped a card called the Five of Wands, which showed a group of men in combat with thick wooden staffs. "From your description, I'd say it was the card you saw in play: the King of Wands' knaves ganging up on some knight. But somewhere along the way, he found an ace, and their plans—literally—went up in smoke."

He rambled on some more but Cat barely heard any of it. She had turned to the next page, which was a layout of Swords. "Wands and Swords," she whispered. "That's how it all started."

"Tell me about it," said Toby eagerly. And, haltingly, she did: everything that had happened from the moment she found herself standing by the heavy-breathing business-man in the Underground. But Toby didn't seem particularly concerned with the knight's fate. He was much more interested in her meeting with the kings and queens.

By the end he was beaming. "I knew it! Ha! You're another chancer, like me."

"Chancer?"

"The Triumph of the Fool. No offence or anything; it just means you're a bystander who accidentally altered the

State of Play. That makes you part of the Game without being, like, an official player. It means you can move around the Arcanum without belonging to a court. Which means—"

"Toby—"

"But what you have to—"

"Toby, wait—"

"We can—"

"SHUT UP! Shut up and listen." Cat took a deep, steadying breath. "OK. Here's the deal as I see it. A bunch of messed-up thrill seekers act out what's on Tarot cards: murder, arson, assault, whatever. Which is sick. Probably the sickest thing I've ever heard. And you don't even seem bothered that that man I met is probably *dead*. Even so, I get it. I can see how something like that works. But what I don't get is how all this is somehow taking place in a crazy parallel dimension that the rest of the world can't see." To her shame, her voice had started to crack. "Meanwhile, you're chattering away like we're swapping tips on freaking *Monopoly*. You say we're the same, but how do I know that? How do I know *anything*?"

Toby looked stricken. "I'm sorry. Sorry. Hell—I can see I've gone about this all wrong. I'd forgotten what a shock it is—finding out, I mean. And I'm not a sociopath or anything . . . I promise." He blushed furiously beneath the freckles. "But I'd been dreaming of finding something like the Arcanum for most of my life."

Cat bit her lip. "The Arcanum—is that what you call the . . . the . . . place where I saw the tramp and the fire? And the inside of Temple House?"

"The Arcanum is where the Game is played: the Game's board, you might say. It's going into the Arcanum that brings a player's card to life. If it'll make you feel any better, it's not technically a different world from ours. At least, I don't think so."

"But—"

"Picture it as the reverse of a card." Toby sounded relieved to be returning to practical matters. He picked up the greasy menu on the table and turned it over in demonstration. "Or the two sides of a coin. The same thing, just a different view."

Cat's brain felt blurred by the enormity of what was happening. She shook her head in frustration. "If the garden I was looking at belonged to the Arcanum side, I don't understand how I was able to see it without . . . I dunno . . . saying the magic words or going through the magic door or . . ."

"Sounds like you weren't actually in the Arcanum proper, more like looking in. I expect that's because you were so close to Temple House, which is common to both our side and the Arcanum—and not wholly belonging to either. There's bound to be an overlap, especially if a card's in play there."

"So how do you get in . . . properly?"

"You toss a coin."

"Seriously."

"I am serious. Find a threshold, then toss the coin that'll appear. Thresholds are like switches to flip you over to the other side. You come across them wherever there's the sign of the wheel." He held up the palm of his right hand, and she saw that he too bore a faint circular mark divided by four spokes. "This gets going when you're close to one; like a compass, almost."

Cat stared at her palm, remembering how it had burned as she'd clutched the garden railings and looked into a world that shouldn't have been there. She shook her head in frustration.

"But when I met the knight being chased in the street, I wasn't in the Arcanum—I couldn't have been. Neither was he. The King of Swords said he'd 'left his move.' "

"You first saw him in the Tube, right? Well, there must've been a threshold to the Arcanum in the station. From what you've told me, it sounds like as soon as the knight realized what the Ten of Swords had in store for him, he lost his nerve and tried to back out. But it was too late for second thoughts, and the Knaves of Swords came after him anyway. Once a player takes his card into the Arcanum, he has to at least attempt to win it."

"Even if his move will end in *murder*?"

"Nothing shown on the cards is inevitable. It's how a player reacts to the challenge of the move that counts."

The Knight of Wands—Anthony Linebeg—had asked her for help, and she . . . Nausea rose in her throat.

"The knight I met might have escaped," she said unsteadily, "if it hadn't been for me."

Toby looked at her solemnly. "He should never have involved you in the first place. It was a stupid risk and you had no way to know. The only people with blood on their hands are the King of Swords and his knaves."

Cat thought of Alastor's sleepy smiles, his tousle-haired charm. Her face hardened. Toby was right.

"So the knaves are the kings' and queens' hit squad."

"Knaves are players who've tried to cheat. They might have got bystanders involved or attempted to sabotage other players, caused trouble at the Lotteries . . . that sort of thing. They have to pay a forfeit by acting as servants to the courts. Sometimes this only lasts for one move, sometimes for a whole round or longer."

She shivered. "Knights . . . knaves . . . I don't get why any of them would gamble their lives on some crazy trial by ordeal."

"Duh! They do it for the prizes, of course. Don't you understand? Once a triumph is awarded to a knight, its powers become *real.*" His eyes shone. "Think of what those cards represent! They can heal the sick, reverse time, make people fall in love, turn a person into a millionaire or a super-model. . . . And that's just for starters."

Cat thought back to the prize-giving after the Lottery, when the Knight of Pentacles had been given a silver die by the King of Swords. *The powers of the Devil will be yours.*

"What does that mean for the girl who won the Devil last night? Sex, drugs and rock 'n' roll, you said."

"Exactly. She's going to enjoy a lifetime of debauchery without any of the side effects. No more hangovers or trips to rehab."

"And the woman who did the Lottery . . . the one who wanted the Triumph of the Moon. What would she get out of it?"

"Inspiration. If she wins that triumph, she'll finish her book or painting or whatever it was, and it will be a guaranteed work of genius. Whatever you want, whatever you dream of, the Game can make it true." He paused. "As long as you're a knight, that is."

Toby's eager expression faded. "We chancers can wander around the Arcanum, but we can't really play—not for prizes anyway . . ."

"So how did you know I was one of these chancer types and not a knight?"

"I arrived at Temple House just behind you. I saw you hand over your invite—the Fool—but lost you after I entered the party. As you probably found, that place is weirdly disorienting. Maybe it's a side effect of being on two sides of the threshold at once."

"You seem to be quite the expert."

"But I'm not," he said earnestly. "I'm an amateur, really, trying to pick up stuff here and there. That's why it's so great I met you. Chancers are rare, but now the two of us have teamed up—"

She laughed sourly. "If you think I'm getting any more involved, then you're even crazier than those royals of yours."

"What?" Toby was incredulous. "Look, I realize you're probably still in shock and everything, but you need to give the Game a chance."

Cat got to her feet. "There doesn't seem any point if I can't win a prize."

"But you can still experience the Arcanum! The prizes are only part of what it has to offer."

"Magic? Mystery? Adventure?"

"Absolutely." Toby didn't seem to notice the sarcasm in her voice. His cheeks were flushed and his eyes bright. "Chancers don't have to work through the cards' obstacles like knights do, or serve the courts like the knaves. We're free agents."

"In that case, I'm free to walk away. None of this has anything to do with me; it was a mistake from the start."

For once, Toby didn't shuffle or fidget, but stared back at her levelly. "That's a load of crap and you know it." She opened her mouth to protest but Toby swept on. "You might've been drawn in by accident, but you still *chose* to get involved. You followed the Knight of Wands. You went to the Lottery. You asked your questions. When you left me at Dark Portal, you went straight to Temple House. So you're obviously not as detached from things as you pretend to be."

"Yeah, well, if I'd known what I was getting into, I would've detached myself a hell of a lot earlier."

"Would you? Can you look me in the eye and tell me that this isn't the most amazing thing that has ever happened to you—will ever happen to you in your entire life?"

"That's not the point," she said, but her voice was uncertain.

Toby's face was alight with missionary zeal. "Come with me into the Arcanum. Just one visit to one move. We'll get ready for it together, go in side by side. After that, if you still don't want to be involved, I'll leave you alone. I swear."

There was a long pause. "I'll think about it," said Cat, and then she left him.

CHAPTER FIVE

IT WAS STILL EARLY in the afternoon when Cat got back to the flat, and she was sure she was too wired even to sit down. But the moment she closed the door of her cupboard-sized room, she sank onto her bed and into a dreamless sleep. When she woke up, groggy and disoriented, it was to find she'd been out for nearly six hours.

By the sound of it, the Saturday-night revelries were already well under way: music throbbed, engines revved, catcalls and laughter floated up from the street below. For a moment, she lay there drowsily, and it was as if she was still the old Cat, the Cat from before. The feeling only lasted for a few seconds, though. Knowledge came jolting back and she sat up, breathless.

"Well then," she found herself saying out loud, "I guess it's time I made a move."

She didn't quite know how she'd reached this decision,

but it came as a relief. *The Wondrous World of Tarot,* Toby's present, was poking out from under her bed, and she gave it a contemptuous kick. To hell with Toby—she didn't want a chaperone. She was the Cat who walked by herself. Once I find a threshold, I'll keep it quick, she promised herself. In and out. New energy surged through her and she found she was humming a recent chart hit in the bathroom, then grinning to herself as she rummaged through the fridge. What did she need to take with her? The usual collection of wallet, keys, phone? God, the whole thing was *crazy.* . . . "Crazy, crazy, crazy," she chanted to herself as she clattered out of the flat and into the street.

After half an hour of wandering around, however, her newfound recklessness began to desert her. She kept checking her palm but the skin was unmarked. She felt cheated. Toby had said that thresholds popped up anywhere and everywhere, but what if there wasn't one in this part of the city at all? The obvious thing to do would be to try Temple House again, but the memory of the ring of fire filled her with dread.

Then, finally, she felt it. A pins-and-needles sensation in her palm as she approached Seven Dials, a small junction between Covent Garden and Soho. The streets running off it were busy and brightly lit, and the column in the center of the crossroads served as a gathering point for people swigging from cans and chatting on phones. She walked up to the pillar, heart thumping. It was in fact a sundial about fifteen feet high, on a circular base with shallow steps. Just above the base she saw that the mark of the wheel, three inches or so in diameter, had been carved into the stone pedestal. Now what? Toby had said a coin would just "appear," but the only money she could find was a penny lying beside a discarded cinema ticket. Feeling slightly foolish, she gave it a flip, and didn't know whether to be relieved or disappointed when nothing happened.

Cat looked at the carving again. The closer she got to it, the more her palm tingled. Hesitantly, she reached out a finger and traced the lines of the wheel. Four spokes and a circle. As she closed the circle, she had to snatch her hand away, for the print of the wheel on her palm was now a burning silver scar. Instinctively, she straightened out her hand. And then, so quickly that she didn't even have time to cry out, the circle on her flesh throbbed and solidified into a disc of metal.

It was blank-faced and heavy, made of some dully gleaming black metal. It looked just like the coin the doorkeeper had thrown to her on the night of the Lottery. The only marking on it was a little icon of a sword.

Cat knew that if she hesitated now, she would lose her nerve. And so, before she had time to think, she tossed the coin high into the air.

Though she'd thrown it clumsily, the coin landed in the center of her palm. The wheel there burned beneath it, flesh and metal merged into one, and the next second her hand was both empty and unmarked. She looked up and saw, with an incredulous jolt, that the world had changed.

It appeared to be dawn, for a primrose light was just

breaking overhead. After the wintry night she'd come from, the air felt softer, fresh. It was eerily quiet—no traffic, no people, not even any birdsong.

Otherwise, her surroundings corresponded almost exactly to the ones she'd left behind. Even the shop fronts were alike, though their signs were unpainted and the windows bare or else boarded up. And yet . . . Her mother had had a kaleidoscope, like a little bronze telescope, which was now Cat's. She had been fascinated by it as a kid, the way the shifting glass beads transformed into a myriad of different patterns as you turned the wheel. Looking at this other street, in this other city, was like giving the kaleidoscope the gentlest tap, the tiniest turn—the pattern of things was only slightly altered, yet completely different. Like the column: on her side, the stone was a light and rather grubby gray; here it was black marble and only had four dial faces at its top. But the carving of the wheel was the same, and when, with a trembling hand, she began to trace its lines, the burning in her hand told her the same dark coin was ready to appear and take her home.

Cat took her hand away before tracing the final curve of the circle. Then she clenched her jaw, lifted her chin and stepped down from the column into the cool summer's morning of the Arcanum.

It was then that she realized she wasn't alone, after all. A woman was standing under a lamppost about ten yards away, eating a chocolate bar and watching Cat through narrowed eyes. She had a shrewd, snub sort of face and was dressed like she was going to the gym. Now she tossed the chocolate wrapper to the ground and came over. "Who are you?" she challenged.

"I'm, uh . . ." How had Toby put it? "I'm a chancer."

At this, the woman's eyes widened, and she gave a bark of laughter. "Well now," she said, "there's a rarity."

"Who are you, then?"

"Knight of Swords, of course. The mark on your coin could've told you that."

So the coin didn't just flip her over to the Arcanum; it also told her which of the four courts was in play there. "I see. So are you . . . do you, erm, have one of those cards?"

"How else would I have got here? It's *my* card that has made this move. You're just a bystander, so you'd better not interfere."

Cat ignored her sneer. "What prize are you playing for?" she asked.

"The Triumph of the Emperor."

"Oh. Er . . . does that mean you'll get to be a sort of . . . king?"

"I'll get to be the boss. Leadership—that's my prize. Once I've won the Emperor, I won't have to take crap from anyone ever again. There'll be no more glass ceilings to smash or greasy poles to climb. I'll finally be where I deserve to be: at the top."

"But what about the risks?"

"Everything in life is a gamble," the Knight of Swords retorted. "The business world's no different from the Arcanum in that respect." Then she seemed to soften a little.

"Still, here I am in my fourth move. Lady Luck hasn't deserted me yet."

"And if you win your fourth card, you'll get your triumph."

The woman gave another short, hard laugh. "If only. No, you have to play a triumph card to get its power. The fifth and final card in my round will be the Emperor himself. As for this one . . ." She felt in her pocket. "Take a look."

Cat backed away.

"There's no need to be afraid. It's not a bad card to be dealt. Six of Cups, the Reign of Past Pleasure."

Cat looked at the card. It seemed to have a faint glow about it, or perhaps that was just the hazy morning sunshine that had begun to fill the street. The picture showed two children playing in the yard of a great house. They were smiling, surrounded by jeweled cups that spilled over with flowers. The walls of the house behind them were high and golden, the sky a radiant blue. As she gazed at the scene, memories of lost and half-forgotten happiness began to stir.

"Pretty, isn't it?" said the knight. She had a faraway look in her eyes. "For there's beauty in this Game, as well as bloodshed. Wonder and glory, too . . ." Then she gave herself a shake. "But I can't stand around chatting. It's time to face whatever challenge this move offers. Wish me luck, Chancer."

She gave Cat a brisk nod, then walked down the street to a door that Cat hadn't noticed before. It certainly wasn't there on the home side: made from ancient blackened wood and set in a narrow strip of wall between two of the empty shop fronts. It looked as though it hadn't been opened for years. But it swung open at the Knight of Swords' touch and a moment later she was gone.

The place felt even more silent and deserted afterward. Cat looked back at the sundial, but it would be lame to go home now, before she'd really seen or done anything. Her anxieties had faded away; somehow, the mere sight of the card had left her with a sense of peace. And she now saw that there was another door just across the street from the one the knight had gone through. This one was ajar.

Its wood was warm to the touch, as if it had been baking in the sun for a long time. Behind it, she could hear children's laughter, high and clear, and her throat ached with some nameless longing: The Reign of Past Pleasure . . . She pushed the door open and stepped through.

It was as if she'd walked into the card itself. She was standing on a smooth lawn enclosed by high, golden walls. Pale flowers bloomed everywhere, their scent so rich she could almost taste it. Facing her was the front of a great and ageless house built of honey-colored stone. Its windows glittered, but where the rest of the garden should have been reflected, there was only the blue dazzle of sky.

It was beautiful. The most beautiful place Cat had ever seen. But even so, she wasn't able to concentrate on it properly. What she really wanted was waiting for her in the house, calling her name, and the farther she walked, the larger the yard seemed to grow. She knew that this didn't make sense; that there was a city surrounding the garden walls, and another city somehow beyond that, but it didn't matter. For the first time since the strangeness of the Game of Triumphs had begun, she felt that she really could be in a dream.

At last, she reached the paved walkway outside the building. There was a glass-fronted door ahead but, like the windows, the view it reflected was disorienting: fragments of brightness where her own image should have been. As she walked up to it, the sweetness of the flowers and the humming of the bees, the warm blue air and distant laughter, surged over and through her. And somehow the glass surged too, a liquid dazzle that drew her in.

Then, suddenly, she was home. Her first home, her real home, with her mum and dad. The little terrace house that had faded to the memory of a memory, except for a few snapshots and a fleeting reference or two of Bel's. She was sitting at her mum's feet in the living room, and there was a toy truck nearby, but it didn't interest her much because she was busy peering at the carpet. It had very fascinating swirls of cream and brown. Like ice cream. She pushed her finger into the nap and then sucked its tip hopefully, just in case. Something tickled and it was her mother, bending to kiss her, her long hair swinging over Cat's face, shiny and soft and smelling like apples.

"Where's my Kitty-cat?" called a voice.

She stumbled to her unsteady toddler's feet and ran to Daddy, who was standing at the door and swung her up and blew into her neck until she was breathless with squeals. And over his shoulder, she could see the hallway and the little strip of yard beyond, with her orange plastic slide and

Mummy's flowers. Only they weren't there; there was just a muddle, shining, and so bright it hurt to look at. But it didn't matter, nothing mattered, because she was safe at home with Mummy and Daddy like they always were and would always be, always, always, always. . . .

And then it was Christmas, Christmas with a real live tree all goldy-glittery with chocolate money, and a rainbow of greeting cards on every shelf. The money and the cards reminded her of something, but then Mummy came over with lots of boxes, and she forgot again, because the paper was slippery and rustling and she could stomp through it like puddles . . . and after that it was her birthday, and more boxes, with a fat pink cake and candles she wasn't allowed to touch but were the prettiest things she'd ever seen, so Daddy lit them again, and blew them out, and lit them, and blew them out, again and again and again, just for her.

So many times . . . some of them flashing past quick as lightning, others languorously prolonged, but all of them, always, the best and most perfect. . . . Sometimes she was Kitty, tumbling about on the floor, and at others she was Cat, watching herself from a very great distance. Something about this bothered her, but only a little, like an itch she couldn't reach. She knew that if she shut her mind to the itching it would go away, but this didn't feel right, almost as if she needed the itch to be there. . . .

At last, there came an afternoon when she was playing in Mummy and Daddy's room, making hidey-houses under the bed. But someone had been there before her, doing their own hiding: a card tucked into the frame, with a glittery picture on the front. Secret treasure!

There was something important about this treasure, something she wanted to remember, and so she took the card to the window, though the light was usually too bright and muddly to look at. But she did it anyway, and now she was looking through grown-up eyes, reading words that were funny scribbles to Kitty, but of terrible significance to Cat.

The Arcanum
Temple House, Mercury Square

Admits One

Throw the coin, turn the card.
What will you play for?

And afterward, when she looked through the window, the view showed somewhere different, somewhere wrong. Then the shining became so bright it hurt all over, and she dropped the card and squeezed her eyes shut and put her hands over her ears—but even that didn't help because when she opened her eyes again, everything had changed.

At once, she knew something terrible was going to happen, so terrible she couldn't bear it. She tried to tell her mummy and daddy but they didn't understand, they kept on tickling her with shiny-soft hair and swinging her over their shoulders and bringing her boxes and blowing out candles again and again and all the time she knew the terrible nameless thing was coming, just round the corner, and there was nothing she could do. Until there she was, Kitty, huddled on the stairs hours past bedtime, watching through a gap in the door as three people talked in the living room.

"This isn't a game," Mummy was saying, and her voice had a crack in it.

"It is the *only* Game," replied a voice Kitty didn't know. A murmuring voice, with a slight stammer. "And I intend to w-win it."

"What do you mean by that?" her daddy asked.

"I mean that I'm going to t-take what's due to me," said the stranger. "Starting with the Arcanum's card."

Then Mummy and Daddy began speaking at once, high and quick.

"Please. There's been some mistake," Mummy was saying. "We can't—" And Daddy began to shout, shouting at someone she couldn't see, but there was a flash and two cracks and a burning smell, and Kitty crouched on the stairs and Cat floating at a great distance both screamed. Because hair had spilled across the carpet, the hair that smelled like apples and the carpet with the ice-cream swirls, both of which were now speckled with hot sharp red. And her screaming went on and on and into a terrible silence that became a surge of blackness and blindness and splintering glass.

The house reared up behind her, gray-faced, its windows gaping darkly. The paving stones were cracked, and greasy with rain. She began to sob. She was still sobbing as she lurched across the tangle of yellowing grass and briar that had once been a lawn, and shouldered her way through the shards of rotting wood that had once been a door. And she sobbed yet harder as she stumbled up to the sundial, traced the wheel and spun her cold hard coin up, over and away.

ETERNITY

CHAPTER SIX

FOR A WHILE, IT didn't look as if the bouncer at the Palais Luxe was going to let her in. Not that she could blame him: quite apart from the fact that no one under eighteen was supposed to set foot inside a casino, she was finding it extraordinarily difficult to string any sort of sentence together. But after repeating Bel's name for the fifth or sixth time, he did a series of mutters into his walkie-talkie and, suddenly, Bel was standing in the musty lobby. Saying her name. Asking if she was all right. Was she hurt, was she sick, was the flat—

"No," Cat said dazedly. "I'm not hurt. I just . . . I really need to talk to you."

Bel gave her a long look and a short nod. "In you come."

The bouncer was still grumbling about regulations and licenses, but Bel shooed him away with one hand, and hustled Cat up the stairs with the other. The next thing she knew, Bel was shepherding her into the tiny kitchen by Greg's office. There she set about making two mugs of sweet, dusty-tasting tea. It was only after she'd watched Cat take an obedient gulp that she spoke again. "Now then," she said. "What's all this about?"

Cat stared at the clock on the wall. Half past nine. She had been in the Arcanum for less than an hour. The clock ticked, the tea steamed, murmurs and exclamations came from the gaming floor below. Cat had hundreds, thousands, of things she wanted to say, all of them impossible.

"I . . . I want to know about Mum and Dad."

"You . . . what?" Bel frowned. Whatever she'd been expecting, it wasn't this.

"Caroline and Adam Harper. My parents." The clock ticked on: twitch-tock, twitch-tock. "They didn't die in a car accident, did they? Somebody shot them."

Twitch-tock, twitch-tock, twitch-tock. Bel made a small muffled sound. She put her hand to her throat. "How do—? Where—? Who've you been talking to?"

"So it's true," Cat said dully. She saw the spill of hair and blood, swirls of brown and cream. The Arcanum hadn't lied.

Bel's hand was still fluttering at her neck. "I'm sorry. Cat, I . . . God, I . . . I thought it would be better, you see. Better for you not to know. You were so small. . . ."

"Tell me what happened."

"Christ." Underneath the fluorescent strip that lit the kitchen, Bel's face was sallow and tired; the tight polyester shirt she was wearing had damp patches under the arms.

She took a wavering breath. "It was a burglary, see. A burglary gone wrong. The police figured some smackhead was looking for something to steal, and your mum and dad . . . well, they got in the way."

"Did—did they catch the person who did it?"

"No. Could've been any old street scum. Odds are, whoever did it was lying dead in a ditch before the year was out. That's what I like to think, anyway."

Cat pushed her mug away, feeling sick.

Bel went on quickly, nervously. "Maybe I should've told you the truth, but how do you explain something like that to a three-year-old? I didn't want to go scaring you witless about men with guns and whatnot. Jeez, I was practically a kid myself. . . . I did mean to tell you, when you got older, but it never seemed the right time. And what purpose would it serve?"

Twitch-tock, twitch-tock, twitch-tock.

"But I saw it happen," Cat mumbled. "I *saw* them get killed, Bel. I—I remember now."

Bel was very gentle. "No, love," she said. "No, you couldn't have. You were staying round a neighbor's that night, thank God. You probably just, I dunno, overheard someone talking about it when you were little? But . . . I don't understand. Why would you remember now? What brought this on?"

"I don't know. I don't know *anything*. I don't—I can't—I—"

Cat found she was crying again, a dry, almost mechanical heaving that she couldn't seem to control. After that, things became blurred. She had a hazy impression of Bel in whispered conversation by the door, of being gathered up and taken back to the flat, where Bel undressed her and tucked her up in bed like a little kid, murmuring her name over and over, like a lullaby. And although Bel's hug smelled of cheap perfume and cigarettes, it was the scent of apples that drifted after her into dream.

Sunday morning was the most painful waking she had ever had.

The truth was, if she'd found out about her parents' deaths in the ordinary course of things—overheard gossip, an ancient newspaper clipping—she wasn't sure how badly it would have affected her. She would have been angry, of course, and sad, but it would almost have been like over-hearing a story from somebody else's life. After all, she'd worked hard on forgetting her loss, until she became used to telling people that she couldn't miss what she'd never known. She almost believed it, too. But the Six of Cups had given back memories that were too glowing and abundant with love to ever be lost again.

And if she trusted those memories about Christmas trees and cake and the rest of it, she had to trust the other one. The one she shouldn't—couldn't—have. The memory of the third person she'd heard in the living room that final night, the man with the stammer. *It is the only Game. And I intend to w-win it.*

If she closed her eyes, she could see the cozy darkness under her parents' bed again, and relive the thrill of discovery as her chubby toddler's fingers closed on the stiff colored paper with the gold trim. What was the card doing there? Did one of her parents plan to play the Game? The idea sickened her. Because their life had been *perfect*; the Six of Cups had proved that. Caroline, Adam and Kitty Harper had everything they could ever want. Her parents wouldn't risk all that happiness in pursuit of some weird otherworldly prize.

No. Probably one or the other of them had stumbled on the card without knowing what it was. *There's been some mistake*—that's what her mother had said. How the stranger knew about the card, and what had become of it, was another matter entirely.

News of a twelve-year-old murder would be hard to track down, but not impossible. There was a twenty-four-hour Internet café on Berwick Street. It was, Cat decided, as good a place as any to start.

It was barely daylight when she slipped out of the flat, moving quietly so as not to wake Bel. The Internet café was empty except for a couple of bleary-eyed backpackers, so she had a row of computers to herself. For the first ten minutes she didn't do anything, just stared at her screen. Who was she kidding? She wasn't ready for this. She never would be. All the same, she brought up a search engine and started to type.

She began with her parents' names, the northern industrial town where they had lived and the year that they had died. When that didn't produce anything useful, she looked for a regional newspaper. The website she found only provided news items from a year or so back, but when she checked its archive, she was directed to an online research service, with links to "related articles." There was a free three-day trial offer.

A few seconds later, Cat was looking at the photograph she had framed on her bedside table: Caroline, Adam and Kitty Harper, picnicking in a sunlit park. Above her parents' smiling faces was the tabloid headline: "Double Murder— Young Couple Slain!"

She braced herself to relive the horror she'd witnessed in the Six of Cups. But the real pain of reading the newspaper reports was how bland they were: a clichéd mix of sensationalism and statistics. Neither the national nor local press suggested that the crime could be anything other than a robbery gone wrong. The Harper family had lived on a respectable residential street, but one which was close to an area plagued by drugs and gun crime. There was no mention of Tarot cards or mysterious games. "Broken society" was to blame.

Numbly, Cat read that Caroline and Adam Harper had left behind a daughter, aged three, who was being cared for by relatives. Neighbors agreed what a nice, polite couple the victims were. Police urged witnesses to come forward. The local Member of Parliament wrung his hands. What a shock. What a tragedy. What a bloody shame.

Yet the fact was, her parents' deaths had had little impact on the wider world. They were newcomers to the town, where they had lived quiet lives, absorbed with their child, and each other. Caroline's mother and father were dead;

Adam's lived in Australia. They were dead now, too, Bel said. She and Cat were the only survivors.

Photographs, postcards, a handful of knickknacks . . . her father's hair and her mother's eyes . . . It wasn't much of an inheritance. Cat and Bel traveled light, always thinking ahead, careless of the past. If there had been any other clue to her parents' fate, it had been lost long ago.

Cat stared at her screen with unseeing eyes. She knew that whatever the police or Bel or anyone else believed, her parents hadn't been killed by some crazed drug addict. It had been done by someone in control of themselves and the situation. Someone looking for an Arcanum card.

Three-year-old Kitty and fifteen-year-old Cat . . . neither of them would have seen the murder if it wasn't for the kaleidoscopic shiftings of the Arcanum.

If the crime had been committed in the Game's name, by one of its players, then Cat's only hope of resolving it lay in the Arcanum. Would she be able to see more if she went back?

Seven Dials at half past eight on a Sunday morning had the same air of abandonment as it had on the other side of the threshold the night before. The shop fronts and windows were all shut up, and the streets were deserted apart from the occasional taxi, or all-night reveler plodding off for breakfast and bed. When Cat approached the column, she found she was shaking all over. Grief and anger, but longing, too: the hope of returning to that golden house. Of going home.

So when her palm remained blank, and no trace of

carving on the column could be found, she refused to believe it. But no matter how many times she circled the sundial, alternately cursing and pleading under her breath, nothing changed. The threshold was gone, and the Six of Cups with it.

Toby wasn't as pleased to hear from her as she'd expected. In fact, their initial exchange was a series of grunts on his part. Cat thought she heard muttering in the background. "A *friend,*" Toby said, away from the phone. "Yes, I do have them, OK?" The background voice grew querulous in tone. "It's none of your business who I—" Crackle of static. Footsteps, a slammed door. "Sorry about that. Parents, y'know?"

Cat bit her lip. "Uh, anyway . . . I was thinking about yesterday and I think maybe you're right. About going into the Arcanum, I mean."

This time, his response was more what she'd been expecting. "So," he said in a hopeful rush, "do you want to come over to my place? We can throw some ideas around, draw up an action plan. . . ."

Cat sighed, but if she was going to get any further, she needed a guide. And right now, Toby was all she had. She took down his directions and agreed to meet him in an hour.

"One thing," she said.

"Yes?"

"How do most people join the Game? If chancers are rare, how do normal players—knights—get involved?"

"Ah!" He sounded pleased with the question. "There've always been rumors about the Game: hints and gossip, speculation on the Internet, even. Some people spend their whole lives trying to find a way in. But invitations turn up randomly, so it's completely down to luck.

"Chancers begin with the Triumph of the Fool, but a knight is invited with a Triumph of Eternity card. Then he goes to Temple House and joins the Game—just like you did. Except he gets to choose what triumph to play for. Obviously, he can't play on behalf of whichever court currently holds it, so the other three courts draw lots to see which of them he'll join. Then they explain the rules, deal the cards, and his round begins."

"Right, fine—but back to the invitations—where do they *come* from?" asked Cat.

"No one really knows. I heard there's one book on this one shelf in the Bodleian Library in Oxford, right, which has the Triumph of Eternity tucked in its pages. And there's a story that every time a certain Old Master painting comes on the art market, whoever buys it finds an invitation stuck on the back. On the other hand, there must be people who get a card but don't follow it up." He gave a disbelieving laugh. "As if a ticket to the Arcanum was just another bit of junk mail!"

That might account for how an invitation came to be in her parents' house. Even though it didn't quite explain why the card had been hidden under the bed . . . What was junk to some was a prize worth killing for to others. After she said goodbye to Toby, Cat stared at her palm, thinking of the throb and burn that conjured metal out of flesh and spun the ordinary world out of reach.

Bel shuffled into the kitchen just as Cat was getting ready to go out again. She didn't look as if she'd slept much and she wore a hesitant, most un-Bel-like smile. Would Cat like to get a coffee? Do some shopping? Go for a walk? Or . . . ? Cat felt bad, saying thanks, but no, she kind of fancied being on her own for a bit. But as she went to leave, Bel hugged her, fierce and hard, and suddenly things were better.

Toby lived at the top of a grand redbrick building in North London. As Cat stepped out of the creaking elevator, she prepared herself for olde-worlde splendour, but the flat that Toby showed her into, although large, felt cluttered and uncared for. Books were everywhere, stacked high in teetering piles; dirty mugs, bric-a-brac and bundles of paper covered every surface. "Writers, both of 'em," said Toby, with offhand pride. "It's OK, though. Ma's gone to the library and Pa's holed up in his study. We won't be disturbed."

Cat followed Toby through the hallway into his bedroom. It was much tidier than the rest of the flat, with pride of place given to a tabletop model landscape on which miniature knights and goblins were arranged in battle lines. Some kind of war game, she guessed, remembering the figurines from Dark Portal. There was a shelf of books, most but not all sci-fi and fantasy titles, and a collection of 1950s B-movie posters on the walls.

Her attention moved from a poster for *Revenge of the Mutant Swamp Blob!*—buxom babes versus toxic slime—to a black-and-white print of a fantastic city. The city was a labyrinth of crazy angles and dizzy perspectives, where lizard-like creatures scuttled up stairs that led to nowhere, windows opened to impossible views and figures sleepwalked off precipices.

"A postcard from the Arcanum?" she asked, being flip.

But Toby took the question seriously. "Could be. The Game of Triumphs has been going for centuries. All sorts of people have played, including artists. Escher might well have been a knight. There's always speculation about visionaries and prodigies—da Vinci, Darwin, David Beckham!"

Toby laughed, but the idea that this thing had been going on throughout history sent a chill down Cat's spine. Still, she reassured herself, this was why she'd come over. Toby was the expert.

"So how long have our gang of Game Masters been involved?"

"Nobody knows for sure. Apparently they were ordinary players once. But now, they're said to be immortal. It's one of the perks of the job."

"Immortal," she repeated blankly. "Bloody hell . . . But—but—how did this happen? Were they knights who got promoted or something? Is that possible?"

"Everything's possible in the Game." Toby lowered his voice in the way he did when he was trying to come over all dark and mysterious. "One theory is that if you catch one of the kings or queens breaking the rules, you can take their place. Then there's a rumor that whoever finds the Triumph of Eternity in the Arcanum gets to be the top Game Master of all. But that really *is* just a rumor. Eternity's on the invitation cards, but nobody seems to know exactly what the prize is or how you win it. It's certainly not in the Game Masters' collection. . . .

"Anyway. The official route to royalty is to win all the triumphs held by the courts. But instead of claiming the prizes, you keep the amulets."

"Amulet? Oh . . . the little colored balls? From the prize-giving?"

"The very ones. You cast them over the threshold of Temple House to take a triumph's power. But a player who wants to be king saves them up. And when you have them all, the king or queen you've taken the most from is the GM you overthrow."

Cat was beginning to see how some people might think that winning a triumph was worth the risk of the Game. However, she could hardly imagine what it would take to win *one* triumph, let alone all of them.

"That doesn't sound much fun. All the pain and none of the prizes."

"Ah, but once you get to GM level, you won't have much need for fame and wealth and the rest of it. You're a god of the Arcanum!"

"A supernatural member of the control-freak club."

"But the kings and queens aren't in *total* control," Toby said earnestly. "Yes, they deal the cards and, yes, they enforce the rules. But they can't win the triumphs by themselves: it's up to the knights in their court. And how the cards come to life, and how the knights play them, is completely out of their hands."

Cat's head was spinning. It was all too much to take in—and she still had so many more questions to ask.

"OK. Back up. So knights are dealt numbered cards to play in order to win a triumph card. And once you've played *it,* a share of its power is yours to keep. Right?"

"Right."

"But what about the cards for the kings and queens, and knights and knaves, too? Plus the Fool card for us, of course. Can you be dealt one of those?"

"The face cards represent players, not moves. But they can still be introduced into the Game. Imagine two knights are playing for the same triumph, and they finish the fourth card in their round at the same time. Instead of letting them try to win the triumph in turns, the Game Masters think it's more entertaining if they play for it simultaneously. Knight versus knight, winner takes all. In which case, they'll each be dealt their opponent's card along with the triumph card." He paused. "That's actually how I first got involved in the Game."

"Really?"

Toby looked smug. "I overheard this girl and a teacher at school talking about the Game. It turns out they were rival knights for the same triumph. I saved the girl's life and got made a chancer as reward."

"Doesn't seem like much of a reward to me."

"You don't mean that! We're part of a noble tradition. An immortal contest! Think of all those who have walked the Arcanum before us: poets, soldiers, madmen, geniuses. . . ."

"Madmen sounds about right," Cat retorted. Toby's

starstruck tone annoyed her. "What is it with you people? The Knight of Swords was the same. Wittering on about the Game's wonder and glory."

"Knight? What knight?"

"Oh. Yeah. The thing is . . . I went into the Arcanum yesterday."

"You went *without* me?" He sat there gawping at her, all shocked and wounded-looking. "But I thought we—"

"Look, I just wanted to see it for myself, OK? No big deal."

"What happened?" he asked breathlessly. "What was it like? What did you do? What was the card in play?"

"The woman I met, Swords, had been given the Six of Cups."

"No way! Isn't that the one to do with good times and old memories and stuff? Did you . . . ?"

Cat had no intention of sharing what had happened with Toby. All she wanted from him was information: how to play the Game, how to get back into the Six of Cups, and how to navigate what she found there. She struggled to sound offhand. "It was a trip down memory lane, all right. Like being a little kid again. Tell you the truth, it's a bit of a blur."

Toby's face glowed. "Sounds amazing. I can't wait for my first go."

"What do you mean, 'go'?"

"My first trip into the Arcanum, of course."

Cat thought she had misheard. Or misunderstood. "But you've been doing this for ages."

"I've been in and out of Temple House, yeah, but I haven't tried my luck in the Arcanum proper."

She still didn't believe it. "But—but—you must have. You know how everything works, what to do . . ."

Toby smiled modestly. "*Theoretically,* yes, I like to think I've worked things out. You can pick up a lot from hanging around the Lotteries, and I've spent ages looking for clues and stuff. I've even raised a coin at a threshold, though I haven't gone as far as actually throwing it—the time's never been quite right. But now there's two of us, we can go in together, help each other." He looked at her solemnly. "It was lucky you had such a nice card on your first visit. You could have got into real trouble."

It was all she could to do to stop herself from hitting him. Instead, she got to her feet, her face taut with anger. "What's the matter?" Toby asked, sounding genuinely shocked. "Don't be mad. Look, I'm sorry if you got the wrong idea—"

"Only because you gave it to me. I thought you had answers. Experience. I thought you were a person I could trust."

"But you can! We're in this together, Cat."

"No we're not." The surreal city on the wall, the fantasy books, the toy armies of knights and goblins . . . Never mind his elaborate explanations: the Arcanum was just a game to him. An adventurous daydream. "You have no idea," she hissed, "*no idea* what it's like in there."

But Toby didn't rise to the bait. Instead, he was looking

at her curiously. "The Six of Cups . . . it must have uncovered something. Something buried in your past that you don't understand. And you want to go back into the Arcanum to make sense of it. Am I right?"

"What I may or may not have seen has nothing to do with you."

"Even though you came to me for help?"

"That was only because you'd conned me into thinking you were some kind of Game Guru."

"I can still help, Cat."

"Can you? Can you look me in the eye and say that the little how-to guides you've given me are anything but guesswork?"

"Er, no, but it's a very educated guess—"

"Can you tell me how to find a threshold that's vanished? How to get into the Six of Cups again? What to do when I get there?"

"Um, not exact—"

"Then no. You can't help me."

"At least I've done *some* kind of research," he replied, getting heated. "I know enough not to go blundering into the first threshold I find, without any kind of preparation or backup."

Cat just stared at him stonily. But when she moved toward the door, he stood to block her path.

"OK. Wait. What if I could find you someone who really is an expert? Who might even know how to get back into your card?" Cat paused and he carried on hurriedly.

"Because there's this girl I know from Temple House. She's the only other chancer I've come across—except for you, obviously."

"So?"

"Well, from something she said, I reckon she's been in the Game for years, even though she's no older than us."

"Then why aren't the two of you a team? I would've thought you'd be wearing matching T-shirts by now."

"Because she's even more stroppy than you are! Seriously, I have tried, but she doesn't want to know me. Maybe if you tell her your story, though, and ask for help, she'll change her mind. Female solidarity."

Cat gave an exasperated snort, but she moved away from the door. "All right." She thought for few minutes, while Toby watched her anxiously. "All right. It's better than nothing . . . I suppose. D'you know where to find her?"

"As a matter of fact," he said, "I do. How do you fancy going to church?"

Toby was confident that he'd come up with a winning plan. The girl in question, Flora, attended Mass at a Catholic church in West London every Sunday at five o'clock, and according to Toby, making contact would be a simple matter of intercepting her as she came out later that day. When Cat asked him how he knew to find her there, he looked a bit shifty and confessed that he "might have" followed her "on a couple of occasions."

"You stalked her, you mean."

"No! There's nothing sleazy about it. It was just . . . research."

Cat sighed. She was still angry, but part of her recognized that she was being unfair. The fact remained that Toby did seem to know a great deal about the cards and how they were played, even if his knowledge was mostly hypothetical. She wondered what this churchgoing chancer would be like. If she'd been casually flitting in and out of the Arcanum for years, she was bound to be odd.

But on the way back home from Toby's, Cat was confronted by just how difficult it was to keep a distance from the Game, even if she had wanted to.

It was lunchtime, and the North London streets were almost as quiet as the ones around Seven Dials that morning. As her double-decker bus wheezed to a halt at the traffic lights at the beginning of a long gray road to Holborn, Cat found that she could look right into the second floor of an office. It was part of an ugly modern building whose front was mostly made up of panels of tinted glass. On a Sunday afternoon, the place should have been deserted. But there were two people in there. A pale blonde and an older black man.

With a trembling hand, Cat pressed the request-stop button. She was able to get off the bus only a little way down from the office; a few minutes later, she was standing outside the main entrance, peering up at the second floor. Could she have been mistaken? But no, the woman had moved nearer to the window and was looking out over the street. She was wearing dark glasses and a white suit. It was unquestionably Odile.

The Queen of Cups tilted her head so that she was staring directly down at Cat. Then she turned back to speak to her companion, brushing something—a speck of dust, perhaps—off her sleeve as she did so. The gesture struck Cat as deliberately contemptuous.

Something snapped. At once, all the fear and confusion of the last few days came crashing down. She began to repeatedly jab the bell. After a while she began to hammer at the door. Then there was a click, and somebody buzzed her in.

This was the last thing she expected. Her assault on the door was an act of protest; it hadn't occurred to her that she might actually be admitted. And now here she was, once again hovering on a doorstep she was half afraid to cross. But the thought of those other entrances, the treachery of their thresholds, only made her more defiant. She marched through the reception area and up to the second floor.

It was a big open-plan office, furnished in shades of beige, its rows of desks heaped with papers, mugs and Post-it notes waiting forlornly for Monday morning. In the center of the room, the Queen of Cups and the King of Wands were observing one of the computer screens. "I think she would be unwise to make a break for it," Odile was saying. "The Chariot hasn't even reached the river."

It was like hearing someone commentate on a sporting event. Not with the excitable outpourings of a fan, but the measured tones of the professional.

Cat saw that all the screens in the office were filled with images of indistinct shapes moving through fuzz and crackle. From the tingling of her palm, she sensed that a threshold was near.

She thought of the grainy TV in the room above the pub, and the larger screen in the ballroom at Temple House. The Game Masters must be using them to view moves in the Game, like the modern-day equivalent of a crystal ball. It seemed even Arcanum technology could move with the times.

"I hope the knight is putting on a good show for you," Cat said, as boldly as she could manage.

Leisurely, they turned to look at her. The black king and the white queen. Like two pieces on a chessboard—and just as inscrutable.

"So far, this move has been predictable," Ahab replied, heavy and hard as granite. "But things could change. It appears that another of your kind has arrived on the scene."

Cat glanced at the nearest monitor, where the formerly impenetrable static cleared enough for her to see a figure walking in some kind of rocky landscape. A male figure. *Another of your kind* . . . did that mean another chancer? Did that mean *Toby*? Perhaps after she'd left, he'd gone out and—but no, this person looked taller than Toby, and moved differently. A long-legged, slouching sort of walk, which nevertheless had a sense of purpose about it.

"Ah yes," said Odile in her light, precise voice. "I remember. He claims to be in search of one of your knights, Ahab."

"It appears he is persistent, if nothing else."

Cat's bravado was beginning to seep away. Still, she was determined not to let it show. "Gripping stuff. Tell me, how's the State of Play shaping up these days?"

"As of this round, the advantage lies with Swords, though Pentacles are only two triumphs behind," Odile replied coolly. "Cups gained one triumph but lost another. Wands follow in fourth place."

"And what happens when Swords collect all the triumphs?"

"Naturally, the King of Swords would be the one and only Game Master, and single ruler of the Arcanum."

Odile didn't seem much concerned by the prospect, however. Her next words explained why.

"The scenario is purely speculative," she said. "Should one court show signs of being overdominant, the other three unite against it."

"See, this is what I don't understand," said Cat, struggling to keep her voice steady. "If that's true, your little competition doesn't count for squat. None of it matters—not to you, anyhow. You're not the poor saps risking life and sanity out there. It's just point scoring for you lot. One-upmanship. What's the point of a game that can't be won?"

"Oh, the Game can be won," Ahab replied seriously. "It is the founding principle of the Arcanum."

"But she just said that whenever one of you starts to get close, the other three gang up to stop them!"

"Indeed. But there is another means of winning. A prize that bestows dominion over all other cards and players— even Fortune herself."

Cat tried to look unimpressed. "Yeah, I heard about the Eternity card. The triumph that's gone AWOL."

He smiled austerely. "Eternity is a prize above all others, and so only a king or queen, a player above all players, may win it. It is true it has been lost in the Arcanum for a long, long time. Who can say, though, what the next turn of the Wheel may bring?

"I am not the first King of Wands, nor, perhaps, the last. Yet I believe the time will come when one Game Master surpasses all others. And once he or she has reclaimed Eternity, a new Game will begin, under that Master's sole rule."

Ahab's manner hadn't got any less intimidating, but it struck Cat that in one respect, at least, the kings and queens weren't all that different from the gamblers at the Luxe. They too were hooked on the lure of the big win that was always just around the corner. "I see. You four reckon that if you stay in the Game long enough, the odds'll change."

Odile pushed her glasses to the back of her head. It was the first time Cat had seen her without them; the eyes revealed were a milky blue so light they were almost colorless. Set in the perfect pallor of her face, the effect was uncanny.

"The odds are of little account. Even if none of us are to have the final victory, our place in the contest is reward enough. For when the players have gone from a move, taking its threshold with them, we wander through the cards at will. We walk the Arcanum's checkerboard, we command its creatures, and we play our games. That is a prize above any triumph." She moistened her lips delicately. "Though I imagine you might feel differently. . . ."

And suddenly all the monitors were showing her, Cat, standing before the door to the garden in the Six of Cups. This time the image was in color and crystal clear. The expression on her face as she moved across the lawn and toward the house—her glow of hopeful happiness—was somehow shameful in its intensity.

The picture moved to a brown and cream swirly carpet. A pink birthday cake. Her mother's face, smiling, as she held out her arms. A hand raising a gun.

Cat let out an animal whimper. She reached out, futilely, to touch the screen. And as she did so, the blur of static returned with an earsplitting crackle.

"You *bastards*," she choked.

Ahab regarded her levelly. "We may umpire the Game, but the Arcanum works according to its own mysteries. What you find there is your affair."

Odile put her hand up to her mouth, making a small smothered sound. Laughter. They were toying with her, that was all. Cat had achieved nothing by being let in here; in fact, she'd only succeeded in giving them yet more power over her, as they reeled her in with their ghostly screens and their enigmatic comments. And now they were watching, waiting, for her to crumble.

It was at that point that Cat made a resolution.

Enough.

No more tears, no more dramatics. She wouldn't give them the satisfaction. Not now, not ever. She was going to leave these people with her head high and her step steady.

Grief and rage would be replaced by cold hard calm. Only then would she be able to do what she had to do.

Whatever it takes and whatever it costs, I will get my answers, Cat told herself as she walked out of the building. Starting with the girl at the church.

CHAPTER SEVEN

CAT WAS GETTING THE HANG of navigating London, but on her way to St. Bernadine's she got off at the wrong Tube stop and arrived at the church nearly fifteen minutes later than she and Toby had agreed.

She found him hovering by the railings, his tweed jacket accessorized with a skull-and-crossbones baseball cap and an immense purple-striped scarf. "I was beginning to think you weren't coming," he said plaintively. "And that maybe it was a mistake not to get here early and actually go to the service."

"Please. There's a limit to the number of creepy ancient cults I can cope with in the space of one weekend."

Somewhat to her surprise, he laughed. "You know, when you're not being uptight, you're quite funny."

She thought that was pretty rich, coming from someone as twitchy as Toby, but she let it pass. And in the next minute, the doors to the church were opened and people started straggling out into the courtyard.

St. Bernadine's was in a smart residential district and built in the elaborate Gothic style beloved by cookie tins and Christmas cards. Its congregation was mainly elderly, all were well-heeled, and Cat was uncomfortably aware of how out of place she and Toby looked. It didn't help that Toby had edged behind a nearby mailbox and was combining chewing his nails with peering around in a furtive manner.

"That's her," he whispered excitedly, nudging Cat as an elegant middle-aged couple and a blond girl came out of the door. But now that the moment had come, Cat found herself overwhelmed by the sheer embarrassment of the situation. Staking out a church! What was she supposed to do now? Rush up to this stranger and start babbling about the Wondrous World of Tarot?

Making contact, however, was easier than she'd expected. It was only six days before Christmas, and people were lingering over their season's greetings and farewells. While their target's parents stayed to talk to the priest, the girl went ahead to wait by the railings. Cat seized her chance.

"'Scuse me," she said. "Are you Flora?"

The girl turned and gave a cautious smile. "Do I know you?" She was blandly pretty: blue-eyed, blond, with a small heart-shaped face, and was wearing a long wool coat with a fur collar. Cat thought the fur was probably real. She looked the type.

Toby cleared his throat. "Uh, hello there. I—uh—you remember me, right? Toby? And this is Cat."

"Toby," repeated the girl vaguely. "Oh yes . . . I thought you looked familiar." There was an awkward pause. She glanced over at her parents but they were still deep in conversation. The pause lengthened.

"Sorry to interrupt," said Cat, "and I know we haven't got much time, but I was wondering if . . . well, it's about the Game."

"And what game is that?" asked Flora, knitting her brows in polite bewilderment.

Cat's eyes flicked to her right hand. Flora was wearing gloves. She tried again, more brusquely this time. "Look, I know you don't know me and there's no reason why you should help, but Toby here says you know a lot about the Arcanum and I was wondering—"

"I'm frightfully sorry," said Flora, with what sounded like sincerity, "but there seems to be some mistake."

"I don't think so. We all know what I'm talking about."

"You've got the wrong person. I'm sorry I can't help."

Cat met her eyes. Their expression was as cool and steady as her own.

"Everything all right here, sweetheart?"

A distinguished-looking man with graying hair and an easy smile had just arrived. "I'm fine, thanks, Daddy." Flora twisted a strand of honey-blond hair around her finger. "Let's go."

⁂

"That's what she's always like," said Toby gloomily, as soon as they were alone. "All polite and polished and impossible."

Although Cat didn't want to admit it, Flora had impressed her. There was steel behind the sweetness. Even without Toby's introduction, Cat felt that she would have recognized her as someone who had also walked the Arcanum's streets, and that an implicit acknowledgment of this had passed between them. "It's not over. If she won't talk to us here, she can't keep playing dumb among the wands and cups and whatsits. You said you first saw her in Temple House, right?"

"Yes. She's nearly always there for the Lotteries."

"Then we'll try that next. But—wait—how will we know when one's happening?"

"Aha . . . sooner than you'd think. Look at your palm."

"It's normal. There's nothing there."

"Look at it. Focus."

Cat stared at where the sign of the wheel had been imprinted on her flesh. She found that by concentrating she could bring it up through her own will: a gray circle, faint as smudged ink. But this time, the four spokes had been replaced with a small black *X*.

"Fortune's the tenth triumph in the deck. Clever, huh?" Toby's expression was as smug as if he'd put the mark on her hand himself. "You'll get into the habit of checking for it, after a while. And it's much easier than signing up for a mailing list."

There was just no escape, Cat thought, rubbing her

right palm resentfully. Even when she couldn't see or feel it, the knowledge that the mark and coin of the Arcanum was always there, lurking, set her on edge.

"Lotteries are fairly frequent," Toby was saying, "but even so, another one coming so soon after—"

"Let me get this straight. There's another party tonight and you reckon Flora will be there?"

"Most likely."

"Then why the hell didn't you say so before? Why are we wasting time skulking in churchyards?"

But Toby looked troubled. "The thing is . . . Flora . . . well, she's even harder to approach when she's involved in the Game. She's not even polite there. . . ."

"Look. You were the one who was so desperate to recruit some buddies to the cause. Are you backing out on me?"

Toby flushed. "I never said anything about backing out."

"In that case, I'll see you outside Temple House tonight. When does it open?"

"Er, usually about eight."

"Fine. I'll see you then."

This time it was Toby who was late. His parents had been delayed leaving for a book reading, and he was in full fret about being back in time for their return.

Cat had scant sympathy. She herself was feeling guilty about going out again since Bel, who had Sundays off, had proposed a girls' night in and had even arranged to borrow Greg's DVD player. And yet when Cat said she was off to the cinema with a girl from school, she got the sense that Bel was relieved. The emotions of last night were too raw for either of them to feel entirely comfortable around the other.

Not that she shared any of this with Toby. She wasn't planning to report her encounter with Ahab and Odile, either. It was her own business—if he wanted to help her, well and good. That didn't make them allies.

But as soon as she and Toby turned in to Mercury Square, all other preoccupations were forgotten. It was like Friday all over again. Warm light spilled onto the pavement; the hum of talk and laughter drifted down the street. She could even hear the piano, which this time was playing a sprightly jazz number.

The same withered doorkeeper was on duty at the entrance, but gave no sign of either recognition or challenge as they passed through the curtain and into the hall beyond. The place was as grand as Cat had remembered, if not as crowded, and the echoing buzz of party noise was just as disorienting. She tried to shake the cloudiness from her head, and said with more energy than she felt, "All right then, Flora. Here we come."

They started with the room to the right of the stairs, where Cat had watched the poker game on her previous visit. This time it was empty. She went straight to the windows and opened the shutters to reveal that the scene outside had changed from a bitter December night to a purplish midsummer's dusk. The trees in the garden were in full leaf; tiny white lights twinkled in their branches and along the railings. It appeared the majority of the guests were outside strolling in the street, or idling beneath the trees.

Cat turned to Toby wonderingly. "Can we get out there?"

"Course. I'll show you." They went back into the hall and past the golden curtain. The front door was ajar, revealing a glimpse of the wintry London square they had come from. Toby turned to the doorkeeper. "Hi there. Do you think you could please let us out? Into the other side?"

The doorkeeper stared at them impassively but didn't say anything. Instead, he drew a blank card from the stack to his left. When he passed his right palm over the face of the card, it left an illustration in its wake: three figures dancing and drinking in a bower of fruit and flowers. "Three of Cups, Reign of Abundance. It's the party card," said Toby with a grin. And this time, the door opened onto a view of leafy trees and a purple-dappled sky.

Toby had said that there was often a degree of overlap between the two sides of Temple House, but this time Cat could see only a flicker of the other square and the other night: the beam of a car's headlights, the bare branches of a shrub, a pedestrian struggling with a broken umbrella. . . . None of it seemed real.

It might have been the world's most exclusive club, but their fellow guests were more varied than Cat remembered from her previous visit. Just inside the gate to the garden a Goth girl with multiple piercings was in animated conversation with an older gentleman in a morning suit.

A group of young men with close-cropped hair and baggy trousers were sprawled on the steps of one of the houses, swigging from bottles and watching the scene with bright quick eyes. Two glamour-model types, one in a sequined cocktail dress, one in denim hot pants, pouted by the railings.

Players in the Game, yes, but ordinary people, too, Cat reminded herself. Real men and women with real lives in the real world. Like Anthony Linebeg, the IT consultant who lived alone . . . or her parents, she thought, with a twist of her gut. Not for the first time, she wondered what ambitions and desires had led these people here, and what strange trials by ordeal awaited them.

Then her eye was caught by a waiter, proffering his tray of drinks to a girl nearby. The girl accepted a glass, and twirled a strand of blond hair round her finger.

"Look—over there," Cat hissed, clutching Toby's arm. "That's her!"

But it took another few moments of scrutiny for her to be sure. Flora looked older, for one thing, perhaps because she had put her hair up and was wearing makeup and a flimsy camisole. Nothing surprising about this, it was a party after all, but there was something a bit disheveled about her appearance that was very different from the artfully Bohemian look rich girls sometimes went for. Her eyes were outlined in smudgy black, and she had a flush of red high on her cheeks.

When she caught sight of Toby and Cat, she downed her drink in a quick, angry jerk. "Oh. It's *you*."

"I'm glad we've found you," said Cat quietly.

"Stalked me, you mean." Flora shot a black look at Toby.

She helped herself to another drink and raised it as if in toast. "Today *is* an anniversary, after all." A private joke, presumably, for the smile she now turned on Cat was a parody of social charm. "But dear me, I'm forgetting my manners. I gather you're a new recruit to our delightful little club. Isn't it all too, too, utterly mah-vellous?" She flung out her arm to encompass the party, slopping the liquid in her glass as she did so.

"Not particularly," said Cat.

"Hmm," Flora looked at her in a speculative if fuzzy manner. "A skeptic. Oh well, you'll soon get used to it. *Regnabo, regno, regnavi, sum sine regno,* as the saying goes." Then she gave a sneering sort of shrug and walked away.

Cat was about to go after Flora and try again, when a bell began to chime, and she saw people stop what they were doing and look around expectantly. The chime was high and very sweet, and a sense of excitement rippled through the air. Flora, too, was standing still and looking up, her mouth slightly open.

The doorkeeper had come out at the top of the steps to Temple House, and raised both his arms to address the scene. "Ladies and gentlemen, princes and vagabonds, players all," he began, his old cracked voice carrying with surprising force, "I bid you welcome and announce that the Lottery is about to begin."

Applause broke out, along with murmurs and coos of anticipation, and everyone began moving toward the house. Flora was among the first to the door.

"Come on," said Toby.

"I don't want to see it," Cat replied.

"Why not? Nobody does anything while a Lottery's taking place. All play is suspended; it's the rules. And anyway, it's exciting."

"So were those old Roman shows with gladiators." Now that she knew what was at stake, the idea of watching some knight sweat as the wheel spun made her feel queasy. "You go keep an eye on Flora. I'll wait by the stairs and we can corner her as she comes out."

Toby didn't need telling twice, bounding up the steps of Temple House to catch up with the other spectators. Cat moved more slowly. She came to a halt on the second floor and watched as the big black-and-gold doors swung behind the last arrivals.

No sound escaped from the room once the doors were shut. Cat decided to visit the picture gallery again to take another look at the Triumph of Fortune and the images set within the wheel's rim. They appeared to be of the various triumphs in the Greater Arcana, and she wanted to compare them to the Tarot cards she'd seen. But she grew uncomfortable under the painted gaze of the other pictures, and moved across the hall into the book-lined study after only a little while.

Two other people were playing truant from the Lottery there, talking intently by the fireplace. A game of chess lay abandoned on a table beside a still-warm coffeepot. Cat helped herself to a cup and went to look at the shelves, on the off chance she'd find some kind of Game rule book or guide. A slim volume entitled *The Queen of Spades* looked promising, but it was just a boring novel about Russian gamblers. The next row along had a collection of poems called *The Waste Land* propped next to a Latin text, *De Consolatione Philosophiae*. Cat yawned, and began to flick through a first edition of *Alice's Adventures in Wonderland*.

Browsing the shelves had brought her nearer to the room's other occupants. Then she caught a snatch of their conversation, and moved closer still.

"Of *course* my forfeit's unfair," the woman was complaining. "It was an easy mistake to make."

The muscular young man standing next to her laughed. "You tried to bribe another knight to swap her cards with you! Personally, I think you got off lightly. Only three moves to serve as a knave, and then you can resume your round."

"I can't afford to be at the beck and call of the courts," the woman said crossly. She was small and chic, and looked even smaller next to her companion's bulk. "I do have a life outside the Game, you know. And Odile hasn't even told me my duties yet! I've been summoned to see her after the Lottery, worse luck. . . . Serving time at these wretched parties is all very well, but running round the Arcanum doing the GM's dirty work is another matter."

Cat couldn't keep quiet any longer. "Can't you say no?" she interrupted. "Refuse to do it?"

The couple looked around; the young man amused, the woman irritable.

"And spend the rest of my life paying the price?" the woman scoffed. "No thanks."

"Rebel knaves don't last long outside the Game," the

young man said, seeing Cat's confused expression. "Not with all the bad luck they carry with them. It's as if the Arcanum condemns them to a permanent losing streak." He reached out to shake her hand. "Knight of Swords. My friend here is—for the moment—a Knave of Cups."

"I'm a chancer."

The knave smiled unpleasantly. "Then you'd better watch your step. There's no Fool like a forfeited one."

"What d'you mean?"

"Work it out for yourself." The knave tossed her hair, and headed out of the room. "I haven't got time for spoon-feeding."

Game players were a bad-tempered bunch, thought Cat, who was still smarting from her encounter with Flora.

But the knight took pity on her. "Chancers can only enter the Arcanum on the condition they don't do anything to help or obstruct the other players," he explained. "Intervene in the Game for a second time, you'll end up a knave yourself—for as many rounds as the Game Masters choose."

With her back to the fire's sleepy flicker, Cat felt herself go cold. It occurred to her that Alastor had mentioned something about this in their first encounter. But it hadn't meant anything to her at the time.

"The kings and queens don't miss much," the knight continued. "They've got their own methods of surveillance. But the knaves are their eyes and ears." He lowered his voice. "A knave that catches a chancer interfering gets set free from his or her forfeit. So I'd keep out of their way, if I were you."

Sudden clatter and chatter from outside made both of

them start. The Lottery was over. "OK. Thanks for the tip," Cat said, moving toward the door. "What are you playing for, by the way?" It seemed only polite to ask.

"Triumph of Strength."

"You don't exactly look like you need it."

"Ah, but I've got the Olympics to train for." The athlete grinned. "Not to mention a world record to defend."

Cat reached the hallway just as Toby arrived. His face lightened when he saw her, and he pointed to where Flora's blond head could be seen at the top of the packed staircase. Progress downstairs was slow, and their quarry remained only a few feet in front. But there was a sudden rush as people reached the ground floor and began to disperse into the reception rooms or out to the square, and they remained stuck in the line as Flora slipped through the crowd and ducked around the corner under the stairs. Cat pushed ahead, dragging Toby in her wake. "Hurry up," she said impatiently. "We can't lose her now."

Flora had gone through a little white-painted door that Cat hadn't noticed before. The corridor behind had a shabby, neglected sort of air and led to the back of the house and a wide paved courtyard surrounded by high walls. Incongruously, there was what appeared to be an old-fashioned slot machine in the middle of the yard. But no Flora.

"I can't believe it! I could've sworn she came this way."

Toby looked nervous. "She did. Um, I think she's gone into the Arcanum."

"But we're already—"

"I mean that she's left Temple House to enter play." He

indicated the door at the end of the courtyard. "I don't know where this exit leads. But if Flora just wanted to go home, she'd have left by the front."

Both felt the wheel mark on their palms begin to tingle. A lilac glow lingered over the roof behind them, and Cat could still hear the piano somewhere deep inside. Past the high walls of the courtyard, however, was the sludgy orange of London's night sky, where the lights of an airplane were winking toward Heathrow.

The tops of the walls were lined with a thicket of iron barbs, and the door was solid steel. It was also locked. This was no ordinary threshold.

They went back to inspect the slot machine, an antique model made of dark wood. A Wheel of Fortune had been painted onto the pearly glass panel above the reels. There were three reels, each printed with a strip of assorted symbols: laughing faces, frowning faces, and wheels.

Close up, they saw that the rim of the wheel on the glass panel was marked with Roman numerals up to twenty-one plus a zero. In the four divisions created by its spokes, the signs of the courts were painted: a pentacle, a sword, a cup and a wand. There were two bronze pointers, like the hands of a clock. The smaller one was aligned along a spoke and didn't appear to be pointing to anything, but the other was positioned on *XVIII*.

"Eighteen! That's the Moon: the eighteenth triumph in the Greater Arcana," Toby exclaimed. "Because, look, if you wanted to choose a card in the Lesser Arcana, you'd use the little arrow hand to point to its court sign. Pentacles or

Swords or whatever." He tapped the painted wheel. "I think it's showing us the card we'll find on the other side of that door. Maybe this is Temple House's route into all the moves in the Arcanum."

Odile had said that the Game Masters liked to wander around the Arcanum in their spare time. Searching for their long-lost Eternity, presumably. This contraption might allow them to visit cards that didn't belong to their particular courts. And now Cat, too, could get into whichever card she liked. She immediately reached to turn the smaller hand to the picture of a cup and the longer one to *VI*.

But the bronze arrows wouldn't budge.

"Hell." She kicked the machine's base in frustration.

Toby shook his head. "It's probably only the Game Masters who can select the cards. I just can't work out how Flora got the door open. . . ."

Cat sighed. "It has to be connected to the slot machine. The obvious explanation is that we need the pictures on the three reels to line up. That's how these contraptions work, right? First you feed in your coin. Then you pull the lever to rotate the reels. If all the pictures match when they've stopped spinning, you've hit the jackpot—or in our case, the door opens."

"And we go visit the Moon!" Toby's eyes widened.

"Didn't you say the Moon triumph had to do with art and creativity and stuff? That can't be too bad."

"Yes, but that's the Moon as a prize. The card itself draws on all sorts of lunar myths and legends. It's illustrated with two towers and—hey, what are you doing?"

"Playing the one-armed bandit." Cat was already tracing the painted wheel's lines, feeling the throb as a coin materialized in her hand. "My aunt told me how your chance of winning on an ordinary slot machine is over two hundred thousand to one. But I bet a player with an Arcanum coin is going to hit the jackpot every time. Here goes."

As soon as the coin went into the slot, the painted glass panel lit up. Cat pulled the lever and the reels began to spin with a soft clicking sound. When they stopped, the symbols revealed were three identical wheels. Toby whooped. The panel began to flash.

Cat hurried over to the door. Sure enough, its handle turned.

"Right," she said. "I'm going through. Thanks for helping, and all that, but there's no reason for you to come. This is my business."

"Are you kidding?" Toby's foot was tap-tapping, and he had ruffled his hair into little agitated tufts, but he gave her a lopsided grin. "Of course I'm coming with you. You were right, that stuff you said about research not really counting. It's just . . . well, this is a big thing, y'know? I mean, wow, I've been dreaming about this for such a long time, right, and now it's actually here—"

She grabbed his arm and pulled him through, before either of them could change their minds.

At first, Cat thought they had got it wrong and the door led to somewhere in the "home" side after all. The dank overcast night belonged to the evening she'd left behind when she'd entered Temple House, just as the concrete jumble hemming them in had a mundane familiarity. Towering apartment buildings of grubby gray reared up to either side, their windows stretching from earth to sky. In spite of the pallid glow of an occasional streetlight, and the scribble of graffiti across the walls, the place seemed utterly abandoned.

"Jeez," Toby muttered, "I thought it would be a bit more, y'know . . ."

"Glamorous?" Cat said it sarcastically, but actually she knew what he meant. She thought of the soft primrose morning the other side of Seven Dials, the glowing rooms of Temple House.

To their dismay, the door they'd come through only opened one way. Here it was the front door of one of the towers, with a narrow grille at the top and a row of buzzers to the left. Toby was going to try the buzzers but Cat, made uneasy by the CCTV camera above their heads, stopped his hand.

"Doesn't matter. We'll just keep walking until we find a threshold that'll take us out of here."

"And look who's here in the meantime. Score!" Toby pointed across the scrubby open space, slightly smaller than a football field, that lay before them.

There was Flora, walking unsteadily but determinedly toward the underpass of a wide concrete bridge. As they watched, she stopped and took a swig from the bottle of champagne she was dangling from one hand.

Toby and Cat exchanged glances, then hurried to join

her. Large greasy-looking puddles pockmarked the yard, and as they crossed its expanse, the concrete seemed to swallow them up and the towers grow higher. But at least one of their problems had been solved: feeling the pins and needles on their palms as they approached the bridge, they knew a threshold must be close, somewhere in the walkway beneath it. Perhaps that was what Flora was heading for. When she saw them coming, she shook her head slightly and began to laugh. "Batgirl and Robin ride again. Haven't you two got a garden party to go to?"

"Hey, Flora. Sorry to, uh, keep bothering you, but we could really use some advice here. You see, Cat wants—"

Cat cut in. "I'm looking for something."

"Aren't we all." Flora's eye makeup had run down one cheek, her voice was slurred and she was shivering in her flimsy camisole. Still, her insouciance made Cat envious.

"It's true though, isn't it, that you've been coming to the Arcanum for years?" Toby asked eagerly.

"Sure. I used to divide my time between here and Narnia—till I got tired of the talking lions, that is." Flora took another swig, and hiccuped. "Oops." She smiled coyly. "These days, there's just the one world in my wardrobe."

Cat had tired of the All-Knowing Badass act. "Leave it, Toby. She's too wasted to talk sense even if she wanted to."

"*Excuse* me?"

Cat shrugged expressively, and turned away. As she did, her eye was caught by a blurred figure moving quickly across the yard, toward the corner of the building on the left, where he or she seemed to crawl up the wall. Then she realized that whoever it was must be climbing a ladder attached to a fire escape.

"What's that?" Something in Flora's voice made Cat turn round again.

The three of them were standing in front of the bridge. To the left was a set of steps leading up to the road; to the right was a lone streetlamp, whose glow barely penetrated the mouth of the underpass. But now Cat could see a pair of yellow eyes gleaming in the sour-smelling dark within. There was the click of nails on concrete and a heavy panting sound.

Instinctively, the three of them moved closer together. "Just a dog," said Toby, but he sounded uncertain.

Though it was hard to tell in the gloom, it looked a bit like a German shepherd, but bigger and shaggier. From deep within its throat came a low soft growl.

Cat felt Flora's arm tremble against hers. In unspoken agreement, they began to back away, while the dog crept forward, slunk low on its belly, its teeth bared. The snarl swelled and throbbed. Yet when the animal reached the threshold of the underpass, it went no farther. Crouched as if to spring, it waited, motionless, staring after them with baleful yellow eyes.

Every nerve, every muscle screamed *run*. Cat could hear the others' ragged breathing. Steady. Steady . . . The three of them continued to move backward in a clumsy, almost comical half walk, half jog that gathered in speed the farther they got from the bridge.

Then, just as they were in the shadow of the towers and were beginning to feel calmer, the animal leaped into the light of the streetlamp, flung back its head and howled—a long, shivering cry that echoed through the blood.

At once, they burst into a scrambling dash, and would probably have scattered if Cat hadn't remembered the figure she'd seen only a few minutes earlier. "This way!" she choked out. "Up!" In a frantic swerve, already imagining the beast snap at their ankles, the other two ran after her toward the lower bars of the fire escape. At the last moment, Flora stumbled. She gasped, lurched forward, tripped again, before Cat came back and dragged her on.

Toby got to the ladder first, swinging himself onto the platform above with a screech of rusting iron. Together, he and Cat half pulled, half pushed Flora after him. Cat scrambled up last, expecting to feel hot breath and stinking jaws close in on her at any moment.

But the wolf hadn't come after them. Huddled on their perch, about twelve feet off the ground, they watched as it prowled before the bridge, ears pricked.

"The Triumph of the Moon," breathed Toby. He gestured at the two towers, the gray waste before them where rainwater had pooled, and the wolf lifting its muzzle to the sky. High above, scudding clouds briefly cleared to show the white disc of light. "It's *just* like the picture on the card!"

Cat stared at his rapt expression in disbelief. Flora, too, seemed to have recovered her composure. Sticking her twisted ankle out in front of her, she leaned back against the building with a wince and a sigh, as if settling in for the night. She took another swig from the bottle, which she'd somehow managed to hang on to. Catching Cat's eye, she passed it over.

The champagne was flat and tepid, and a sudden clanging noise from above set Cat spluttering. Whoever had gone up the fire escape before them was climbing higher. Craning her neck, she saw a smudge of face looking down on them, before the figure swung into an open window three or four flights up.

"Is that the knight, d'you think?" Toby asked, still unfeasibly chirpy.

"No," Flora said, pointing. "*That's* the knight."

There was a woman running along the top of the bridge, her figure in silhouette against the sprawl of city lights beyond. Cat felt a lurch of sickness. It was the Knight of Cups she'd seen play the Lottery, on her first night at Temple House. She must have won her next two moves and was now making her final gamble.

As they watched, another howl shivered through the air, not from the wolf they had seen—which had disappeared into the night—but from somewhere farther off. Farther, but not far. The woman froze at the sound, then staggered on. Briefly, she disappeared from view. Then there was movement in the darkness to the left of the bridge, and they saw her head bobbing as she descended the steps.

A moment later, and she had reached the yard. Although the moon had gone behind the clouds again, they could see that she was dressed in a long white nightgown. Her bare feet kept tripping on the hem, and her dark hair had come undone from its knot. In the vast silence of the place, they could hear her sobbing breath; on the crest of the bridge, black shadows massed.

Cat scrambled to stand up, to call out to the fugitive so she could head for the safety of the ladder. Before she could open her mouth, sharp nails dug into her arm.

"Don't move," Flora hissed. "Don't say a word."

"But we have to help her! She'll be torn to pieces by those animals—Toby!" Cat looked to him for appeal.

"She's right. We have to do something," he whispered back, wide-eyed.

"Idiots," said Flora in an urgent yet contemptuous undertone. "Don't you understand? We're chancers. We're not allowed to intervene—not without paying the forfeit."

Cat's words of protest died in her throat. Her conversation with the knave and knight in Temple House had come back to her with horrible clarity.

As they were talking, first one, then two, three, four wolves had slunk out from the underpass and darted ahead of their prey, cutting off her flight. Meanwhile, those on the bridge poured down the steps, as swift and silent as smoke. Eyes gleamed, tongues lolled, hot animal breath steamed in the air. The knight was encircled. Cat's whole body crawled with horror.

Flora still had her arm in an iron grip. "Wait," she said. *"Wait."*

For the woman's face was suffused with a kind of radiance as she gazed up at the sky. With a cry, she plucked at the neckline of her gown, raking her throat and breast with her nails, as she swayed and muttered. The next moment, the clouds parted to reveal the moon, and the landscape was flooded with cold, dead light. The woman lifted up her arms, let out another wail and sank to the ground.

She seemed to shrink into the drapes of her gown, twitching and shuddering, her long black hair spilling over her face and down her back. It grew longer and shaggier, shot through with shimmers of gray. There was a terrible moaning noise. And somehow, in a matter of seconds, the tangle of folds and hair and flesh had vanished, leaving a great silver wolf baying at the moon.

At once, the rest of the pack surged to meet it. It was twice the size of the other animals and its cry was louder and wilder, and more desolate, than any they had heard before. With one mighty bound, it leaped ahead, racing across the forecourt and between the two towers.

Cat, Flora and Toby shrank back on their platform, hardly daring to breathe, as the wolf pack streamed after it and under them and beyond. And sometimes Cat saw the wolf, and sometimes it was the woman, with bare feet and flying hair, running ahead, and urging them on.

For a while afterward, nobody spoke. It felt as if they were eternally locked into this dead landscape, the creaking iron and the damp wind.

Eventually, Toby cleared his throat. "What do you think will happen to her?" he asked.

"Depends," Flora answered wearily. "We don't know the

conditions for winning this triumph. It could be that changing into the wolf is the knight's only chance of survival. Or it's a temporary transformation, which she'll use to complete her task." She looked at the other two meaningfully. "*Her* task, *her* move. Whatever the outcome, it's nothing to do with us. Not if we want to stay chancers."

"That's pretty harsh," Toby muttered.

Flora pursed her lips. "I don't make the rules."

There was another long silence.

At last, Cat swung around so her feet were dangling off the edge of the platform. "Well, I'm going down," she told the others with more firmness than she felt. "We can't stay up here forever."

Leaving the comparative safety of the fire escape was a drawn-out process. They all halted on the final rung of the ladder, ears straining for the sound of padding feet or panting breath, and once they were on the ground, nobody wanted to be the first to break away from grabbing distance of the rails.

Given the choice, Cat would have preferred to make a run for it, one final sprint to the threshold under the bridge. But Flora's ankle, though not badly sprained, meant they had to compromise on a scuttling sort of shuffle around the edges of the forecourt, flinching at their own shadows, hardly daring to breathe.

Somehow, though, they made it. Once more they stood in front of the mouth of the underpass, feeling the sign of the wheel prick their palms and fear prick at their necks.

But this time the darkness within appeared to be as lifeless as the wasteland they'd just crossed.

Toby felt in his pocket and drew out a mini flashlight. "Thought it might come in handy," he said, a bit self-consciously.

First Toby, then Cat and Flora stepped under the arch and followed the flashlight's thin beam. They had gone about seven or eight paces into the tunnel when Flora made a small, exclamatory noise.

"Are you OK?" Cat asked, struggling to keep her voice steady. Flora was farther behind her than she'd realized and Cat could barely make her out in the darkness.

Silence.

"Flora?"

"Yes . . . sorry." Her face suddenly loomed into the glow of Toby's flashlight, pale as a wraith. "Look, we've found it. There."

Sure enough, the slope of the wall to her left had been spray-painted with a fuzzy red outline of the wheel, its curves vivid against the tidemark of graffiti all around. Flora was already reaching out a hand to trace the markings. In a few seconds, her palm gleamed metal. "We only need one," she told them, peering down at the disc. "But you have to be touching me." And in a flash of her coin, it was all over.

The home side of the underpass wasn't much of an im-provement, smelling of toilets and littered with fast-food wrappers, but after where they'd come from, the motley row of liquor stores and discount shops ahead looked almost welcoming. All three hurried out toward the street.

Just before they got there, somebody shouldered past Cat, so roughly that she stumbled. "Hey!" she called out to his retreating back, and he momentarily turned, his face a gray blur beneath his hooded sweatshirt. She remembered the youths in Mercury Square, the slouching boy glimpsed in the static of a computer screen, the climbing figure in the Arcanum. But he was already gone.

According to their watches, it was only half past nine. Even on a rainy Sunday night there was plenty of traffic about, and a kebab shop across the street was doing brisk business. Cat glanced back at the bridge and saw the two towers rear into the night, their stories spangled with lit windows.

"Whoa," said Toby, shaking his head. "I mean, wow. How cool was that?"

"Cool?" repeated Cat. *"Cool?"*

"Aw, c'mon. I thought it was meant to be one of those female fantasies: 'women who run with the wolves'—you know—empowering."

Cat looked at him incredulously. He coughed and changed the subject. "Er, right, we need to think about getting home. That's Canary Wharf over there, so—hey, where are you going?"

Flora was limping across the road. "Taxi," she said without looking back. Then, reluctantly, "I suppose you can come too, if you want. . . ."

They went to join her. Flora was a mess, her hair straggling, makeup smudged, bare arms covered in goose bumps, but she gave instructions to the cab driver with crisp assurance. Then she sank back into the seat and fell asleep. Toby, meanwhile, wasted no time in getting into an animated—if one-sided—chat with the driver about the local hip-hop scene.

Cat couldn't believe it. Flora's indifference was one thing, Toby's carelessness quite another. She remembered his airy and, as it turned out, completely false assurances that chancers were free to do whatever they liked within the Game. Yet once faced with the realities of the Arcanum, he seemed more inclined than ever to treat it as one big adventure.

She leaned back in her seat, half listening to Toby's chatter, interspersed with grunts from their driver and the burbling of the radio. Outside, the quiet Sunday streets slid past, streaked quicksilver in the rain.

"This is me," said Toby, and Cat blinked, realizing that she had been close to nodding off herself. His voice seemed to come from very far away, though she was blearily aware of him saying that he could get home from here, that he'd see them soon, wasn't it great, bye guys, bye, bye. . . .

"We can get the driver to drop you off wherever you want," Flora offered, once they were on the move again. Her voice was no longer slurred, just very sleepy-sounding. "I've got plenty of cash."

I'll bet, thought Cat. "I'll get out at Oxford Street," she said shortly. "We're nearly there."

Flora was about to say something else, but the trilling of a phone interrupted her. She extracted a slim metallic-pink phone from her pocket. "Yes? Oh, Georgia, hi . . ."

Cat closed her eyes and tried to zone out again. The conversation ended on a brightly social note—"Morelli's at eleven, then. Brilliant. See you tomorrow!"—and the next moment, the cabdriver was pulling up beneath a set of Christmas lights, whose flashing reindeers formed an arch between two department stores.

Cat climbed stiffly out of the cab. Flora was now setting her smeared face to rights with the aid of a makeup compact. She raised a hand in brief farewell, then went back to combing the tangles from her hair.

And soon, thought Cat, as she began the chilly trudge back to the flat, Flora would go home to where her parents were waiting. It would be a big old house, most likely, where light glowed from behind velvet curtains and the streets were quiet all night long. The blond woman from the church would open the door and hold out her arms. "Thank goodness you're home," she'd say. "Everything all right, sweetheart?" the kind-faced man would ask.

"I'm fine, thanks, Daddy," Cat whispered into the darkness of the city. "Everything's fine."

CHAPTER EIGHT

THE NEXT MORNING, MONDAY, Cat had three or four calls from Toby. She ignored them, just as she ignored Bel's anxious looks over the breakfast table. More fool him if he imagined yesterday had been the beginning of mutual magical escapades. Even so, she was—on balance—grateful to the guy. Flora too. For all its craziness, last night had been very instructive, she reminded herself as she flicked through the Yellow Pages. Moira's Bar, Morden House, Morelli's . . .

It turned out to be a coffee shop just off the King's Road. Flora and her friends had taken over most of the ground floor, sprawled elegantly on the oversized sofa or perched on the chairs. The girls' lattes were skinny to match their jeans, their lips as glossy as their hair. There were a couple of floppy-haired, drawling boys dotted among them.

Flora, sipping daintily from a glass of water, didn't seem any the worse for wear from the night before. Her skin was peachy-smooth, her eyes clear blue. She was wearing a cream cashmere sweater, and a tiny gold cross glinted around her neck.

"Hello, Flora. Got a minute?"

Conversation halted and glances were exchanged. "Do you *know* this girl, Flo?" frowned the fair-haired boy sitting next to her.

Flora gave a sweet, helpless shrug. "Well . . . we do seem to keep on bumping into each other." She blinked up at Cat with the polite bafflement she did so well. "You know, I'm afraid this isn't a good time."

"But the future of the world is at stake!" Cat turned to the others and grinned broadly. "See, we're both members of the *Lord of the Rings* Role-Playing Society. Flora here is one of our most adventurous gamers. But now we're coming up to a critical strategic point. . . ."

Flora's eyes flashed. Two of the girls were spluttering into their lattes; the rest of the crowd looked torn between confusion and hostility. Cat pressed on remorselessly. "Orcs against Elves: the final showdown. So, Flo, are you coming? Or maybe I should just pull up a chair and—"

"No need," said Flora smoothly. The boy next to her caught at her hand. "It's fine, Charlie. Honestly. I just need to sort out this . . . mix-up. I won't be long."

She followed Cat out of the coffee shop, limping slightly, and over to a bench across the street. They both sat down warily, not quite looking at each other.

"I really don't appreciate being put on the spot like that," Flora began. "How did you find me, anyway?"

"Your phone call in the cab. How's the ankle?"

"It's not too bad, thank you."

"Could've been worse. You could be picking werewolf teeth out of it."

Flora wrinkled her pretty little nose, as if to say she found the remark in bad taste. "I don't mean to sound rude, but what do I have to do to get you to leave me alone?"

"Talk to me. About last night . . . among other things."

"Last night? Really? I wouldn't have thought there's much to be said."

"It was lucky for you we came along, though, wasn't it? Else I'm not sure you could've got up that fire escape. Dodgy ankle aside, you were so smashed you could barely walk straight, let alone outrun the beasties." Flora's breath hissed but Cat just smiled blandly at her. Two could play at that game. "Is that what the Arcanum is to you?" she continued, still in a conversational tone. "Party central? A place to get off your face where Mummy and Daddy need never know?"

If Cat was hoping to get a rise out of the other girl, she was unsuccessful.

"I wouldn't have lasted very long if that were true," Flora replied tightly. She began fiddling with the tassels of her scarf. "Not that it's any of your business but . . . yesterday was a bad day, that's all."

An anniversary, Cat remembered her saying. She pushed the thought to one side. "You're right: it's not my business. Fact is, I couldn't care less about what you get up to in there. I'm just here for your expertise."

"Your sidekick seems well informed."

"Toby? He's an amateur. Not like you."

Flora didn't say anything for a while, staring out at the street with unseeing eyes. Then she sighed. "What do you want to know?"

Cat took a deep breath.

"The first time I went into the Arcanum, the Six of Cups was in play. But when I went back to find it again, the threshold had gone. I want you to tell me how I can get back into the card."

"It is a dangerous card."

"I thought it was one of the better ones."

Flora made a small, impatient gesture. "Every card has its tricks. People can disappear in that one, wandering endlessly around in the past until they forget their present selves. After all," she said quietly, "there are few things more seductive than lost happiness."

For a moment, Cat caught the sound of distant laughter, the scent of flowers and sunbaked earth drifting in the air. Once upon a time, there had been a family: Caroline, Adam and Kitty Harper. But their happiness hadn't been lost—it had been stolen.

She clenched her jaw. "I don't want to go there so I can be a rose-tinted kid again. I want to go back because I saw something there that I don't understand. Something important. Unless . . . unless it's just a trick?"

"The Six of Cups only shows the truth." The other girl's face was blank. Cat wondered if Flora, too, had walked across that velvet lawn, into the maze of memories beyond.

"So how do I get the threshold back?"

"You can't—a threshold disappears once a move is finished and the players have left. Then another one appears somewhere else, for another knight. What lies on the other side will depend on the card dealt to the knight in play."

"Well, once I've gotten into the Arcanum, can't I go from one card to another?"

"No. Each move is played within its own self-contained space. Like the squares on a chessboard. If you kept on walking, before long you'd find you were hitting dead end after dead end."

"But the Six of Cups is my only chance—"

"Then you have two options," Flora replied evenly. "Either you keep going into the Arcanum, time after time, threshold after threshold, in the hope that you stumble on what you're looking for, perhaps in the Six of Cups, perhaps in some other card. Or . . ."

"Or?"

"You walk away. Forget any of this ever happened, ignore the prickling on your palm, shut your eyes to the signs on the thresholds. Look for your answers in the real world."

"I can't do that."

"No." Flora gave a half smile. "None of us can. It's ironic, really. A chancer can't play for a triumph. We're part of a game we're not allowed to win. And yet the temptation's the same."

"What temptation?"

"Of finding your heart's desire, of course." She spoke with bitterness.

There was a burst of laughter from across the street: Flora's friends had come out of the coffee shop and were taking up the pavement in a lively gaggle. She got to her feet and straightened her clothes. "It's time I got back."

"OK then. Thanks and . . . uh, see you around some-time."

Flora gave another of her polite, bland smiles. "Maybe."

Cat watched as she walked back to her friends, who pulled her in, laughing, exclaiming, shaking out their glossy hair. The boy called Charlie slung a careless arm around her shoulder. The group moved on.

When Cat got back to the flat that afternoon, she realized she was too exhausted to think, even to feel. After every-thing that had happened, the numbness came as a relief.

She spent the next couple of days holed up in her bed-room with *The Wondrous World of Tarot* and an ordinary Tarot deck, trying to familiarize herself with the cards so that she could recognize their Game of Triumphs equivalents. The il-lustrations were reasonably similar and so were their mean-ings, as far as she could tell. But it was impossible to guess what kind of strange life the Arcanum might give them.

Some cards were easier to remember than others. The Fool was the chancers' card; Fortune, the one that called a Lottery. Four aces, one for each of the four elements. The Greater Arcana's triumphs and the Lesser Arcana's court cards . . . Cat presumed that the court cards showing groups of people in various activities, often involving combat, were the moves where knaves were likely to be involved.

There was one triumph that she kept coming back to, which was illustrated by a stern-faced woman holding a sword and scales. Justice. With Justice on her side, Cat would be able to find her parents' murderer, and make him pay. But she was a chancer, and this was a power she couldn't win.

Please, her mother's voice entreated in her head, *there's been some mistake.* And the other voice, the third voice, the one that was just out of reach . . .

Out of reach in the ordinary world, yes, but in the Arcanum it was a different matter. There, where time and distance blurred, she might find all kinds of impossible things—forgotten voices, secret truths, her past happiness. She might even find the person who had taken it from her. In which case, Cat wouldn't need any triumph. Cat would deal out justice herself.

She told Bel that she felt she might be coming down with something. Neither of them had yet made any direct reference to the revelations of Saturday night. It was as if they had suddenly become shy of each other, Bel especially, and Cat found Bel's nervousness deeply unsettling. For the moment, Bel could understand that she was still coming to terms with the true circumstances of her parents' death, but Cat knew that from here on, the enormous, impossible secret of the Arcanum would always be between them.

By Wednesday afternoon, however, Bel had decided enough was enough. When Cat slunk into the kitchen to get some toast, it was to find the place festooned with tropical-fruit fairy lights. Luridly glowing bananas, pineapples and bunches of grapes dripped from the walls; a fringe of red and green tinsel hung in the doorframe. Her aunt was sitting with her feet up on the table, wearing a paper crown from a Christmas cracker and eating brandy butter from a jar.

"God almighty," she said, looking Cat up and down, "you look like crap."

"Compliments of the season to you, too."

"How d'you like the bling?"

"Tinsel-tastic . . . Can I have some of that?"

"Help yourself. It's about time we had a bit of Christmas spirit round here. And speaking of spirit," Bel continued sternly, jabbing her spoon for emphasis, "you, puss, are growing old before your time. Old and dull. And I'm no better. We need to get out of this hole of a flat and have some fun."

Cat grinned through a mouthful of brandy butter, mostly from relief that things appeared to be back to normal between them. "What kind of fun?"

"The high-rolling kind."

Bel explained, gleefully, that Greg had used his connections to wangle them tickets to a charity poker tournament being held in a Mayfair hotel that night. There would be bright lights and glamour. Free booze and designer canapés. Cat couldn't think of anything worse.

"Sounds like a bit of a busman's holiday," she tried. "For you and Greg, I mean. And gambling's for mugs—everyone knows that."

It was true Bel thought of the Luxe's clientele with a kind of genial contempt. "Poor old dopes," she'd say, "down to their last chip, hoping their final throw's going to save the mortgage or the marriage or whatever it is. And even if it does, the next round takes it off them all over again." But she always added that pity was a waste of time, given the way gamblers got abusive when their numbers didn't come up.

Now she waved off Cat's remark. "Yeah, but this is different—a good cause and all that, for people who can afford it."

"Sounds heartwarming."

"'Sides, you and me are going for the social scene, not the bleeding poker."

It occurred to Cat that maybe that was what the evening was about for Bel: a fantasy version of her job, where the champagne fizzed and the music played, where everyone was a winner and nothing important was at stake. Which made it all the more difficult for Cat to explain why she didn't want to go. In spite of her fear and resentment of the Game, it was all she thought about. She just had to decide her next move.

Greg's connections weren't high enough to get them through the front of the Martingale Hotel; instead, they were sneaked through a service door at the back. Since the entrance fee for the event was three hundred pounds for players and two hundred for spectators, they could hardly complain, although Bel, who'd been hoping for marble and chandeliers, was a little disappointed by their surroundings. Everything was sleek and minimalist, luxuriously restrained.

As they entered the reception area, Cat found herself thinking back to Temple House. The party-going hum was the same, and the air tingled with the same sense of privilege and expectation. All around them, women were greeting each other with cooing air kisses, the men exchanging slaps on the back and barks of laughter.

She could see Bel sizing the place up with amusement. Bel's flashy dress and brash brightness should have been incompatible with everything else about the evening, and yet the heads she turned were mostly admiring. The male ones, anyway; Cat was rather touched by the proprietary way in which Greg ushered her to a table in the bar. His dusty tux made him look more drooping than ever. Not that she could talk. In her plain black shift—one of Bel's castoffs—she could almost have passed for one of the hotel staff.

Cat had known from the start that she was feeling too fidgety to sit down and too prickly for company. She told the other two that she was going to the main room to check out the tournament, but it didn't take long for her to realize that as a spectator sport, poker came somewhere between bowling and watching paint dry. From there, she wandered into another lounge area, where a jazz band was in the process of setting up.

It was also the place where the few guests who were near her own age had assembled. The way they looked and talked reminded her of Flora's friends. In fact, there was a blond girl in a lace cocktail dress who—

"Cat? I don't believe it! You know, I'd been hoping I'd run into you again."

Cat had seen Flora the ice maiden, Flora the wild child, but this was a different Flora again. Flora the friendly, all sparkle and charm.

"You have?"

"Oh yes. What luck you turning up tonight!" This made Cat uneasy. She didn't trust luck, or coincidence. Not anymore. "Are you here with your parents, too? Daddy's on the board of the trust. Last year they raised over a hundred thousand pounds, you know. Anyway . . ." Flora lowered her voice, though her expression remained brightly social. "I was thinking that we should meet up. Toby as well. There's something I think you'll be really interested in, to do with what we were talking about the other day. Something I've found."

"To do with the, er, Game?"

Flora smiled. "What else? Listen, how are you fixed for tomorrow? I know everyone's madly busy at this time of year."

Ah yes. The giddy social whirl. "I'll have to check my calendar."

The other girl either ignored or didn't pick up on her ironical tone. "Well, if you're free, perhaps you and Toby should come round to mine. Say, six-ish?" Flora scribbled her address and phone number down on a piece of paper, and Cat found herself folding it away in her pocket. "Wonderful. If I don't see you later, enjoy the rest of the evening!"

Cat was left frowning to herself. Part of her was tempted to tell Flora to shove it—why should Cat come running when she called? But underneath the charm, there had been something a little feverish in Flora's manner, a kind of urgency, which was very intriguing. She'd been waiting for something like this. Her next cue . . .

Bel's voice cut into her thoughts. "There you are! Who were you talking to back then?"

"Just this girl I kind of . . . bumped into, once."

"Looks a right little princess," Bel sniffed. "One of those trust-fund types."

"Looks like it."

"Listen, puss-cat, have you seen Greg anywhere?"

"The last I saw, he was getting cozy with you in the corner."

"Yeah, but then he went off to have a word with his mate, the one who got us into this place. I don't suppose you'd be a star and go look for him?"

"Why can't you?"

Bel rolled her eyes humorously. " 'Cause I'm busy networking, aren't I?" She lowered her voice. "See him over there? Goatee, cigar? Well, he's only the manager of that flash new casino off Trafalgar Square; Alliette's, it's called. This could be my big break."

"I don't see why you need Greg, then. Won't he just cramp your style?"

"Greg might be my boss, but he knows I'm destined for better things than the Luxe. He'll big me up just to keep me sweet. C'mon," she wheedled, "he'll not have gone far. Try the night porter's room—we passed it on our way in."

Cat decided that looking for Greg was marginally more interesting than watching poker. But retracing their back-door route to the party was trickier than she'd thought. Perhaps she should have gone right rather than left at the end of the hall, or maybe her first mistake was going past the last set of double doors. At any rate, before she knew it she was adrift in the back stairs and service corridors. She passed a laundry-sorting room, full of weary dark-faced women; glimpsed a cramped office lined with pigeonholes; heard clashes and roars from the kitchens. Eventually, she found her way to the delivery entrance at the back of the building. A couple of porters were on a break, smoking by the wall.

She was about to go and ask them for directions, but as she turned she stumbled into someone who'd come out with a sack full of rubbish. It slipped from his grasp, disgorging a glut of plastic food wrappings. Cat went to help but he gestured her away, swearing under his breath and stuffing everything back in with irritable jerks. As he looked up their eyes met. There were dark circles under his, their expression hard and mistrustful.

"I've met you before." The words came out before she could stop them.

"Yeah? So many girls, so little time," he said shortly, pushing back a hank of dirty brown hair. She remembered his bitten fingernails.

"From Mercury Square. Outside Temple House?"

"Can't say I've had the pleasure."

He had his back to her as he slung the bag into a Dumpster. He was taller and broader than she remembered, and wearing an apron over ill-fitting overalls. Tall, and slouching.

What had Odile said to Ahab as she looked into the screen? *He claims to be in search of one of your knights . . .*

"You're looking for a Knight of Wands," she said.

At once, he whipped around. They faced each other, his face startled and angry; hers questioning.

"Oi, Blaine!" Someone inside yelled at him to hurry up, followed by a barrage of expletives. And the next moment Blaine was pushing past, back toward the steam and clamor of the kitchens. The way he shouldered her out of his path was familiar, too.

Bel was still talking to the man with the goatee. She was doing her special laugh, flinging back her head to display a swoop of throat and shaking out her hair. They both appeared to be enjoying the performance. However, as soon as Bel saw Cat, she moved away from the bar to join her by the door.

"Cat! I thought we'd lost you! I felt dead guilty; Greg turned up just after you left."

"Where's he gone now?"

"Oh, he'll be back in a sec—he had to take a phone call. Are you all right? You look a bit peaky."

"Yeah, I think I must be still fighting this cold. Um . . . you don't mind if I head off, do you?"

Bel's face fell. "Listen, I know it's a bit stuffy here but Leo"—she jerked her head toward the goatee man—"says he'll introduce us to some people. You should come over and say hello. And there's a band just started up, and we've hardly touched the nibbles."

"Please, Bel, I'm not in the right mood. Not for this sort of thing."

Her aunt looked guilty. "No. No, of course." She took Cat's arm and drew her into the corridor. "It's just that I'm worried about you, puss-cat. After the shock you've had . . . I thought a bit of distraction might do you good. Too much too soon, I guess. But I hate seeing you like this—I really do."

The sympathy was nearly Cat's undoing. Her encounter with Flora and the boy Blaine had unsettled her more than she'd realized.

"I hate *being* like this," she burst out. "I hate being confused and angry and helpless. I hate being so *weak*. . . . Bel, have you ever blundered into something you didn't understand? Something you were better off not knowing? And you wish you could forget it all, that life could go back to before, but it's too late, everything's changed. And you have to do something about it, to take back control, but you don't know how, and—and—"

She ground to a halt at the sight of Bel's stricken face.

"God knows, if I could make things right, I would. I . . ."

"'S'OK.'" Somehow, Cat managed to smile. "Don't worry, I'm all right really. Not like me to go all hysterical; it's the flu germs talking. Honest."

"You don't look all right to me. You don't sound all right, either."

"I'll be fine. I just needed to have a rant, that's all."

"No, Cat, I've screwed up; I can see that. I haven't been

straight with you and now, like you said, everything's changed."

"Things haven't changed between us. That's not what I meant. And anyhow, I won't let us be changed, not by *anything*."

"You really mean that—not anything?"

"I swear it."

Bel looked at her fierce expression, and this time she laughed, relieved. "Right you are, puss-cat. I'll swear to that, too. Look, let's go home, anyhow. Have some peace and quiet."

"No! There's no reason for you to leave as well. I'll only feel worse for making you miss out."

But Cat was overruled, and a few minutes later she and Bel were walking out through the main entrance. A ten-foot Christmas tree dominated the lobby. It was a real tree, though so symmetrical it looked false, its baubles arranged in rigidly coordinated tiers. As Cat brushed past, she caught the spice of pine, a dark sap scent that made her throat ache. For a moment, her vision blurred, and she was three years old again, reaching into the prickling branches for the gleam of chocolate coins.

THE FOOL

CHAPTER NINE

"THINK ABOUT IT," TOBY was saying as they walked to Flora's on Thursday evening. "We can be like the Famous Three or something. The Prom Queen, the Lovable Geek and—"

"You're not lovable."

"Aw, c'mon, haven't you ever heard of geek chic? Instant X factor. Anyway, as I was saying. Team Arcanum: the Prom Queen, the Lovable Geek and the Goth."

"I am not a Goth."

"OK, not technically speaking, no. But you have to admit, you're on the pale and prickly side," Toby said cheerily. "I suppose you could be the Enigmatic Loner, if you'd prefer."

"I'd prefer it if you'd shut the hell up."

Cat's mood did not improve when they arrived at Flora's house, a big white-columned affair on the edge of one of London's most fashionable parks. It was the kind of street where even the exhaust fumes reeked of money.

The door was opened by a blond woman in a silk dressing gown. She raised a perfectly plucked eyebrow in interrogation.

"Yes?"

"We're here to see Flora."

"Are you sure?" The woman continued to look them up and down in a slightly unfocused fashion.

"Mummy." Flora's voice came from the hall beyond. "It's all right, I'm expecting them."

Her mother shrugged elegantly, the movement making the ice in her drink tinkle, then pinned a well-practiced smile onto her face. "Marv'llous, darling. You know how I love meeting your friends. . . . Sorry to be a touch *dishabille*—running late, as usual. I swear the party season gets more exhausting by the year." She laughed, a little too loudly, and raised her tumbler as if to make a toast. Cat remembered Flora in the garden at Temple House, her parody of social charm.

"We're going up to my bedroom. Have fun at the Richmonds'." Flora wasted no time in ushering her guests upstairs. Cat, her feet sinking into thick carpeting, had only a vague impression of the rest of the house, which appeared to be done up in varying shades of white.

Flora's bedroom continued the theme. The bed had a gauzy white canopy, and a gas fire flickered in a white marble fireplace. The pin-board above her desk was covered with snapshots of Flora and her friends at parties, on ski slopes, city breaks and country weekends. A night breeze ruffled the curtains by the window, which looked over the garden and the park beyond.

Their hostess perched on the edge of the bed, hugging a cushion to her chest. "Oh," she said, "I should have asked. Would you like anything to eat or drink?"

"Why, are you going to ring for the maid?" asked Toby.

"We don't call her that. Mina's like one of the family."

Cat turned from the window. "Toby thinks you're the prom queen," she said abruptly.

"I beg your pardon?"

"You know. All the best hero squads have one. You're the token blond cheerleading type, Toby's the geek and I'm the Goth."

"It was only a joke," Toby said, reddening. "There's no need to keep going on about it."

"It's a joke with a point, though. Right from the start, Flora, you made it clear that you wanted as little as possible to do with me or Toby or anyone. Now you've called a team meeting. What's changed?"

"Well, there's no need to make a drama out of it," Flora replied mildly, twirling her hair. "I just came across something that I thought the two of you should know about. Whether you choose to take it any further is entirely up to you."

"So what is it?"

"Something I found—well, stumbled on, really—in that

horrid tunnel under the bridge. When we were trying to find the threshold."

Cat watched as the other girl walked over to her dressing table, took a silver key from one of the drawers and passed it to Toby. It was plain and slim, and the bow—the handle-like part at the gripping end—was a design of a circle enclosing an oval.

"It's a zero! No way!" He turned to Cat to explain. "A zero represents a chancer, because the Fool is outside the sequence of triumphs. Do you know what the key belongs to, Flora?"

"Not for sure." She hesitated. "But . . . there's a door in Temple House that's always locked. Its keyhole is marked with a zero, too."

Cat frowned. "And so you think this key is meant for us?"

"The three of us—and maybe another."

"Like who?"

"When we were in the Triumph of the Moon, there was somebody else there apart from the knight, remember. The other person on the fire escape. Now, there's usually only one knight per move, and there aren't any knaves in the triumph cards. And that person was just as anxious to stay out of the action as we were." Flora took a coin from her pocket and tossed it from one hand to the other. "Here's the thing. You know when you reach a threshold and raise the coin, it's always marked with a sword, cup, wand or pentacle to show which court is in play? Well, when I got us out of that move, my coin was marked with a zero. That's never happened before: after all, chancers can't make moves of their own. Yet the coin showed that the focus of the move was on us.

"So I believe that as well as the knight and the three of us, there was a fourth chancer in the Triumph of the Moon that night. Four chancers in one move! A rarity—definitely. A coincidence? Perhaps. But then a key with a zero literally appeared on our path. And that, I think, is no coincidence at all."

"Like an omen," said Toby in awestruck tones. "Do you know how many chancers there are in the Game?"

"No. Until I met the two of you, I never encountered more than one other at any one time. Of course, there must be a few knaves who began as we did." She gave a slight smile. "It's only when we break the rules that we make a difference; I think that's why the kings and queens like to have us in the Game. There's always the possibility we'll slip up and interfere in such a way as to tip the balance of power from one court to another.

"Now, I could be wrong about this key business. It might not fit the door I'm thinking of. It might have nothing to do with anything. But I thought you should know."

Cat was still frowning. "Why didn't you say anything about the key when you found it?"

"I'm afraid I wasn't thinking straight. We were in such a rush I just stuffed it in my pocket and carried on with getting us out of the Arcanum."

Hmm. Cat wasn't entirely convinced by this. She was thinking, too, of the boy called Blaine, and whether he could be the mysterious fourth chancer in the Triumph of the Moon. But if Flora could take her time deciding what and when to share, then so could Cat. "OK. What do you want to do next?"

"Well, if you're interested, I thought the three of us could go and try the key."

"In Temple House? Right now?"

"Sure—" There came a noise from downstairs, raised angry voices and a crashing sound, and she stiffened. "Wait here a sec."

As soon as she'd left, Toby, who had been fidgeting in his chair, got to his feet and began to pace the floor. "This is a major development, you know. Perhaps we'll find some ancient prophecy! Or a magic weapon. Anything's possible."

"That's what scares me."

But in spite of Cat's misgivings, she was just as curious as Toby. What if the key really did lead to something important, something that could literally unlock the secrets of the Arcanum?

"Hey, Cat, if you could win any triumph, what would it be?"

"Dunno. Haven't really thought about it."

"Yeah, *right.*"

"Whichever's the one for being filthy rich, then," she said, to keep him quiet.

"Ah, the Empress. It's a popular choice. Me, I'd go for something like the Chariot, maybe."

"What's that for?"

"Heroism." He grinned. "I quite fancy being the Clark Kent of the Arcanum."

"The last thing the Arcanum needs is men in tights. It's already quite frightening enough."

Flora came back and Toby tried her—"So which triumph would you choose to win? Cat was saying she'd pick the Empress."

"I'd rather not discuss prizes, if you don't mind," said Flora primly. "Players say that if you talk about getting a prize, you jinx it."

This hadn't been the case with the two knights Cat had talked to. They'd seemed quite happy to discuss their triumphs. However, Flora's dream prize was her own business, and Cat wasn't going to pry. It might invite unwelcome questions in turn. . . .

"Are you ready to go?" the other girl asked. "My parents have just left, so we might as well get a move on. I know a shortcut."

The other two nodded, trying to suppress a flutter of nerves. Their hostess, however, looked utterly composed as she slipped the key into her pocket and made her preparations to leave.

They followed her downstairs and into the drawing room at the back of the house. This was as polished, pale and orderly as the rest of the place, except for the mirror above the fireplace, which had a crack running across the center as if something had been violently hurled against it. Flora made no comment, however, as she led them through the French doors and into a garden glittering with frost.

A gate in the wall opened onto a tree-lined path that

ran alongside the inner railings of the public park. The noise and lights of the city were not far away, but the expanse of grass unfolding through the darkness felt as otherworldly as any scene in the Arcanum. It was bitterly cold.

"No one's supposed to be here after sunset—the main gates are locked at five," Flora told them. "You have to keep your eye out for the park wardens, and sometimes a tramp gets in."

Then she ducked under the rails, her footprints black in the silver grass. She was heading in the direction of a summerhouse, built like a toy temple with slender white columns and a domed roof, and set on a small rise.

As the other two hastened to catch up, they felt a familiar prickle on their palms. Toby pointed to the summerhouse. "I think that's a threshold."

"There's always been one there," Flora said casually, as they walked past. "Well, for as long as I've been in the Game, anyway."

"And how long have you been playing?"

"Since I was ten years old."

God. Cat tried to picture a blond girl-child, adrift among the monsters and marvels. No wonder Flora was a bit schizo. "I thought thresholds disappear once a move is over."

"Obviously, then, the move in play here is still incomplete."

"Have you been into it?" Toby asked.

"No," she said crisply. "Come on."

Reaching the other side of the park, they climbed over the railings onto a busy main road. From there, it was fifteen minutes' walk to Mercury Square.

"You must've been through a lot of cards by now," Cat said to Flora as they made their way through the streets. "Does that mean you know what you're in for as soon as you switch sides at a threshold?"

"I haven't been into all that many moves, as it happens. Regular trips to the Arcanum are bad for the health. And anyway, the Arcanum never brings a card to life in the same way twice—there might be similarities, but no two moves are exactly alike. . . . Turn left, Toby. Yes, it's just down here."

Temple House appeared lifeless, its windows shuttered. As they pushed open the door, the sense of abandonment became even more complete. The gold curtain had gone, and the mat in front of the door was littered with junk mail. The room to the right of the stairs had been stripped bare; in the one on the left, dust sheets sagged in lumpy mounds. The drowsiness Cat had experienced on previous visits still hung in the air, though without the confusion of the crowds it was easier to shake off. However, she noticed that the three of them were moving a little more sluggishly.

Flora led the way up the stairs to the third floor and into the mirrored ballroom. The last time they had been there, it had been brightly thronged; now their reflections in the glass were as dim as ghosts. All the same, Cat wasn't sure she trusted the deserted feel of the place. Eyeing the blank TV screen suspended from the ceiling, she wondered who could be watching them, and from where. Languid Alastor; chilly Odile; Lucrezia with her dark opulence; Ahab, somber as a tombstone.

Flora seemed to know what she was thinking. "It's fine; Temple House belongs to all players. No one's going to interfere. Now, look at this."

They were standing in front of the mirrored wall that faced the doors. Its glimmering surfaces looked as uniform as the others lining the room, but Flora guided them to the central panel, where, peering closely, they saw there was a small keyhole to one side, with an oval—a zero—etched around it in the glass.

"I've been over every inch of this house," she said, "in every room, down every corridor, at times when the place has been heaving with people or as derelict as today, and this is the only door I've never seen open. I've never even seen anyone attempt to go through it, or found so much as a thumbprint on the glass."

"So what are we waiting for?" Toby asked.

Flora didn't waste time on ceremony or second thoughts. She fitted the silver key to the lock and turned it with one brisk movement; there was a click, and the panel sprang open, sliding smoothly over to one side. It revealed a narrow flight of stone stairs.

There was a slightly breathless pause as they took in the steepness of the steps, and the darkness of the waiting shadows below. Toby was the first to recover. "Can I go first?" he asked.

It must be his every dream come true, thought Cat as

she went after him. Hidden chambers and secret passages. Dungeons and dragons . . . ! Then there was a click from behind, and the stairwell plunged into blackness. Flora had locked the door behind them.

"Are you crazy?" Cat hissed. "Now we can't see a thing!"

"I'd just prefer to reduce the possibility of anyone creeping up behind us," Flora replied. "We'll have to feel our way. Unless . . . Toby, what about your flashlight?"

"Er, back on my bedside table. Sorry."

They shuffled on down the steps. And down, and down, and farther down again. Though the walls pressing on either side were cool and smooth, Cat's heart banged hotly against her ribs. She soon lost track of how many floors they must have passed. It seemed as if the blindness would last forever, a descent without end.

But at last the black turned to gray, grew softer and warmer, until they stumbled out into a lit room. The floor was checkered black and white; the walls were wood-paneled and set with alcoves where old-fashioned oil lamps burned. On the wall to their right was a large gilt frame that reminded Cat of the paintings in the gallery upstairs; its canvas, however, was so dark with age or grime that it was impossible to tell what was depicted.

The only furniture in the room was a circular table covered with green felt, displaying a triangular die, and a card with four more cards set around its corners. The faces of the die were blank, and the five cards were similarly featureless, both sides patterned with a design of interlocking wheels. It was as if, thought Cat uneasily, they were waiting for a game that hadn't yet been made, let alone begun. Across from the stairs was an archway hung with a curtain of gold brocade; the lettering above read *regnabo, regno, regnavi, sum sine regno.*

"I shall reign, I reign, I have reigned, I am without reign," Flora said. "It's the inscription around the spokes of Fortune's Wheel." Unlike the other two, she showed no outward sign of nerves, or even much curiosity about their surroundings. Instead, she waited by the archway, impatient to be moving on.

When they drew back the curtain, they saw how far down they had come. They were below even the foundations of Temple House, among roots of ancient stone. Through low arches and squat pillars, a maze of chambers lay before them, lit by more oil lamps set in alcoves along the walls. A faint scent, as of incense, sweetened the air.

"We must be in some kind of crypt," Toby marveled. "Come to think of it, we've already had werewolves, so we're probably due a vampire or two. Or a mummy. . . ."

"Oh, drop the melodrama." Cat was damned if she'd let Toby get to her. "If it was a crypt, there'd be inscriptions. Tombstones. Bimbos in black leather doing kung fu and waving crucifixes."

"Sounds good to me."

"This is a sacred place," said Flora quietly. "Can't you feel it?"

"Yes! It's like that Mithraic temple they excavated under the City." Toby was determined not to be outdone. "I read

155

a book about it once. The ancients built it underground for secret rites. Maybe we're going to meet a pagan god!"

"Yeah, and maybe we'll have to offer you up as a blood sacrifice." But in spite of her flippant words, Cat was wondering who had lit the lamps and put the cards on the table. There was no sign of dust—someone must have been here—yet she had the feeling this place had lain undisturbed for a long, long time.

They moved on, slowly and cautiously, among crude columns and under shadowy vaults, following the path lit by the lamps, until at last they came to a circular chamber with a high domed roof. In the center of the room a tree was growing. At the end of one of its branches was a noose, from which hung the motionless body of a man.

All three drew in their breath. The tree sprang strong and green from the bare stone. Its glossy leaves were rustling, although there was no breeze here in the depths of the earth, and the flame in the lamps burned straight. The limp body weighed down its branch like some kind of monstrous fruit.

Then the man opened his eyes and smiled. "Ave Fortuna, Imperatrix Mundi!"

Cat tasted blood. Without realizing it, she'd bitten hard into her lip. Beside her, Flora was rigid as a statue. Even Toby was, for once, lost for words.

"Do not be afraid," the man said, his voice as peaceful as his smile. "I can do you no harm."

After the initial shock, Cat realized that although his body hung unsupported from the cord around his neck, some invisible force must be holding him up. He was suspended in the air, as if weightless, about three feet off the ground.

The eyes that regarded them were astonishingly wide and a vivid blue, set in a gentle, childlike face. His skin was drained of all color, and his hair, which came down to his shoulders, was neither the blond of youth nor the white of age, but something in between. His clothes were plain black, of indeterminate style, and his hands were bound behind his back.

Toby had recovered the power of speech. "Er . . . shouldn't you be upside down, like on the card?"

Now the man looked amused. "Since the Triumph of the Hanged Man was first created, my fate has known many representations." He sighed, and the tree's leaves murmured as if in response; in the dim light of the chamber they had acquired a coppery tint. His eyes shone innocent and blue. "Would you like to know," he said softly, "how the Game of Triumphs came to be?"

THE HANGED MAN

$\mathcal{C}$HAPTER $\mathcal{T}$EN

"THERE WAS A CITY," he began. "Long, long ago, like in the fairy tales—though it was real enough. A city of art and power and learning, much of which has been lost. And each year, on its great festival day, the city held a lottery, when the people would pay to receive a token. Most of these tokens were blank, but a number of them could be exchanged for prizes. Some of these were practical and others decorative, but a few were precious.

"Many citizens played this lottery, but the leisured classes did not, considering it beneath them. Until one year, the authorities decided to introduce something different. The four leading guilds within the city, the ones who administered the lottery, announced that they were going to include penalties among the prizes. Just a few. Small fines or trials, to be performed in honor of the gods. And to their surprise, subscription to the lottery doubled. To play now required an element of daring and so became a matter of prestige.

"The next year, the lottery was not open to all. Invitations were issued at random. The rewards were more glittering, the penalties more dangerous. As a result, the guilds were obliged to form an order whose purpose was to enforce the fulfillment of the lots, and give worship to the goddess Fortune and her Wheel.

"And with time, the workings of the lottery—or Game, as it was now called—grew yet more elaborate. The heads of the four guilds met in secret for its operation. The symbols on the lots became so complex it was no longer clear what was a penalty and what was a prize, for their making was steeped in mystery. So too was the fulfillment of the fates decreed. Over the years, it was rumored that the gods themselves took their chance in the Game, or that in joining it you could walk through men's dreams and see into other worlds.

"More time passed, and the power within the city shifted away from the guilds. The old religion, too. Some people began to say the Game had become a shameful thing and a wickedness. It ceased to be spoken of, though it was still played.

"Until at last there came the day when the city fell to its enemies. There was great destruction, and most people assumed the Game had perished also. But, somehow, something survived. The symbols devised by its first makers began to appear in different forms—in decks of playing cards, in poetry and prophecy, things sacred and profane. It was whispered that the Game had found new cities and new players ready to venture all."

There was a long silence. In the time he had been speaking, the tree's green had changed to brittle brown and gold, and now the first leaf fell, quivering, through the air.

Toby swallowed nervously. "But—but if you were there when the Game began, then, er, why are you down here?"

"I was once a priest of Fortune; I studied her mysteries and worshipped her Wheel. I created many of the moves within the Game. But when the four guilds grew into mighty courts, and sought control over all players, I opposed them. And so the first Game Masters used trickery to imprison me." He smiled his gentle smile. "My triumph is never sought as a prize. Indeed, it has few enticements. Do you know, though, what it signifies?"

Cat tried to visualize the Hanged Man's card in a Tarot deck, and the things she'd read. Toby, though, was ahead of her. "Knowledge through suffering," he said. "Sacrifice."

"Sacrifice, yes . . . but not a willing one. For as long as the kings and queens have me as their prisoner, their domination of the Game is complete."

Since entering the chamber, Flora hadn't taken her eyes off the man's face. "So if we were to set you free—"

"We can't intervene, though," Cat cut in. "We're powerless."

The Hanged Man laughed softly. "Not so. Accidentals and blunderers you may be, yet the Fool is the agent of Fortuna, Imperatrix Mundi, who presides over all. Her laws are the Arcanum's laws; all other rules are lesser, and false. That is why the four Masters have no choice but to open the Arcanum for you and guide you to the Game. They know the Fool is as integral to its workings as the Wheel, for you too may change the course of a move, shaping a court's luck and a player's destiny."

"But only by paying the forfeit," Cat insisted. "By being taken as knaves."

"It was not always so, nor need it be."

"What do you mean?"

"I mean that my freedom would lead to the freedom of greater and lesser alike."

The three chancers exchanged glances.

"The Game has been corrupted by its Masters. You will have seen how the kings and queens scheme among themselves, hoarding the cards, concerned only with their own winnings. They treat the pains of their knights as a frivolous thing, as if players and playing board alike are toys for their amusement."

The Hanged Man sighed. It seemed his strength was waning with every leaf that fell from the tree.

"The Game I helped create was a thing of joy, and liberty. The players only had to play a single card to win their prize, and were free to move through the Arcanum as they chose. There were no boundaries or forfeits or interventions then, no hierarchy of players.

"If I was free and the rule of the courts overthrown, the Game Masters would be compelled to release their triumphs so that anyone in the Game might play for them. Every card would be free to turn, every die to roll, and every move to be completed. There would be prizes for all."

"Not everyone in the Game is after a triumph," said Flora slowly.

"No, indeed." The man fixed his shining eyes upon them. "There are many hopes sought in the Arcanum. Even the Game Masters are in search of a greater victory, though they search in vain. With the right card for the right venture . . . why, even a fool could play to win."

"Tell us how to release you," said Toby. His voice was strained. It was obvious that they could no more untie him from the tree than pull down the pillar of stone at their backs. The very air they breathed was steeped in the power of the Arcanum.

"Whether by an accident of luck or the design of fate, the key to my tomb is only found when a Suite of Fools has entered play." He sounded profoundly weary. "Where, then, is the fourth?"

"I—we—we don't know."

The floor of the chamber was now a carpet of dead leaves that, even as they watched, turned to filigree and dust. It seemed the man's voice had grown dustier also, his skin like ash. "You must find him. A Fool for every court and a court for every Fool . . . ," he murmured. "Four throws of the die will open your way. My sacrifice is the Twelfth, but my deliverance shall be by the First. When the First of the Greater gives you the Firsts of the Lesser, then I may be set . . . set free. . . ." His voice faded away as his head sank down onto his chest. The last leaf had fallen from the now-barren tree.

As they left the chamber, its spindly branches were silvered in frost.

Their next move was waiting for them in the room with the golden curtain. The card in the center of the table, which had formerly shown no illustration, was now the Triumph of the Magician. Perhaps the Hanged Man still retained some limited powers, or perhaps forces within the Game itself had worked the change. Cat did not want to believe that Fate had much influence on the ordinary world, but the Arcanum's destiny might be a different matter.

The four cards laid out around the Magician had kept their abstract patterning. The chancers went to turn them over, just in case an illustration lay on the other side. As they did so, the motif of wheels merged, reshaping into color and form. Cat gasped as the Triumph of Justice appeared before her eyes. But the next moment, the picture began to fade into blankness, and she let out a groan. Across the table, Flora and Toby also stared with dismay at their vanishing prizes.

To be so close—! Yet Cat wasn't despairing. What had once been a faint hope was now a promise. *There would be prizes for all . . . even a fool could play to win. . . .*

Cat would complete the task and win her prize. They all would. She had not glimpsed the images on Toby's and Flora's cards, but as they tucked the precious cards away, their faces showed the same strength of purpose as hers.

The fourth card remained featureless. "The other chancer's reward," Cat murmured. She slipped it into her jacket, next to her own card, while Flora took the Magician and Toby the blank-faced die. Then they began the long climb up the stairs, and back to the everyday world. They hardly dared speak until they got back to Flora's house.

According to the clock in the drawing room, only half an hour had passed.

"Whew," said Toby, flopping down on the nearest arm-chair. "It looks as if we've got ourselves a quest."

"Or a wild-goose chase," said Cat, though she didn't mean it. Hope surged in her heart. "Let's have another look at the Magician."

They moved under the light to inspect the card. A man in red and white robes stood over a table displaying the symbols of the courts. His right hand raised a staff toward the sky; his left pointed toward the earth, where roses and lilies were entwined. The top of the card was marked *I*.

"Our job's clear," said Flora. "The Hanged Man's the twelfth triumph, and he said his 'deliverance' will come from the first. That's this card: Thoth, the mage and magician. So we need to enter the Magician's move and ask for help."

"Yeah, and then we'll have aces, too," said Toby.

"Aces?" Cat repeated.

"They're the first cards of the Lesser Arcana, of course. *When the First of the Greater gives you the Firsts of the Lesser, then I'll be set free.* So the Magician will give us the powers of earth, air, fire and water—the perfect weapons for a prison break! The Hanged Man'll be out in no time."

164

Cat bit her lip. "But I still don't see how we can get involved in the Game without paying the forfeit. We'll end up as knaves."

"The forfeit only applies if we interfere in another player's move," said Flora impatiently. "But we'll be playing *our own* card. A card that hasn't been dealt by any of the kings or queens. And once we've released the Hanged Man, *everyone* will be set free. Any chancer, knight or knave will be able to walk through the Arcanum and win a prize, and there won't be any stupid rules to stop them." Her face was alight with longing.

Toby had turned his attention to the unmarked die. It was a pyramid with four triangular faces, and made of the same gleaming dark metal as the Arcanum coins. "*Four throws of the die will open your way . . .* This must be to create a threshold for our move." He threw the die up in the air, nearly fumbling the catch. "Gotcha!" With a flourish, he showed it to the others. One of the sides was now printed with a little silver zero, the sign of a Fool. Toby immediately tried again, but did not produce any further transformation.

"Here, let me." Flora took it from Toby's unwilling hand. "Oh!" she exclaimed, as a second side revealed another zero. "Go on, Cat—it's your turn."

A third throw, and a third side revealed its marking. But no matter how many times they passed the die round, the fourth face remained blank.

"It's probably just as well," said Flora. "I don't much like the idea of having a threshold to the Arcanum in our drawing room."

"We need the missing chancer," said Toby gloomily. "The Hanged Man said there should be *a Fool for every court,* remember? The die won't work because we need four chancers for our quest. But tracking him down could take months."

"Not . . . necessarily," said Cat.

"What are you saying?" Flora asked sharply. "Do *you* know this person? Or how to find them?"

Cat waited before she replied. There had been something niggling at the back of her mind and now she wanted to set it straight. "I think so. Maybe. First, though, I want to know why you didn't tell us you'd already tried the key."

"What do you mean?"

"I mean that I was watching you during our trip to the crypt. You seemed quite at home in that room with the card table. Almost as if you'd been there before."

For a moment, it looked as if Flora would tough it out. Then she seemed to think better of it. She even gave an embarrassed sort of shrug. "All right," she said. "Yesterday I went to Temple House by myself and tried the key in the door."

Cat folded her arms across her chest. "And then what?"

"I went down the stairs and into the little room. But the cards on the table—well, they were different. Four Fool cards, one at each corner of the Triumph of the Moon. Then I thought back to the other person we saw in the move, and the coin coming up with a zero, and I realized that this wasn't something I should be doing on my own. When the Arcanum gives you a sign, you'd better listen to it."

She gave a slightly shaky laugh. "In the end, I didn't even look past the curtain. I went straight back up the stairs, and decided to come back only after I'd found you two."

Cat snorted.

"Look, I'm sorry I didn't tell you. I'm used to going it alone in the Arcanum, and that's how I prefer it, to be honest. But as soon as I realized the key, and the crypt, involved all three—four—of us, I knew I'd been wrong not to share it. I didn't want to tell you that I'd started out on my own because I wanted you to trust me. And I am worth trusting. I swear." Flora widened her eyes in appeal.

"OK, fine." Cat kept her voice level. "But if I'm going to try and find our AWOL chancer, and if we're going to take this . . . thing . . . any further, we need to be straight with each other."

"You're right, and I'm sorry," said Flora penitently.

"We're a team now," put in Toby. "Team Arcanum!"

"Exactly."

Cat caught her own eye in the splintered mirror above the mantelpiece. She had already seen where the remains of a broken tumbler had been stuffed into the wastepaper basket, already remembered the crashes and shouts they'd heard from Flora's perfect white bedroom. What prize was Flora playing for, and was it only superstition that prevented her from discussing it? Was Toby, even, as open about his motives as he seemed?

Perhaps Cat wasn't the only chancer with hopes too painful to share.

KING OF SWORDS

CHAPTER ELEVEN

CAT TOOK A BUS back from Flora's, getting out at Oxford Street. It was nearly nine o'clock, but Thursday was late-night shopping night and progress was slow. London crowds no longer alarmed her, at least; she had recovered her knack for losing herself in them without getting lost.

Every inch of pavement was seething with people, their bodies muffled in winter layers, their elbows, bags and feet all jostling for position. Every inch of shop front glittered with fake stars and cotton snow. Their promises were imitation, too: Magic! Romance! The Perfect Present! A Better Future! Set in lights above Regent Street, characters from the latest Disney film gamboled in the air. A roast-nut stand wafted a stale syrup smell through the traffic fumes, along with blasts of fried onions from a hot-dog vendor. "Sinners spend but Jesus saves!" admonished an evangelist with a loudspeaker. "If you shop till you drop, who will catch you when you fall?"

"It seems the End is nigh," came a voice in Cat's ear. It was Alastor, the King of Swords, wearing a long black coat with the collar turned up, and lounging beneath a slew of sale signs.

Cat started, but managed to reply steadily enough. "Doing a spot of bargain hunting?"

"As a matter of fact, I was hoping you'd spare the time for a little talk." He nodded toward an unmarked black car that had just pulled up in the bus lane.

"There's no way I'm going anywhere with you. I'm not stupid." She began to back away.

"Oh, don't worry—you'll be quite safe. I'm as anxious to avoid any rule breaking as you are. Please," he said gently, "I'd be very grateful if you'd get in."

At this, although she wasn't quite sure how or why, Cat found herself climbing into the backseat. The interior smelled of expensive leather, and the driver was shut off from his passengers by a sliding panel of tinted glass. The next moment, the car had moved off into the stream of traffic.

"God, what a slum this place is getting to be," Alastor remarked, settling more comfortably beside her. He winked at her with lazy charm. "So much nicer on the other side of town, don't you think?"

Cat looked out of the window. They had just turned down Regent Street, but the crowds and fumes and garish Disney characters had disappeared. The Christmas lights strung between the buildings were now a cascade of hearts, clubs, diamonds and spades, flashing black and red on white against eerily artificial sunset. As the car purred on, the majestic buildings lining the street slipped past in a seemingly endless curve. She didn't need the prickling of her palm to know that the King of Swords had taken her into the Arcanum.

She felt for the handle on the door. It was locked. At once, Alastor raised his hand in a gesture of reassurance. "I told you I am not here to threaten or obstruct you. A chancer is not subject to the control of the courts."

"You still seem pretty good at pulling our strings."

He arched his brows at her. "Everybody who enters the Game does so freely. Even—or perhaps especially—those who claim it to be by accident."

"I don't reckon accidents figured much in your career. The way I heard it, to get to be a GM, you have to win every triumph in the deck."

"But never enjoy them as prizes, remember. A player who desires the Game's mastery must play round after round, move after move, risking everything over and over. For if just one round is lost, then all triumphs previously won are discounted, and the struggle must start again. . . . Why, Cat, don't tell me you're ambitious to be queen?"

"Not a chance."

Alastor laughed indulgently. "My predecessor was a queen, you know. She had ruled Swords for a very long time; I think she may even have been one of the first Masters. Yet in the final reckoning, it was found I had won more triumphs from her than from any other. Thus her court became mine."

In spite of herself, Cat was intrigued. "When was this?"

"Long before your time, in another city and another age." He gave a graceful shrug. "I was born to a life of ease, yet none of its pleasures satisfied me. I grew weary of the world and my existence in it." Briefly, his face darkened. "And then I found a new world in the Arcanum, and did not rest until I made it mine. . . . Here the gamble is infinite, the Game inexhaustible. Every moment of play has the savor of victory."

"Bet you wish you didn't have to share that victory, though."

"What do you mean?"

"Ahab told me how you're all scheming to be top dog, even though nobody seems to know how to pull it off. He said there's a special prize just for kings and queens. The Triumph of Eternity. And whoever finds it gets to be the one and only Grand High Game Master."

"Well," said the King of Swords softly, "that would be a triumph indeed."

Cat wondered what had happened to the queen whom Alastor had deposed, and about the life he had given up to rule the Arcanum. They're all fools, she thought. For all their swanky speeches and scheming, it's the Game that plays *them*.

She turned and looked out of the window again. The Arcanum's sky was bruised purple streaked with orange. A spiral of hearts flashed before her eyes, spinning into cups at the final moment. Behind, a tumble of spades was now an arch of dancing swords.

"Don't you think it's time you told me what you want?"

"What an abrupt girl you are," he said. "I rather thought you were enjoying our chat. Very well. Let us come to the point: the course of play that you three Fools have embarked on."

So the kings and queens knew about their encounter with the Hanged Man. They must have spied it on some flickering TV screen. Or maybe they'd read it in the cards.

"The next move is yours, Cat. I know you are in search of another chancer to join your cause, and that you know where to find him. But if you do enlist him, and your gamble succeeds, I promise you will regret it."

"I thought you weren't going to make threats."

"This is not a threat, but a warning. The courts may give it only once, so listen well."

The King of Swords leaned forward to rap on the driver's partition. The next moment they were drawing up at Piccadilly Circus.

Cat felt even more uneasy once she got out of the car. The statue of Eros that presided over the intersection had been replaced by an effigy of Justice with her sword and scales. Seated on the steps below the fountain were the other king and queens—Odile in white; Ahab, somber-suited; Lucrezia, swathed in furs—all as motionless as the statue itself. Under the shimmer of the vast advertising panels, where Samsung and Coke had changed to alternating symbols of the four courts, Alastor's languid face pulsed white light and dark shadow, then neon red.

"The Game gives us the chance to make our own luck,

Cat. To change our fate. To win our most secret desires, against all odds. Yet by seeking to overturn its rules, you are set on a path that will lead to its ruin."

"Yeah, and who makes the rules?"

"The Arcanum operates according to its own principles. These will always endure. But without the rules that the courts impose on the Game, there would be no strategy or structure, no restraint."

"No perks for you, you mean. So is this where you tempt me over to the Dark Side? Promise me triumphs? Heroism and happy endings?" she mocked.

At that, he gave an odd sort of half smile, reaching across to lightly touch her hair. "Poor kitty-cat . . . If I drew you for my court, you would make a fine knight, I think. Today, Cups holds Justice. Tomorrow, who knows?" He tilted his head toward the three figures on the steps. "We are *all* Fortune's fools, and it is not my place to halt the spinning of her Wheel. But in this Game of ours, the winners are those who know it is every player for himself. Remember this the next time your friends coax you through hidden doors, or make their promises, or ask you to take their word on trust."

Now the king leaned in nearer, his voice very low, breath sweet as cinnamon, as the sky was lit by the acid dazzle of swords.

"And there is something else you should know. The Hanged Man has another, older name. In times past, he was called the Traitor."

With great effort, Cat dragged her eyes away. The world

reeled and sparkled but somehow she managed to straighten her shoulders and shake her head. "If he betrayed the likes of you and your mates, then good for him. Because the courts don't deserve my loyalty—every player for herself, that's what you said."

Black, white and red flared against her eyes. Alastor laughed softly. "Then face the odds and take your gamble, as we all must do." He took out a coin and spun it high in the air.

And by the time the coin returned to his palm, she was standing under the Statue of Eros, once more alone in the crowd.

Friday was Christmas Eve. Cat got up early, filled with new determination. The King of Swords' warnings had showed her that the Hanged Man was right: she was neither powerless nor insignificant within the Game. Her years of watching and waiting, of slipping around the edges of life, had come to an end. She would find the missing chancer, and change the Arcanum's fate as well as her own.

Cat began her search for Blaine at the service entrance to the Martingale Hotel. At seven o'clock in the morning, the yard was bustling with the arrival of those on morning shifts and the taking in of deliveries. Cat decided to try a burly man who was supervising the unloading of crates of fruit from a grocer's van. " 'Scuse me, I'm looking for someone who works here. His name's Blaine and—"

"This isn't a lost and found, sweetheart. Nor a dating agency."

"I only want—"

"'I want' doesn't get; didn't your mother tell you? So unless you're here on official business, you can clear off. Go on—hop it."

"Miserable old grump," muttered a woman walking past with a clipboard. "Blaine, was it?"

"That's right."

"I know—does some washing up occasionally. Strictly off record, of course." She winked broadly. "If you can wait a bit, Malek will be coming off shift. He might know. I'll ask him to have a word."

Cat did the rest of her loitering in the street. A quarter of an hour later, a small man in a cleaner's uniform, his dark face tinged gray with fatigue, stopped alongside. "You look for Blaine?"

Cat nodded.

"Why you want?" he asked warily.

"He . . . he did some odd jobs for my uncle a while back. Stocktaking. We might have a bit of work for him, that's all."

Malek didn't reply at once, but continued to look her over carefully. Whatever he saw seemed to satisfy him. "OK. Blaine he sometime stay in Langdon Street by Turkish shop. Place down the underground."

In the basement, presumably. Cat felt a rush of optimism: Langdon Street was in Soho.

The air by the Turkish coffee shop was warm and fragrant; mounds of pastries glistened in the window within a garland of red tinsel. To one side was a small hardware store, to the other a boarded-up office. Judging by the layers of flyers and posters plastered on every inch of surface, it looked as if it had been empty for some time.

However, in the dank little space down by the basement stairs Cat could see chinks of light between the boards and hear, faintly, the sound of voices. She knocked on the door.

Immediately, the voices stopped. She knocked again.

There was a minute or so's wait until the door eventually creaked open a few inches. It was Blaine. The recognition on his face was instant, and almost as instantly wiped clear. "Yeah?"

"My name's Cat."

"So?"

"Malek—from the hotel—said you might be here." His hostile expression didn't waver and she had a flashback to Flora, playing dumb in the church and badass in the Arcanum. She wasn't going to let herself be stonewalled again. "I want to talk to you."

"What about?"

"This."

She thrust the fourth card from the Hanged Man's crypt into his hand. The movement took him by surprise and he took the card before he'd realized what it was. As the interlocking wheels shifted into an illustration Cat couldn't quite make out, his face abruptly changed, its wariness replaced by something hard and resolute.

"You OK there, bro?" Someone else had come to stand

behind Blaine: a very thin, very tall white guy with dreadlocks that had been dyed a startling flamingo pink.

Blaine cleared his throat. His sleeves were pushed back, and Cat noticed a ragged scar along the outside of his right arm. He hadn't taken his eyes off the card, though its face was now blank. "Yeah. Just some kid."

Cat felt a flash of annoyance: this boy didn't look more than a year or so older than she was. She fixed him with her chilly gray gaze. "So, are you going to talk to me or not?"

He shrugged. "Looks like I don't have much of a choice."

Same here, she wanted to say. The Six of Cups had seen to that.

Cat had arranged to join the others at the greasy diner Toby was so fond of. Their meeting wasn't meant to be much more than a progress report; she had not expected to find Blaine so quickly, and though she knew the others would be surprised and elated by her success, the closer she and Blaine drew to the café, the more apprehensive she felt.

Meanwhile, Blaine loped along in silence, hands thrust deep in his pockets, hood pulled low. Despite her own reticence, she was surprised by how much his unsettled her. She had kept her explanations as short as possible, as if brevity could reduce them to something manageable and matter-of-fact. But he showed little or no reaction to her account, and accepted her offer to meet the others with a terse nod.

Even so, her curiosity got the better of her. "I know you were in the Triumph of the Moon," she ventured. "Does that mean you were at the Lottery, too?"

"Lotteries are a pile of crap."

"But Temple House—"

"Temple House is an even bigger pile of crap. Garden parties! Fairy lights! Chitchat over the canapés." He snorted. "Makes me want to vomit."

"I know what you mean."

"Do you now?"

"I know that everyone involved in this is either desperate or a lunatic or both. And it's stupid to pretend otherwise."

"Yeah? So which are you?"

Cat ignored the remark. "If you didn't get to the Moon through Temple House, you must've found its threshold in the city. The one we used to come back, in the underpass."

Blaine gave a grudging nod. Then, somewhat to her surprise, he went on to explain. "I go out looking for them. I had this idea. I thought if I found enough thresholds, I might be able to work out a pattern. For where and when they turn up."

"And have you?"

"No." He grinned, and the shadows in his face briefly lightened. "But since when does this Game of ours go to plan?"

They were approaching the diner now, and Cat could see Toby and Flora in the window. Toby was talking and gesturing excitedly while Flora, pretty in pink, daintily sipped a cup of tea.

Toby was the first to spot Cat and who she had brought with her. "I can't believe you've found him already!" he exclaimed. "Wait—I mean—this is *him*, right?"

"Blaine, meet Toby. Toby—Blaine. And that's Flora."

Flora was staring, fascinated, at his frayed cuffs and dirty fingernails. However, she soon rallied. "Pleased to meet you, Blaine," she said in her most winning manner. "It's awfully good of you to come."

Blaine turned to Cat. "Is she always like this?"

Flora's airs and graces might annoy her, but Cat wasn't ready to exchange conspiratorial asides about them. She compromised on a noncommittal shrug.

Toby broke into the increasingly awkward pause. "Look, why don't you two sit down and we can get some coffee or . . ." He looked doubtfully at Blaine's thin wrists and dark-rimmed eyes. "Would you like, er, something to eat . . . a hot meal?"

"How kind. Maybe you can knit me some socks and take round a collecting tin while you're at it."

The air of embarrassment grew stronger. Blaine stretched and yawned enormously. "But seeing as you're offering, I'll have bacon, eggs and home fries. And a large tea."

". . . so, basically," Toby finished, "we need to create a threshold to play the Magician's card. Then he'll help us get the aces we need to set the Hanged Man free, and it'll be prizes all round. Cool, huh?"

The dour waiter plonked Blaine's plate down with a disbelieving grunt, and went off shaking his head.

Blaine didn't look too impressed, either. In fact, he seemed more interested in concentrating on his food, shoveling it in with speed and efficiency. When it appeared they were going to get no further response from him, Cat stepped in.

"See, we figure the die will only work after you've activated the fourth side. And once that's done, we can get into the Arcanum whenever and wherever we like. We won't be tagging after some knight. We'll have our own move."

But again, Blaine showed no reaction and Cat ground to a halt.

"If it's all the same with you," said Flora, who had moved on to inspecting her own fingernails, "I'd prefer to put off any excursions until after Christmas. Would it be frightfully difficult for people to get away on Boxing Day?"

Conversation descended into the wrangling over places and timings that occurs when any kind of group outing needs to be organized. Blaine didn't contribute to this, either. But as the others were debating Cat's suggestion of meeting at Piccadilly Circus at three o'clock, Boxing Day, he turned from staring out of the foggy window.

"There's no sense rushing things," he said suddenly. "It's not like the future of humankind is at stake. We don't even have to save the world from the Forces of Darkness."

"Well, no," said Toby, "but rescuing the Hanged Man—"

"Let's not kid ourselves we're doing it for his benefit."

Nobody had anything to say to this, aware of the cards they each carried, held close as a promise. Blaine looked slowly round the table. "How did you lot get into this gig, anyway?"

Caught off guard, Cat found herself stammering. "It—it began when I sort of—of—stumbled into someone."

"I . . . erm . . . overheard a conversation," Toby said reluctantly, feet tap-tapping under the table.

"By following a thread," said Flora, eyes defiant. "And you?"

"I read a book." Blaine pushed his plate away and got to his feet. "Full of information, aren't we?" he remarked sardonically. "See you later . . . team."

"So you *are* going to join us?" Toby asked.

Blaine didn't turn round. "I'm going to think about it."

The other three stared after his departing back. "Looks like you've got some competition for that Enigmatic Loner tag, Cat," Toby observed. "Funny, he doesn't particularly sound like a street kid."

"And how're street kids supposed to sound?"

Toby ignored the question. "Do you reckon he's in a gang? I'm sure that was a tattoo I saw on the back of his neck."

"It was probably dirt," said Flora, wrinkling her nose. Then she looked at Cat. "The two of you seem to have some kind of . . . rapport. I think you should go after him."

"And say what?"

"Whatever it takes. We have to be certain he's going to help. This is too important for second thoughts."

❧

Cat felt she had already done quite enough running around after Blaine. To be running after him on Flora's orders was to add insult to injury. But of course Flora was right: they did need him. After her encounter with the King of Swords, Cat knew that better than anyone.

She caught up with Blaine at the end of the street. When he saw her, he raised his brows. "You're eager."

"No. Just desperate, remember?"

He laughed.

"Don't play games with us," she said abruptly. "There's already more than enough of that in the Arcanum." She drew him away from the pavement bustle, into the doorway of a closed-up shop. "Tell me straight: are you going to help or not?"

"I don't know, do I? I don't know anything about you. Or your friends."

"All right, so ask me some questions."

"You can start by telling me what you're playing for."

She took a deep breath. "Justice."

"Hmm. And why's a nice girl like you in need of law and order?"

"It's not for me. It's for my parents. Somebody . . . somebody shot them. Killed them for an invitation to the Game."

He stared at her. "Jesus."

" 'S'OK," she said awkwardly. "I mean, no, it's not OK, obviously. But it was twelve years ago. Anyhow, winning Justice is my chance to make sense of what happened."

"Yeah . . . There's a lot of bad stuff in this world that goes unpunished. Unnoticed, too." He was tracing the line of the scar on his right arm. Cat suspected the gesture was unconscious.

"And you're looking for someone?" she said. "A Knight of Wands?"

Grudgingly, he nodded.

"And what do you want from him—payback? Because of what he did to your arm?"

Blaine looked down at the scar, as if surprised to find it there, and pulled his sleeve over it irritably. "My arm doesn't matter. No. It was because of the . . . the other things he did. And not just to me."

Cat felt a shiver that wasn't from cold.

"Payback's only part of what I want from that bastard." He was speaking quickly and angrily, all reticence gone. "He's my stepfather. He's a bully and a liar and a thief. He's the reason I left home. The reason I became a chancer, too . . . Anyway. We're both in the Game, and I've been looking for him in the Arcanum. He's hiding there. Or stuck in some move."

"What will you do when you find him?"

"I don't know. I know what he deserves. But first . . . There're questions he has to answer, people he has to face. He needs to be forced to admit what he's done. *Then* they'll have to believe me. Then I can go back to my old life."

Cat didn't ask who "they" were. The expression on

Blaine's face seemed to forbid it. Instead, she got down to practicalities.

"If he's a knight and you interfere in his round, you'll be in danger of forfeit."

"That's a risk I'm willing to take."

"But you don't have to," she said earnestly. "Not if we manage to change the Game like the Hanged Man says. We'll be free to do what we want in the Arcanum. We'll each get our reward."

"And we can trust this guy on the tree, can we?"

Cat remembered the shining blue of the Hanged Man's gaze, how his voice had faded with the falling leaves. The gentleness of his smile. She had no words to describe the solemnity of the crypt—its sense of mystery, and power.

"The Hanged Man's triumph is the card of sacrifice," she said at last. "He was there at the beginning of the Game. He knows how it works and what's wrong with it. What's more, the kings and queens have found out we're trying to help him, and it's got them rattled.

"Alastor even tried to stop me finding you. He called the Hanged Man a traitor because he wants to spoil their Game. United, the four of us are a threat. So, yeah, I believe in my prize and, yeah, I believe in the man who promised it."

Blaine looked at her and slowly nodded. "OK."

"As in OK, you'll help us?"

"Sure." He shrugged. "Fact is, I was always going to give it a shot."

Cat stared, exasperated. "So why—?"

"Maybe I just wanted to put you through your paces. See how persuasive you could really be."

Their eyes met, and he gave her a crooked sort of smile. Then he stepped out of the doorway. "Happy Christmas, Cat."

ACE OF PENTACLES

CHAPTER TWELVE

CAT AND BEL'S CHRISTMAS began the same way it always did: not with stockings, but with working their way through a stack of Christmas crackers—jumping when they snapped apart, putting on the paper crowns, and laughing over the terrible prizes. Greg was spending the day with his elderly mother out in Rotherhithe, so it was just the two of them. For their ready-made lunch—hoisin duck and pancakes for Bel, roast chicken and trimmings for Cat—they turned on the stereo to drown out the interminable drum 'n' bass from next door, and drew the curtains so that they ate under the glow of the fruit lights. Rain pattered cozily against the windowpanes.

Cat felt treacherous for wondering how this Christmas could have been different—how it might have been if she still had her mum and dad. Bel would be there too, of course. They'd all be squeezed up close round the table, chatting and laughing. There would be stockings and home-made pies and a real tree. A family Christmas, Disney style. Rose-tinted thinking, Cat told herself. Get over it.

Bel was in a very good mood. She'd bought them both feather boas, pink for her and purple for Cat, and insisted they get dolled up, adorning Cat's face with swoops of silver eye shadow. She also made Cat wear her present from the Secret Santa at work: a sparkly four-leaf clover on a chain. Afterward, she produced a set of keys with a flourish. "Greg left them with me. I reckon it's time you had a backstage tour of the palace."

"I thought you said it's a hole."

"Hole, sweet hole. But there's a karaoke machine left from the Christmas party, as many potato chips as you can eat, and widescreen telly in the bar. It'll be fun. Like sneak-ing round school after hours."

For the second time in a week, Cat was shown into the Palais Luxe's dingy lobby. This time, however, they headed to the gaming floor, which was dominated by three black-jack tables and three roulette wheels. A plastic Christmas tree leaned drunkenly against a rank of slot machines. The paisley carpet was dark with grime, the ceiling low and the air stale with a lingering smell of sweat.

Bel turned on the lights and sound system, flooding the room with Andy Williams crooning about Paris skies. The slot machines twinkled into life. "Our own private party palace," she said cheerfully, going to the bar to help herself to a rum and Coke. She came back with a can of lemonade for Cat and an armful of snacks. "C'mon, what do you fancy? Roulette? Poker? James Bond brooding in a corner?"

"Game of tiddlywinks is all I'm fit for."

"We'll see about that." Bel flicked her feather boa over her shoulder and sashayed over to the nearest roulette wheel. "Would Madam care to place her chips?"

Cat gave in. She opened a packet of peanuts and placed three on the betting table to the side of the wheel. A straight inside bet, number eight. Eight was the Triumph of Justice.

Bel spun the wheel in one direction and launched the ball in another. "No more bets!" she called, as the ball got ready to drop from the outside track of the wheel toward the numbered slots. It whizzed around some more, bounced and settled. "Unlucky," she said, placing a marker on the green *0* square on the layout and scooping up Cat's peanuts. "Try again."

But Cat was still staring at the wheel, where an image of the Lottery at Temple House had flashed before her eyes. "No," she said, with sudden vehemence. "That's enough."

Her aunt laughed. "All right, puss-cat. You keep hold of your peanuts. There was a bloke here yesterday—bloodshot eyes, probably hadn't changed his clothes all week—and I watched him lose ten grand in an hour. Ten grand! Course, you can't stop them, and they wouldn't thank you if you tried." She frowned, her effervescence suddenly fizzing away. "You know what I heard? Back in the old days, Lady Luck was a girl called Hecate. That's the Queen of Witches."

Cat's mouth felt dry. "Who told you that?"

"Oh . . . just someone I used to know."

"A gambler?"

"Yeah. They're a superstitious bunch." Bel cleared her throat. "Got a meeting with Leo set up after the holiday—you remember, from that charity poker night? The manager at Alliette's. Anyhow, he reckons there might be an opening for me there."

Cat looked at the opposite wall, and its posters of soft-focus couples laughing as they placed their bets. They didn't bear much resemblance to the solitary, dead-eyed figures she had seen waiting outside the Luxe's doors. "D'you think it'll really be that different? I mean, it would be bigger and flashier. Obviously. But underneath, it's . . . it's all the same, isn't it?"

Bel acted as if she hadn't heard. She moved toward the blacked-out windows, flexing her hands restlessly. "When you first start handling the chips, it stretches your fingers. Makes them ache. I don't even notice it now. . . ." She was still frowning. "I'm a good dealer, Cat: slick with the cards, quick with numbers. The gamblers like me. At Alliette's they have proper training programs, for management and that. There wouldn't be so many night shifts. And after all the moving around and starting over . . . well, it could be my lucky break. Our lucky break, you know?"

"Yeah," said Cat softly. "I know."

On Sunday, Cat got a call from Toby about an hour before they were due to meet the others. He sounded unnaturally subdued. "There's something I want to talk to you about,"

189

he said. "I'll be at Piccadilly Circus in five—can you come and meet me?"

She sighed. It had not been a good night. *The odds are ag-gainst you,* murmured the stranger in her dreams, and she had woken up to find her eyes swollen and gluey, as if she'd been crying in her sleep. But although it was a relief to get out of the flat—where Greg and Bel were drinking gin and jeering at the television—the gray quiet of the city, deep in its post-Christmas torpor, felt just as oppressive. Toby's serious tone had shaken her more than she liked to admit.

"What's all this about?" she asked as briskly as she could make it.

Toby took a while to answer, hunched over himself and frowning. "I need to tell you how I got into the Game."

"Something to do with saving a girl's life, you said."

"That's right. But something just happened, something . . ." He paused and then shook his head. "I'd better start at the beginning.

"So I board at this school called Hargrove, right? It's just outside London. Anyway, there was this secret club: the Chameleons. They gave people dares."

"Dares?"

"It was silly to begin with. The challenges were connected to film titles; anyone who got *Mrs. Doubtfire* had to turn up to assembly in drag—that sort of stuff. Toward the end of last term, though, it was becoming . . . well, there was one called *The Invisible Man,* and the girl who got it wasn't allowed to speak to anyone and nobody was allowed to speak to her for a week. It was like she didn't exist. Even the teachers seemed to stop noticing her."

"Sounds kind of twisted."

"Yeah, but it was also exciting. Boarding school is a really regimented, claustrophobic world, and those dares were a chance to throw out the rules. To see the old conventions turned upside down. Enjoy a bit of risk. Like the Hanged Man's Lottery, I suppose.

"OK. Anyway . . . there was this girl . . . a couple of years older than me, part of the popular crowd. Mia wasn't a snob, though. She was different from the rest. In fact, she was really nice." Now he was blushing beneath his freckles. "One evening I was in the art studio, late. And I'd just turned off the lights in the back room when I heard her and the art teacher, Mr. Marlow, come in the main door. Mia sounded really agitated. She was saying she was in over her head, and that she'd never thought it would come to this. Then they started talking about how this last move had to be a fair fight. And that whoever lost it would have to start all over again, with a new round."

"So . . . they were both knights, competing for the same triumph?" Cat asked. She remembered Toby telling her that in such cases the Game Masters made their fifth and final move into a competition.

"Exactly. But at the time, I assumed it was something to do with the Chameleons and their dares. It wasn't that surprising that Mr. Marlow was involved. He was this sleazebag who thought it was cool to smoke dope with students.

Anyway, in the end they agreed to meet at midnight in the clock tower.

"Now, the clock tower was way on the other side of the playing fields. It was out of bounds and all spooky and rickety, the perfect setting for a secret society. I thought this was my big chance to see who was in the Chameleons, how the dares were organized and so on.

"I got to the tower before midnight and crept up the stairs to the room at the top. I heard shouting behind the door, followed by a crashing sound. Marlow was yelling and Mia screamed, so I burst into the room. Mia had a gash on her head. She was clutching something in her hand and Marlow was grabbing for it. Later, I realized it must have been an Arcanum coin. On the wall behind them, you see, this weird circle design had appeared. A threshold wheel. So I think Mr. Marlow had tried to knock out Mia, or even kill her, before she could enter their move."

Cat frowned. "Isn't that cheating?"

"Probably. He must have decided it was worth a forfeit if he got his triumph at the end. Or maybe the rules are different for when knights play against knights.

"Of course I didn't know anything about this at the time. I didn't have time to think. Mr. Marlow had ahold of Mia. So I just hurled myself at him. He was a big man, but I took him by surprise, and somehow managed to get him off her. A moment later, he was back on his feet, and literally flung me out of the room.

"I knocked my head on the wall, not hard, but enough

to make things go fuzzy. I remember a ripping sound, though. Like a piece of paper being torn, but louder.

"The next thing I knew, Mia was dragging me downstairs. She was screaming that we had to get out. 'My God,' she said. 'He'll kill us! *The Ace*—'

"Just as we got outside, the tower began to shake. The bricks didn't look solid anymore. They sort of . . . trembled in the air, as if the whole building was made of silk. Then there was this awful groaning, cracking noise, and the roof of the tower collapsed."

"With—with the teacher still inside?"

"No. Afterward, there was no sign of him. He must've escaped into the Arcanum in time."

"Whoa."

"Yeah. It must've been the Ace of Pentacles. Root of Earth, you know? Creating earthquakes is part of its job. And aces are the only cards that have power on *both* sides of the threshold."

"What happened next? What did you do?"

"I just stood there gawping. People were already coming out of the school, raising the alarm and so on. Mia kept her cool, though. She said I had to go back to my dorm and not tell anyone what I'd seen. She said I'd understand later. And that she'd take care of explanations.

"And she did. She said Mr. Marlow had lured her out to the tower and tried to attack her. When she fought him off, he'd run away. The building was structurally unsound, so nobody really questioned how the roof had fallen in. Of course she was immediately carted off to the hospital to be treated for shock and stuff, and after police inquiries were over she didn't come back to school. It was the most tremendous scandal. . . . I don't even know if Mia got her triumph in the end. I've never seen her at Temple House.

"Nobody connected me to what had happened. I barely knew what had happened myself. But the next evening I went back to the tower. It was fenced off with big KEEP OUT and DANGER signs, and there was a woman standing there, all dolled up in a leopard print coat and high heels. It was the Queen of Pentacles.

"She said, 'I thought I might find you here,' and gave me a card. The Fool. And, well, you can imagine the rest."

Cat couldn't help comparing his story to her own initiation into the Game. Whereas she'd contributed to a man's death, Toby had actually saved the knight whose move he'd intervened in. She was grudgingly impressed.

"Didn't what you'd seen scare you?"

He shrugged. "I was nervous about getting in over my head. Of course I was. I knew I couldn't afford to make any mistakes; that's why it took me such a long time to try out the Arcanum.

"Look, it's obvious you and the other guys each have your own top-secret mission with a Very Important Prize at stake. And I'm just a—a hanger-on. I do see that. But it's not so terrible to want to be involved, is it? With something bigger than me, I mean. Something bigger and better and more exciting."

Yes, she could see it all. The princess in her tower, rescue and romance . . . Which was all the Game would ever mean to him. However hidden their motives, it was clear Flora and Blaine were acting out of the same kind of desperation as she was. Meanwhile, Toby just wanted to play heroes.

And yet Cat was oddly touched that he had shared this story with her. She wasn't used to heart-to-hearts or receiving confidences.

"Why are you telling me this now?"

He started twisting his hands. "Because—because after we said goodbye on Christmas Eve and I was going home, I saw Mr. Marlow, walking down the street.

"He was moving very slowly, with a cane. His left foot was dragging behind him, and the leg didn't look right. All stiff and crooked. He used to be quite good-looking, in a slimy sort of way, but now he just looked ill.

"We recognized each other at the same time. Marlow went even paler than he was before. He . . . he clutched my arm and—and said in this horrible rasping voice, 'You can't win. *You can't win.*'" Toby licked his lips nervously.

"Then what?" Cat prompted.

"Then I ran off. But . . . now I . . . I can't stop thinking about it. It felt like an omen. Or a warning."

Cat shook her head. "It's no secret that chancers can't win prizes. And it's no wonder the man's pissed at you. You ruined his move."

"I guess. But it was a weird coincidence, don't you think? Meeting him just before we start our quest."

"Maybe the kings and queens *arranged* for you to bump into him, just to scare you."

She told Toby about her meeting with Alastor. "We've obviously got the GMs worried," she said in conclusion, "and that's a good sign."

Toby's expression brightened. "True. Once we've changed the Game, knights like Marlow won't be driven to kill other players. *Everyone* can be a winner."

Cat was pleased that Toby had got over his misgivings so easily, but she felt a little envious, too. Whatever lay ahead, she knew she couldn't face it with his kind of optimism. And what had happened to the others? They had arranged to meet at three, and it was nearly quarter past.

But the next moment, a taxi drew up and Flora got out. "Gosh, I'm so sorry I'm late," she said breathlessly. "We had one of Daddy's golf cronies over for lunch and it went on and *on*. Did everyone have a nice Christmas?"

Although he hadn't announced himself, Blaine had also appeared, just behind Cat and Toby. His hood was pulled low over his face and he was swigging from a can. At Flora's words, he spat on the pavement.

Flora wasn't easily cowed. "Hello, Blaine," she said sweetly. "How was your day?"

"Super. I robbed a little old lady and spent the money on crack."

Her smile didn't slip. "If you're trying to shock me, I'm afraid you'll have to do better than that."

"That's assuming I give a toss about what you think." He chucked his can into the gutter. "Now we've got the Season's Greetings over with, isn't it about time we made our move?"

Cat had assumed that their meeting point would be where they'd create the threshold. She liked the symmetry of it, too: Piccadilly was where she'd first met the Knight of Wands, and where the King of Swords had taunted her with the effigy of Justice. However, she wasn't the only one who wanted their threshold's location to have some scenic or symbolic significance. It emerged that Flora wanted to move up to Mercury Square while Toby preferred to walk down to Admiralty Arch—"I've always thought it's got a triumphal sort of feel about it."

"Give us a look at the trinket," Blaine said abruptly.

"Careful," said Toby. "Once you've thrown it, the faces will be complete and—we hope—ready to work their magic."

Blaine flicked the die into the air. Sure enough, as soon as he caught it, the final face was marked by a zero. "Nice. So all we need to do is give it a roll and, Open Sesame, a threshold appears."

"I think so, but we don't want—"

Too late. Blaine had already stooped to send the die skittering down the pavement. Its triangular shape meant that it moved oddly, more of a bounce than a roll, yet the motion had a strange sense of purpose to it. As they watched, it tumbled over from edge to edge in a rough circle, before coming to a stop. This time, each felt an unmistakable throb on their right palms, as the four faces of the die glowed silver, then returned to blankness. Now it was just a lump of dark metal.

Flora's breath hissed. "You irresponsible *jerk*."

"Oh, get over it. If I'd left it to you lot, we'd be debating locations till next Christmas."

"So where's the threshold, then?" asked Toby. "And can I be the one to raise the coin?"

"Be my guest." Cat pointed toward a fast-food outlet a few feet away on Shaftesbury Avenue. The lit-up HOT FOOD sign in the window had a wheel worked into the first *o*. A few seconds later, Toby was proudly brandishing his coin.

"Look, it's got our zero on it as well! OK—time to rock 'n' roll."

"What, no big speeches?" Blaine jeered. "No gathering round for a team pep talk?"

"You want to make a speech, go ahead," Flora replied. "Please. I'm sure it would be most inspiring."

Cat looked up from where she'd been staring at the pavement. "I dunno about fancy speeches, but it seems to me that if any of us are having second thoughts about this . . . thing . . . we're doing, now's the time to say so. Because once we throw the coin, it'll be too late."

She waited. A motorbike roared past, a woman giggled into a phone, pigeons pecked for crumbs in the gutter. Nobody spoke. Slowly, carefully, they met each other's eyes. Slowly, carefully, they each gave a brief nod.

"All right then. We're off to see the wizard."

CHAPTER THIRTEEN

THEY WERE IN A CITY of ruin: of ragged walls and blind windows, bones of buildings in a starless night. Even the air tasted stale. The only sign of life came from the threshold, and the glow of the burger bar's menu—an incongruous token of the other side.

But they had only been peering around them for a moment or two when a jumble of light and music began to seep into the night. It seemed to be coming from what had once been Great Windmill Street. Close, Cat realized uncomfortably, to her own flat.

"Sounds like a party," said Toby, setting off in its direction.

Cat was the last to move. The flat, with its plasterboard walls and damp ceiling, might not be much, but she didn't want to see it reduced to rubble. She was even more uneasy once she'd turned the corner and was faced with the Palais

Luxe, lit up like a schizophrenic Christmas tree. Only it wasn't the Luxe anymore: according to the ultraviolet lettering above the door, it was a club called Hecate's.

Its sooty brick façade was the only intact structure on the street. A dance beat pumped out of windows pulsing with Technicolor, and an enormous bouncer stood guard outside, his arms folded menacingly across his chest. "No card, no entry," he growled.

His expression didn't soften when Flora held out the Magician card in her best party manner. However, after clearing his throat in a resentful sort of way, he condescended to unhook the rope from across the entrance.

Before Cat could go in, Blaine stopped in the doorway. "There's a redhead who works at the Luxe. She's some kind of relation of yours."

"My aunt. How did . . . ?"

"Soho's a small neighborhood." He stepped into the lobby. "You never know; a bit of insider's knowledge could come in handy."

It was true that, thanks to Bel's tour, Cat was familiar with the layout of the Luxe. But although Hecate's might have had the same basic structure—and the same shabby paisley carpet in the entrance—that was where the resemblance ended.

For one thing, it was packed: a smoky fug of people, some of whom were in costume. A Japanese geisha, a trio of men in Second World War RAF uniform, a woman in an elaborate powdered wig, an old gent in a toga . . .

"Who are all these people?" Toby asked.

Flora shrugged. "Optical illusions. Ghosts of players past. God knows. They're just part of the scenery; it's the Magician who *counts*."

"For illusions, they feel pretty solid," Cat grumbled, as a girl in leather hot pants crashed past, squealing endearments at a man on the other side of the lobby. "Somehow I don't reckon Mr. Abracadabra will look much like the mug shot on his card. Which means we'll have to work our way through the rooms and hope we'll know him when we see him."

They began with the basement, which had been set up with a stage where showgirls writhed in costumes of tattered feathers and diamanté. Puffs of dry-ice mist swirled around the tables that crammed the floor. If the Magician was there, he was keeping a low profile, and after five minutes of knocking into tables and getting sworn at for obstructing the view, they retreated back to the stairs.

As they moved up the building, the din intensified. What had been the Luxe's gaming hall was now an amusement arcade, where shooter and racer games were packed alongside pinball and slot machines. Everything blared with noise and color as players pushed coins into slots, pulled levers and furiously hammered on buttons.

"This is completely *insane*," Flora called out, pushing back a strand of sweaty hair. There was something about her expression—something glinting and reckless—that reminded Cat of how she'd been the first time they met at Temple House. Perhaps the excitement of the place was catching. At any rate, Cat couldn't take her eyes off all those whizzing, blinking panels. Her heart raced and ears rang. Was this how the gamblers at the Luxe felt as they waited for the roulette wheel to spin? For a confused moment, she could have sworn she saw Bel, tilting her head back and laughing, and she had to steady herself against a slot machine. Focus, she told herself, focus.

"What's the matter with you?" It was Blaine, glowering at her.

"I thought I saw someone I knew. Just for a second." Come to think of it, one of the dancers in the basement had looked very like the blonde from the strip joint down her street. And that fat man lighting a cigar was a dead ringer for her old geography teacher.

"Me too. It's not real, though. Don't let it get to you."

Blaine's hood had been pushed back, and under the glaring lights Cat saw the remains of a bruise on one cheek. She was gripped by the absurd notion that if she were to put a fingertip to it, and the purplish smears under his eyes, she could rub out the markings, as lightly and easily as if she were using an eraser on pencil.

"What?"

She realized she had been staring and looked away, confused.

The upstairs dance floor was the source of the techno beat thudding through the building, yet the couples beneath the glitter balls swayed in sleepy embraces, as if moving to a melody that only they could hear. On the other side of the floor was the way through to the bar. Behind a mirrored counter, bartenders juggled bottles and glasses with dizzying ease. Cat grabbed a tumbler of ice and held it against her hot cheeks.

It was less busy here than in the rest of the club, with most of the crowd concentrated in the center of the room. Some sort of demonstration or performance was taking place. A man in a top hat and tails was presiding over a card table while his audience called out instructions and encouragement, interspersed by raucous cheers.

Cat thought she recognized the game. She'd seen a version of it played on street corners, where gullible passersby could be waylaid, and a quick exit made at any sign of trouble. It was known as Follow the Lady. To begin, the dealer would place three cards face down on a table. He'd nominate one of the cards—usually the Queen of Spades—as the target card, and then quickly rearrange the cards to confuse the player as to which was which. The player was invited to choose one of the three cards. If it turned out to be the Queen, he'd win an amount equal to the stake he bet; otherwise, he lost his money. Of course, thanks to the dealer's sleight of hand, and all manner of misdirections, the only sure thing was that the player would lose.

"Care to place a bet, my friends?" The man looked at them craftily. His eyes were black and very bright, his face creased and yellowish. "It's the easiest game in the world!"

He spread out the Three of Clubs, Seven of Diamonds and Ace of Hearts and waved a red silk handkerchief over the table. Now they were their Game of Triumphs equivalents. "Three! Seven! Ace! But where's the Lady?" With a wink, he reached behind a pretty girl's ear and pulled out the Queen of Spades. He tossed all his cards in the air; when they fell face down on the table, there were only three again. "Pick a card, any card!"

"The Twelfth," said Blaine.

The whole room seemed to freeze. Heat, noise, movement all drained away into a ringing silence. Then, as if at the flick of a switch, the party resumed, although the Magician's smile had vanished. "No more bets!" He gave a hasty bow before backing away from the table. "The entertainment is over, ladies and gents, and the game is played! Thank you for your time!"

Pushing through his former audience, the Magician headed for a door marked STAFF ONLY at the side of the bar. The four chancers hurried after him, into a storage space stacked with crates of bottles. Ahead of them was a set of steps leading to another exit, through which their man had disappeared in a whisk of coattails.

They found themselves on the roof, in a small flat space between the gables. It was furnished with a bench and a sprinkling of cigarette butts. A string of tropical-fruit fairy lights sagged overhead. The Magician was standing at the very edge of the roof, staring across the skeletal city.

"Excuse me, sir," Toby began. "The four of us are chancers, right, and the Hanged Man gave us your card—in a manner of speaking—so we were hoping . . ."

"I know, I know," he muttered, gnawing at his lip. "The Twelfth on his tree. And you wish to bring him down from it. . . . Well, well. If the Wheel has turned that way, then I must follow it. *Fortunae te regendum dedisti, dominae moribus oportet obtemperes.* . . . So it was at the beginning, so it has always been."

"And you were there at the beginning, weren't you?" Flora said, looking at him intently. "Thoth, the mage, and first maker."

His forehead creased, as if he was trying to remember something. "I was once, perhaps. . . . But I have had many names, and the cards many makers. The man of whom you speak I first met by the gates of Atlantis. Or was it Babylon? There was a temple in Thebes, I recall, and an apple tree. *Haec nostra vis est, hunc continuum ludum ludimus—*"

"Yeah, whatever," said Blaine roughly. "Question is, will you help us release him?"

At this, the Magician shot him a sly look; the showman's gleam was back in his eyes. "I must do as I am bid, young sir. Oh yes indeed. See how my Lady plays her tricks: once I was a god, now I am a charlatan. Still, I have kept a few trappings of my craft. Behold!"

He opened out his coat to reveal all manner of pockets sewn into its faded scarlet lining. From one he produced a shot glass, from another a steel letter opener. Patting his outer pockets, he drew out a cigarette lighter and, digging deeper, a plastic poker chip.

With a flourish, he spread his red handkerchief on the bench and laid out his trophies. "As above, so below," he told them, with one of his quick crooked smiles.

They might have looked like a load of junk, but the objects did correspond, in a skewed sort of way, to those shown on the Magician's card.

"Four aces, my friends—that's what you'll be chasing, if you wish to bring about Yggdrasil's fall."

"Yggdrasil . . . is that a demon?" Toby asked breathlessly.

The Magician laughed. "It is a tree, young master, and one you saw in the place of sacrifice. Axis Mundi. Yggdrasil. Etz haChayim. It has nearly as many names as I, for many seeds may fall from the one fruit. To reap its harvest will take the powers of the earth and air, fire and water."

"The first cards of the Lesser Arcana," said Cat.

"Bravo. A big hand, please, for the lady in the corner!" The Magician mockingly tipped his top hat in her direction. "Behold the Ace of Pentacles, Root of Earth." Taking the poker chip, he spun it on the bench. When it settled, they could see the disc was no longer plastic, but made of clay. "Ta-da!" He spun it again, faster and faster, until its blur crumbled into a little scoop of dust. A puff of his breath and it was gone. "Next Cups, Root of Water." He held up the shot glass, which transformed into dripping ice that melted in his hands. "Swords, Root of Air." At this, he picked up the knife and threw it over Flora's head. Instinctively she ducked, but as it flashed through the air, it turned into a white bird that swooped upward and away. "And lastly, Wands, Root of Fire," he announced, flicking open the long black lighter. The next moment it shot skyward in an explosion of rainbow sparks as the Magician took a bow and looked round for applause.

"Uh, that's really cool," said Toby at last. "But . . . er . . . we do need the actual cards. Can't you give them to us?"

"Aces are not common cards. Even the Game Masters cannot control them, for they are dispersed and renewed within the Arcanum itself. A player who finds one is fortunate indeed.

"So no, I cannot deal you the cards. But I can gather the elements they unleashed the last time they were each played and save them for you in this new form. That will be power enough, I think."

Four blank faces stared back at him.

"Tsk! Do you still not understand? The objects you saw just now were only the image of what you seek. I have shown you their shadow; you must capture the substance. Just as the tree you saw in the Hanged Man's crypt was only the shadow of a greater tree—as above, so below. Remember."

"But . . . where . . . ?" stammered Flora.

"Ah yes, that is one more service I can offer you. In order to play my card, you had to roll a die, did you not? I would like to see it."

After a slight hesitation, Blaine passed it over. "I don't think it works anymore. The little symbols vanished once the threshold showed."

"Hmm." The Magician took off his top hat, put the die inside, and placed the handkerchief over the brim. He then passed the hat to Cat. "Click for luck."

Feeling like a kid at a birthday party, Cat snapped her fingers over the red silk.

"Expertly done." With a wink and a smirk, he brought out the die again. "Ta-da!" All four sides were once more etched with a silver zero.

"Now then," he said briskly, "I have loaded this die so that each throw will take you to the time and place where an ace's power can be found. And four aces to gather means four moves to play. The fifth and final roll of the die will take you out of the Arcanum."

"What do we do once we've found them?" Flora asked.

"Why, then you will return to Yggdrasil and plant each root." The Magician smiled. "I have shortened the odds for you, my friends. Now you must throw your die and take your chances.

"Since you do not belong to a court, the kings and queens may only oppose you through the rules of forfeiture. So have a care that your task does not interfere with the progress of any other players who you meet. Other than that, your path is clear. Follow the aces, ladies and gentlemen! Follow the aces!"

Blaine glanced at the other three, shrugged, and bent to roll the die for a second time. As soon as its strange circular tumbling was over, a threshold wheel flickered into life on the door behind him. This time, however, the corresponding symbols on the die didn't disappear. "No point hanging around," he said.

"Indeed not." The Magician's gaze had drifted back to the ruins all around. "So many fair cities, and their endings all the same," he murmured. "Players too, and yet . . . *Tu vero volventis rotae impetum retinere conaris?* The show is over, and my part is done."

ℭHAPTER ℱOURTEEN

THE OTHER SIDE OF the Magician's threshold was a park. This wasn't much like the orderly lawns behind Flora's house, however. They had come from ruin, and here was wreckage of a different kind. Fallen trees were tumbled on every side. A baby carriage had been caught in one of the toppled giants' branches; the flotsam and jetsam of trash cans and abandoned picnics were strewn like grubby confetti across the grass. Swollen black clouds glowered overhead, though here and there a frail blue was beginning to peep through.

"It looks like the Ace of Swords has done its worst," Flora observed. "Which means the Magician's bird must be around here somewhere."

"I can't hear any birdsong," said Cat. "The place seems dead."

"Maybe we should try over there," said Blaine.

As usual, he was standing a little apart from the other

three. Now he pointed toward a hill about half a mile ahead. Something was glinting on its top: a greenhouse or conservatory. Its ornate structure looked out of place in the middle of a wasteland, but the Arcanum was full of things far stranger, and by unspoken agreement they set off in its direction.

Before they got there, however, there was another hill and what looked like the remains of another greenhouse. Smashed windowpanes glittered in the watery afternoon light; the hothouse plants trampled in the mud were already smelling of rot. A cracked cherub statuette pouted in a puddle.

Toby surveyed the wreckage, unimpressed. "I still think the Magician could've given us the aces if he'd wanted to," he grumbled.

Flora raised her brows. "That wouldn't have been very epic-worthy. I thought you were a fan of impossible quests."

"Bird catching isn't epic," Toby retorted.

"Wait till we see the aces in action," said Cat. "I'll never forget my brush with the Ace of Wands. The knight tore the card in half and—*kaboom*. A towering inferno in seconds."

"Well, I hope he put it to good use," said Flora. "You'd only play something as powerful as an ace if you were in serious trouble."

Blaine grunted. "So why was this one used?"

Nobody had an answer for this. And as they resumed their walk, Cat found she was hanging back again. It wasn't just because of Flora's remark about trouble. Their destination—an octagonal conservatory crowned with a cupola—

appeared to have weathered the storm unscathed. Glossy leaves and flowers bloomed within; its floor-to-ceiling arched windows were gilded by the emerging sun. The flowers, the sunshine, the shining glass . . . it reminded her of the Six of Cups, and not in a good way.

As with many places in the Arcanum, the conservatory's interior was bigger than it had looked from the outside. A black-and-white mosaic path wound its way through the beds and bowers; classical music was playing somewhere, and mingled with the tinkling of a fountain. The air was warm and deliciously perfumed. There could be no greater contrast with the bedlam of Hecate's, or the desolation they had walked through before and after.

Flora, Toby, Blaine and Cat filed along the path, under branches swathed with pink blossoms. By the time they had reached a circular space below the cupola, they all had a scattering of petals in their hair.

"My dears! I am so very pleased that you could come!"

An elderly lady was smiling up at them from a wicker armchair. She had an elegantly faded face and a great quantity of silver hair, held up in a chignon. It looked as if she had been doing some gardening, for a pair of pruning shears and a basket of cuttings were next to her slippered feet.

Cat eyed the teapot and four cups on the table beside her. "You were expecting us?"

"Of course. After all these years, I like to be the first to welcome visitors. Offering a little refreshment is the least I can do."

"It might be poisoned," Toby muttered.

The old lady's laugh tinkled as merrily as the hidden fountain. "Poisoned! Whyever would I want to poison you? It's not often that I receive guests, you know—and when they do arrive, it's always such a treat. Now, do stop fussing and sit yourselves down."

In the end, they each accepted a cup of tea, though nobody intended to risk drinking it. Flora perched gingerly on the other wicker chair, the others hunkered down on the little wall winding around the flowerbeds. Blaine looked especially awkward with a dainty china cup balanced on his knees.

"Please," Flora tried, "we're looking for a bird. A white one. Have you seen it?"

"Dear me . . . let me think. Well, the only birdie I've seen round here is the one on our card."

"*Our* card?" Toby repeated.

"To be sure. We're all in the same move, aren't we?"

He frowned. "So you are—were—a knight? A knight playing for a triumph?"

"I suppose I must have been. What a bother and aggravation it all was! Really, I'm much better off as I am. It took me a while to settle in, of course, but there are my plants to keep me busy, and the occasional guest for entertainment. You'll see." She nodded and smiled. "But you were asking about my card. Now, where did I put it . . . ? Here we are. The Nine of Pentacles. Isn't it pretty?"

It was, indeed, a pretty picture. A richly dressed lady was enclosed in a luxuriant garden, with a bird on her arm.

"How time flies," their hostess said with a chuckle. "It's hard to believe I was only a few years older than you when I was dealt it."

"And speaking of time . . . ," Cat muttered.

Flora took the hint. "Thank you for the tea. We'd love to stay and chat, but I'm afraid we really must get on with finding our bird."

"Young folk these days, forever dashing about!" The old lady tutted. "It was the same with my last guest. Ah well. If it's really so important, I'd best put you in the right direction. People do tend to lose their way among the paths."

They got to their feet, Toby taking the opportunity to tip his tea into a potted lily. Their guide led the way, somewhat stiffly, to the foot of a miniature wrought-iron bridge. The little pool below was sequined with darting fish; the path on the other side led to a brick wall and a white door, similar to the one they had come in by. "That's where all my visitors go. Are you quite sure you won't stay for another cup?"

"I'm afraid we can't," said Flora. "But thank you very much."

"Goodbye, my dears." She stood on the other side of the stream, waving at them fondly. "So lovely to have you!"

The door led to another conservatory. There was the same faint melody of violins and splashing water, and the same mosaic path meandered around a profusion of leaf and blossom.

Pleasant as it all was, Cat was beginning to feel slightly

claustrophobic. The interconnecting wall between the two buildings was the only section of the octagon not made of glass, but from where they were standing, the windows to either side were half obscured with foliage, half misted up by the moisture in the air. She pushed her way through the greenery, toward the view of open skies and rolling heath. Except the view had changed.

"Uh, guys . . . I think we have a problem."

Their conservatory was no longer connected to the old lady's. It was on its own little hill. One hill, among many. One conservatory, among many. At least a hundred self-contained bubbles of glass, glinting and winking in the sun.

At once, Blaine hurtled back to the door they had just come through, closely followed by the other three. It was nothing more than a painted panel nailed to the brick. A marble nymph peeped out from the shrubs nearby. Blaine seized the statue and, staggering slightly, flung it against the nearest window.

The glass wasn't even scratched.

They were trapped.

At first they refused to accept it. They went round each of the conservatory's eight sides, inch by inch, like flies buzzing against a windowpane. But by the time they ended up where they had started, they hadn't found so much as a chink or chip in the glass.

"That evil witch!" Toby fumed. "I knew we shouldn't have trusted her! A sweet old Arcanum granny—of course it'd be a trap!"

"She said that she'd been dealt the Nine of Pentacles when she was only a few years older than us," said Cat weakly.

Flora's eyes darted among the three others in horrified disbelief. Cat knew what she was thinking. These same people in this same place. For the rest of my life.

"Oh God." Toby had had the same thought. His face went blotchy. And in spite of everything, in spite of the claustrophobia, and the bewilderment, and the surging fear, Cat felt a tiny stab of satisfaction. It was about time Toby realized the Game wasn't such a glorious romp.

Blaine was silently, and ferociously, stripping the petals off an azalea.

"Ugh!" Flora suddenly smacked her forehead with the palm of her hand. "We're being idiots. It's fine. I mean, we're not fine exactly, but we have the die, remember? We can create a threshold to the next move whenever we want to."

Of course! How could she have forgotten? Cat felt almost faint with relief; from the looks on the others' faces, they felt the same.

"But," Flora went on, "this move here is our only chance to get the Ace of Swords. If we don't find it before we leave, we might as well give up on the whole thing."

Toby nodded, though he was still looking a little green. "At least we know what its powers were used for—the knight in play here must have used the ace to blow down his greenhouse." Then his face brightened. "Hey, is that what I think it is?"

He pointed to an orange tree behind Cat. A small gilded

cage hung from one of its branches. The latch was open, and a single white feather clung to the bars.

As if on cue, a bird trilled from within the undergrowth. It seemed to Cat that the sound had a faintly taunting note.

"Time to go catch us an ace." Blaine got to his feet.

"Wait—where are you going?" Cat asked. "The sound came from that way."

"No, it didn't, it came from behind us," said Toby.

"I'm sure it was in those bushes over there," said Flora. They stopped still, listening.

Silence.

"You know," Cat said reluctantly, "splitting up is probably a bad idea but . . ."

"It's not like we have much of an option," finished Toby. "OK. Last one back to the birdcage is a loser!"

But before he could charge off, Flora took hold of his arm. "Just a minute. Before we all disappear in different directions, perhaps we should take a moment to consider—well, to consider our various responsibilities."

"How do you mean?" he asked impatiently.

"Oh, well, only that it might be a good idea to check exactly who's looking after what. In case anything goes wrong, you know." She smoothed down her hair, keeping her voice carefully casual. "For example, Blaine's still got the die. . . ."

Blaine gave a bark of laughter. "What, you think I'm going to run off with it into the bushes and never come back? Sneak ahead to grab all the aces, then sell them half-price down Temple House?"

"Of course not; I only thought we should—"

"Fine. I get it." He felt in the pocket of his sweatshirt, and threw something at Cat. "Catch."

It was the die. "Hey, *I* don't want it."

"Tough. Her Ladyship seems to think it belongs in more trustworthy hands."

"For goodness' sake! You're *deliberately* misunder—"

But he had already sauntered into the flowerbed behind them, whistling, "Here, birdie birdie . . ."

Flora pursed her lips before heading up the path in the opposite direction. Toby and Cat were left looking at each other.

"You want to take the left or the right?" he asked.

"Whichever."

She ended up going right, and at first made good progress. She could hear cooing only a little way ahead, and once or twice she was sure she glimpsed a flutter of white feathers. The sounds of the others blundering about faded as she went farther into the greenery. The plants in the beds grew denser than she would have thought possible; in fact, the glass dome of the conservatory was almost completely obscured by the mesh of branches overhead.

Maddeningly, the piped music was playing a melody with flutes in it, whose ripples were very close to birdsong. She couldn't hear the fountain anymore and the black-and-white check of the path had also disappeared from view. The air grew more humid, its sweetness darkened by the scent of compost and decay. Her feet squelched over fallen fruit. Bugs squirmed, flies buzzed.

Soon she was sticky with sap and sweat; her hands were torn from when she'd had to struggle past a tangle of crimson roses. The wretched flute music had stopped, at least, but now she was aware of all sorts of uncanny noises—little rustles and scuffles and creaks in the undergrowth. She called out, hoping to hear Toby, or Flora, or even Blaine, but nobody answered.

At last, she came to a thicket that seemed impenetrably matted. She hunkered down in a small hollow among a clump of ornamental ferns. The earth here was dry, and very soft. If she could just get her breath back, have a little rest . . . she would worry about finding the others later . . . she would worry about everything later. . . . Cat curled up and closed her eyes.

Twoo-tweet . . .

It was her ears playing tricks again. An echo of something that wasn't there.

Twoo-tweet, twoo-tweet . . .

Tweet, tweet . . .

Her eyes snapped open. Preening itself on a branch just the other side of the ferns was a small white bird.

Hardly daring to breathe, making her movements as slow as possible, she sat up. Cat and bird regarded each other. Its feathers were snowy, its eyes beads of red. An albino.

Twoo-tweet . . .

Her quarry half hopped, half flew to the ground. Now it was less than three feet away. Oh God. Any sudden movement or noise and it would fly off, out of sight and out of reach. What she really needed was a net. Perhaps she could lure it to her with something. But with all these seeds and berries, it wasn't likely to be hungry.

And yet . . . the way the bird was cocking its head, the tentative little hops as it sidled along. It seemed almost as interested in her as she was in it.

A thin shaft of sun had filtered through the canopy, making something on her shirt sparkle. The pendant from Bel's Secret Santa! She'd forgotten she was wearing it; up until now, it had been hidden by her collar. It was just a bit of plastic: a four-leaf clover on a chain, coated in gold glitter. Glitter that twinkled in the sun.

The bird hopped closer.

Weren't magpies supposed to be attracted to shiny things? This wasn't a magpie; it wasn't any kind of ordinary bird. But it was worth a try.

With agonizing slowness, Cat inched her hand up and around her neck to undo the clasp of the chain. Very slowly, very gently, she lowered the pendant into her hand. "Like the bling, don't you?" she crooned, soft and coaxing. "Come and get it then, you little horror. Because I'm going to take you down; yes, you and your mad king and all his loony court."

And the bird swooped into Cat's opened palms.

She gasped in shock, but reflexively closed her hands around its body. The bird didn't struggle. She could feel its heart beating, warm and steady within the frail puff of feathers, as it looked up at her, its eyes bright as blood. The Root of Air was cupped within her hands.

Shakily, she stood up. To her immense relief, the foliage jungle had thinned, and she could see the path only a few steps away. Cat stepped out from under a canopy of jasmine, to find the other three also emerging: scratched, sweaty, bleary-eyed.

It seemed impossible that they could ever have lost their way among these fragrant bowers and neat paths. The orange tree and cage were as they'd left them; the water still babbled and the music played. Cat walked up to the cage and carefully placed the bird inside. Her captive seemed perfectly content, cooing softly as she fastened the latch. Close up, she saw that the cage was octagonal, to match the conservatory, with a little dome on top.

"One down, three to go," Cat said to the others, her voice trembling a little as she refastened the pendant around her neck. Then she took out the die. "Let's get the hell out of here."

CHAPTER FIFTEEN

THE CLOCK HAD STOPPED at five minutes to midnight. Moonshine illuminated the glass panels of the giant dial, which, at about twenty feet in diameter, dominated the bare brick tower room.

"OK, so this is weird," said Toby. "Weirdly familiar, I mean."

"You know this place?" Blaine asked.

"A very watered-down version of it. The clock tower at my old school got pulled down by the Ace of Pentacles. I guess the Arcanum side of the threshold survived the quake."

"Well then," said Flora, after a slightly confused pause, "given the scenery, I suppose the card here could either be the Triumph of Time or the Tower."

"If it's Time, then I think its clock needs some new batteries," Cat observed. The bird in its cage cooed, as if in agreement.

The Nine of Pentacles already felt far away. After Cat had thrown the die, they had found the threshold sign carved in the bark of the orange tree. Here, it was welded to the axis of the hour hand. This was made of wrought iron, as were the Roman numerals around the clock's rim. It didn't look as if it had moved in a long while.

Broken cables—presumably once connected to the bells at the top of the tower—lay in a tangle of plaster and fallen masonry. The inner workings of the clock were housed in the room below, and a spiral staircase ran between the shafts that attached the mechanism to the hands on the dial. The section of the stairs that continued up to the belfry had either rusted or been wrenched away and came to a jagged end about two feet off the floor.

Toby peered out of the clock face. A number of panes were missing; beneath the tower, bare sands spread in every direction. "At least now I know what prize Mia and Marlow were competing for," he said to Cat. "It has to be Time; it's a really popular triumph. Whoever wins it gets the chance to turn back the clock and change something about their past. Useful, huh?"

Flora had overheard. "Useful but limited," she said. "It's only your own past actions you can alter. Nobody else's."

Cat shifted the cage under her arm. She didn't want to think about the past, or all the things she longed to change about it.

"Look," she said. "There's writing around the frame of the dial. More Latin slogans."

" 'Infima summis, summa infimis mutare gaudemus,' " Flora

read aloud slowly. "'We make the lowest . . . turn to the top, the . . . highest to the bottom.'"

"We delight," said Blaine.

"I'm sorry?"

"*Gaudemus.* We delight." Blaine's voice was deliberately colorless. "Fortune, the 'royal we,' or Time, *delights* in making the downtrodden rise and the stuck-up fall."

"Um . . . yes. Right. How . . . ?"

He smiled slightly. "So now I know what it takes to shock you."

After a brief hesitation, Flora swept on as if she hadn't heard, although her cheeks had reddened. "We need to get on. Toby thinks the Ace of Pentacles has been played here, which means we're looking for the Magician's poker chip."

"I'll check the other room," Toby volunteered, his hands already on the broken rail of the stairs. The other three continued to poke around the dial but there wasn't much more to see, and a few minutes later Cat went to join him.

She descended the rickety spiral very cautiously, her movements hampered by the birdcage she was carrying. The stairs ended in a platform over the middle of the clockwork, with ladders down to the floor.

Cat wasn't the technical type, but even so she was impressed by the size and complexity of the mechanism, an intricate system of weights, wires, wheels and drums. It was contained within a cast-iron frame that took up most of the space in the room.

"Impressive, isn't it?" Toby had got out his mini flashlight and was shining it across the frame. "See—there's three series of interlinked gears: the time train, the striking train, and the chiming train. That one should be connected to the bells. And there's the handle for winding it all up."

Cat ran her hand along a dusty brake shaft, imagining what the works had been like when in motion. A sharp-edged engine of ticks and turns: not just for measuring time, but driving it . . .

"Got anything?" Blaine thumped carelessly down the stairs and along the creaking platform.

"Toby's giving a lecture on gear trains."

"And talking of lectures," Toby said, "what was with all the gaudy/gaudier/gaudiest stuff back there? Had you seen the slogan before?"

"No."

"So you really could translate it?"

Blaine looked about to snap back, then seemed to think better of it. "I used to live with a Latin teacher," he said shortly.

"Whoa. That can't have been much fun."

"You could say that." He absentmindedly rubbed his right arm.

"What's this for, Toby?" Cat asked, sensing the need for distraction. She gestured to a ten-foot rod with a circular weight at one end.

"It's the pendulum." He pointed his flashlight, and they saw the weight had two neat stacks of coins on top of it. "Pennies! That's how they adjust the timekeeping in Big Ben's clock. You add or subtract coins to speed up or slow down the pendulum; it's not the weight of the coins that makes the difference, but the height of the stack. It moves the center of gravity, you see."

"Fascinating," Cat yawned.

But Toby was looking thoughtful. "Coins . . . It can't just be a coincidence. I wonder if . . ." He leaned forward and shone the flashlight directly on the stack. "Aha. The one on the left isn't a coin at all! It's our Ace of Pentacles!"

"Toby, wait. We should—"

It was too late. He was already reaching to pick it up. A second later, the pendulum began to swing and the gears shifted into life.

Toby looked confusedly at the small clay disc in his hand. "But it shouldn't make any difference—it's not the pendulum that drives the clock."

"Since when did the Arcanum make any sense?" Cat snapped. She had a bad feeling about this. "We've got the second ace, so it's time to make our exit. Flora!" she called, as her free hand fumbled for the die. "Let's get out of here!"

"All right, all right, I'm coming," said a voice from above. "What on earth have you done to the clock?"

Flora began to climb down the spiral stairs. When she was about three or four steps from the platform that bridged the clock work, a bell began to toll. First one, then two, then a whole cacophony. Midnight.

Toby didn't need to tell anyone that this shouldn't be happening. They'd all seen the broken cables. And the sound of the bells themselves was wrong, too: harsh, discordant, thunderous.

Flora cried out as the stairs began to shake, reverberating

in time with the clanging bronze. There was a sound of smashing glass from upstairs, and a sandy wind came whipping through the clock face. For a few moments, she clung to the rails like a sailor in a storm, before there was a great screech of metal and the stairs pitched out over the mechanism.

Somehow, Flora had managed to keep on top of the crush of iron, but the slightest movement on her part could bring everything down into the thrumming, spiky mass of machinery below. All the while, the bells rang on, louder and louder.

"We have to jam it!" Blaine shouted.

The next moment, he had climbed onto the frame that enclosed the clockwork, leaning dangerously far out to make a grab for a pole that was broken and dangling after the stairs' collapse. Flora's white face stared out from the wreckage. Even if they could use the pole to seize everything up, there was no way of knowing how long the brake would hold. The mechanism, like the bells, had acquired a crazed life of its own.

Blaine lunged at the pole, and missed. Only Toby grabbing at his waist kept him from tumbling into the clockwork himself. But with the next lunge he caught the end of the shard. Cat and Toby pulled behind him, adding their weight. By now, the noise of the bells was almost unbearable, and their faces were stinging from blown sand. The bird thrashed within its cage, half maddened with fear.

Somehow, with the three of them tugging, they managed to wrench the pole down so that it stuck, quivering, into the center of a gear train. With a shudder and shriek that could be heard even over the bells, the machinery ground to a halt.

"Cat—be quick—raise a threshold," Blaine gasped.

As she fumbled with the die, the stairs gave way and Flora leaped for the platform. Blaine was there to gather her in.

The clockwork might have stopped, but the bells, if anything, got louder. The noise was like a hammer striking at the flesh and brain, bursting through the blood, swelling unstoppably through the body. Sand was pouring in from the room above in a blizzard of grit. Cat could barely open her eyes to see a silver wheel glowing on the brick behind them. But she managed to trace the circle, throw the coin, and a few agonizing seconds later it was all gone.

CHAPTER SIXTEEN

AT FIRST, THEY WERE afraid the bird was dead. Its eyes were closed and it was bunched up stiffly in a corner of the cage. But when Cat tapped on the bars, it croaked faintly and opened a crimson eye.

The bird wasn't the only one feeling battered by their last move. Everyone was ashen-faced; for a while they just swayed on their feet, waiting for their heads to clear and their ears to stop ringing.

They were in a stony mountain valley, under a sky blazing with stars that were much brighter, and more thickly clustered, than any they had seen before. Tiny white flowers formed the sign for the threshold and were scattered underfoot. A series of pools glimmered before them.

"I think I know where we are," Flora said dazedly. "This looks like the Star, the triumph for health."

"It does seem sort of refreshing," Toby agreed, sniffing

the air. It was very cold, but invigoratingly so. "I already feel a lot less tired than I should be."

"That doesn't mean there isn't a nasty surprise in store," said Cat.

"And here it comes," Blaine muttered, as a stumbling figure came into view.

He was a tubby, youngish man in a pinstripe suit, clutching a small stone urn to his chest. When he saw the four chancers, he gasped, and staggered.

"No—you can't stop me!" he choked out. "Stay away!" He clasped the urn tighter and began to back away, his eyes darting fearfully. "Did the King of Swords send you? Because the courts can't intervene, not now. I played my ace fair and square."

The four of them exchanged glances. "What did the ace do?" Toby asked.

"A—a wave appeared, from one of the pools. A flood that turned to ice . . . I didn't *want* to use it." Now the man looked almost petulant. "The Ace of Cups was all I had! It was him or me, two rivals for the same triumph. The Game Masters set us against each other. The other knight gave me *no choice* . . ."

"It's all right," said Cat. "We're not going to interfere."

"I wouldn't let you!" he said defiantly. "If I fail, I have to play a whole new round."

"What's in the pot?" Blaine asked.

"Spring water, from the grotto. Whoever takes the urn and pours its water onto the threshold wins the triumph."

"The gift of health," said Flora softly.

"Not for me—my wife. She's ill—the doctors are useless—and I—I promised her—there was *no choice.*" He dragged one hand over his face, groaning. "God forgive me . . ." But with his next words, the whine of defiance was back in his voice. "If he'd had the ace, Swords would've acted as I did. You would have, too."

Then he turned his back on them, and lurched on down the valley.

After five minutes' walk in the opposite direction, they found what the ace had been used for.

They had already passed two shallow pools, their surfaces silver with starlight. The third, however, was solid ice. Its depths were clear enough for them to see the man encased within: his hands petrified in a futile gesture of defense, his face frozen in a twist of fury and fear. His eyes stared out from his prison; it was horribly difficult to drag their own away.

"Do you think he's still . . . alive?" Cat faltered.

"I dunno," said Blaine. "But since the Magician turned our ace into an ice cube, I reckon it's in there with the knight."

"We could hack the ice with a rock or something," Toby suggested.

Flora shook her head. "It will take more than that to undo the Ace of Cups."

"So what'll we do?"

"The knight had an urn of spring water. That's what they were fighting over, he said. And since this is the triumph for miracle cures, that water probably has some kind of healing power. . . ."

"And we might be able to use one kind of watery force to cancel out the other." Toby nodded. "It's worth a try. Well, the knight came from this direction, so if there is a spring, it must be somewhere up in the rocks over there." He reached into his jacket pocket and brought out a hip flask with a Magician-like flourish. "We can carry the water back in this."

"Got any more tricks up your sleeve?" Cat asked.

"Sure. Flashlight, chocolate rations, compass, whistle . . ."

Blaine snorted. "Camping stove, encyclopedia, kitchen sink."

Actually, Cat thought that Toby had the right idea. The flashlight had already come in handy, and she found herself wishing she'd equipped herself with more than a few tissues and a packet of chewing gum. "OK, let's go climb some rocks."

"Um, if you don't mind," said Flora, "I think I'll wait for you here." She smiled apologetically. "My ankle is still a little weak from when I twisted it the other day, and I wrenched it again on the clockwork."

"We can't just leave you! Look what happened when we split up in the other move," Toby protested.

"I'll be fine. The Star is one of the most benign cards in the deck."

"Tell that to Mr. Freeze."

"C'mon, it won't take four people to fetch a bottle of water," Blaine put in. "Us two will go find the spring. Cat and the bird can stay with Flora."

Toby passed Cat the whistle. "In that case, you'd better have this. Blow twice for a distress signal, and me and Blaine'll come to the rescue."

"So you get to be Boy Scouts, and I'll play nursemaid," she said, but under her breath. The truth was, she'd be glad of a rest.

By unspoken agreement, the two girls moved away from the tomb of ice, settling instead by a pool where the water was clear and fringed with flowers. Flora went down to the water's edge and set about washing her face and hands. Then she took a comb from her pocket, smoothing out her hair and tying it back in a neat ponytail. Finally, she applied a slick of cherry lip balm.

Cat watched in fascination. There was no doubt they were all in a state: grimy and disheveled, speckled in scratches from the Nine of Pentacles, gritty with sand from the Triumph of Time. But given the circumstances, Flora's grooming routine struck her as perverse.

Flora caught her eye and passed over the lip balm. "Granny always told my mother, 'Put some lipstick on and you'll feel better.' And actually, I think she was right." She laughed humorlessly. "Of course, gin is Mummy's pick-me-up of choice."

Cat remembered the wild shouting. The crack across the mirror, ugly as a scar. . . . She swallowed, tasting the faint scent of cherry on her mouth. "Is that why you're in the Game? Because of—of your parents?"

There was a long silence, and she thought Flora wasn't

going to reply. Perhaps she was angry at being asked. But when the other girl did speak, her voice was calm. "No," she said. "I'm in the Game because of my sister."

She tilted her head toward the star-studded sky. "You know, I've been in this move before. It looked different, of course, but the principle was the same."

Cat didn't follow the change of subject, but she nodded anyway.

"I went to the spring that time," Flora continued. "I even got some water and took it home across the threshold. I brought it to my sister. I thought it might help."

"Is she . . . ill?"

"No," said Flora. "She's sleeping. She's been asleep for five years."

"Grace is seven years older than me, and beautiful. Clever, too. All the time she was growing up, she had that . . . shining quality, a kind of radiance, which people are drawn to without quite understanding.

"With such a big age difference, you might have thought that she wouldn't have much time for me. But it wasn't like that.

"When I turned ten, Grace invented a special story-telling game. We pretended that there was an enchanted land waiting around the corner, where there were fabulous cities and creatures, and dreams came true. Grace said the only way to enter the land was with a magic coin. I couldn't go and play there—I was too little, she said. But she used to draw me pictures of the adventures she had had, and tell me stories of kings and queens, knights and knaves. A world of complex rules and fabulous quests.

"I was too old for make-believe, really. Far too old to believe my sister was having adventures in a different world. Even so, I was obsessed by her stories. She made them sound so real. I used to go through her things, looking for a magic coin. I waited up for her when she was out late; I even tried to follow her a couple of times. Needless to say, I never got very far.

"In the week before Christmas, Grace seemed unusually preoccupied. Even our parents noticed that she was on edge. I think they thought it must be something to do with a boy. On the evening of the nineteenth, she came to find me in my bedroom. She was excited: fizzing with energy. But she was nervous, too.

"'I've been lucky so far,' she told me. 'I'm good at this game, and the cards have been kind to me. And I'm so close, Flo—so close!'

"Then she started pacing up and down, biting her lip. 'I've got a bad feeling about this next move, though. I don't know. . . .'

"I was just happy she was playing our game again. She hadn't talked about it for a while; I was worried she had become bored of it.

"When she found me, I was doing some homework on the Greek myths. We had to read the story of Theseus and the Minotaur. 'Theseus had a test,' I told her. 'He got lost in a maze and had to fight the Minotaur. But the princess gave him a thread to show him the way, and he killed the monster and escaped and became king. You'll be like him: like a hero.' Grace shook her head and smiled. 'Sometimes the heroes came to bad ends,' she said. I didn't beg her to take me on this new quest. I knew that wouldn't get me anywhere. But as a joke—though I meant it half-seriously—I gave her some red embroidery silk from my ribbon box. I told her it would help her find her way home.

"My sister laughed and hugged me, then left me to my book. She was supposed to be going to a party that evening. A midwinter ball. Our parents were out, too; I was staying at home with the housekeeper.

"I couldn't sleep that night. In the end, I got out of bed and went to the window. It had started to snow, and I saw that the door at the bottom of the garden was ajar. I knew it shouldn't be left open, and all of a sudden I was afraid.

"Even though I didn't want to be alone in the dark, I felt I had to face this by myself. Like the heroes. So I put on my boots and coat over my nightgown and went to the end of the garden, and through the door into the deserted park. There was something—someone—lying by the summerhouse on the hill. It was Grace, all spread out in her scarlet evening dress. The snow was already settling on her face.

"I can't remember much of what happened immediately after. Everyone seemed to arrive at once: my parents, the paramedics, the police. The only thing we knew for certain was that Grace was in a coma. Nobody knew what she was doing in the park or what had happened to her, except that she never turned up to the ball. She had no injuries, no signs of illness, alcohol or drugs, though they tested her for everything. She was . . . untouched.

"I didn't show anyone the card I had found by her side, a picture of a woman bound and blindfolded inside a cage of swords. I knew it was Grace's secret and that she wouldn't want me to tell. At first, you see, we thought she would wake up.

"My parents left me at home while they went in the ambulance with Grace. And that morning, very early, I went down to the garden and out into the park again. It had snowed heavily during the night and everything was covered in white. I was carrying the card I'd found with my sister, trying to work out what it could mean. Then I saw something red fluttering by one of the columns on the summerhouse.

"It was a broken strand of silk. The same silk I'd given Grace when I told her to use a thread to find her way home, like Theseus in the labyrinth. She must have tied one end to the summerhouse before she used the threshold there. I don't know why. A superstitious impulse, perhaps. Or maybe she only did it to please me.

"A young man and a blonde were sitting on the other side of the summerhouse, drinking hot chocolate. I remember thinking how beautiful the woman was, all wrapped up in white fur. 'I'm glad you could make it,' she said, and took my card.

" 'What have you done to my sister?' I asked.

" 'She took a wrong turn,' the man replied. 'Her move is

incomplete.' That's all they would tell me about Grace. Then, or ever. And they said that because I had intervened in their Game, I could now join it. But not like Grace. Not as a knight. I was just a fool.

"Grace's last move was the Eight of Swords. It is a card of imprisonment. I think my sister was trying to escape some kind of trap, and she used my thread to guide her home, but part of her—the living, laughing, waking part—is still captive in the Arcanum.

"My parents think their daughter has spent the last five years in a coma. They have given up hope. They've stopped talking about the day when she will come back to us. I know better. Every time I go past that threshold, I feel my palm burn, and I know my sister is waiting for me on the other side. I just need the right card to take me in and complete her move.

"And as long as the threshold remains, I know my sister can still be saved."

Flora's narration had been so matter-of-fact as to be almost expressionless. Cat didn't know what to say; it might have been easier if Flora had broken down and cried. At least then she would have had a cue.

Cat thought of the Arcanum's other victims and wondered what all-consuming hopes and fears had driven them into the Game. Then there were the people they had left behind, never to know their loved ones' fate. She understood what Flora was playing for, but what about Grace, the girl who had everything? And what about her own mum and dad? If they had had the chance to play, what prize would have been worth the risk?

It struck her that she and Flora were not so different after all. In spite of the glossy friends and doting parents, Flora was someone else who walked alone. Perhaps Toby was right to say that the burdens and mysteries of the Arcanum were better shared. Her own wariness was defensive; recognizing another's, and reaching past it, was something new.

"I'm sorry," she said at last, and inadequately.

Flora didn't seem to hear. "Of course I've kept looking, but not as hard as I could have. I'm afraid, you see, that if I go into the Arcanum too often I'll discover why my sister loved it so." Then she gave her head a shake, as if to wake herself up. "Really, Cat, I can't think why I'm boring you with all this. It's certainly not your problem."

"My parents were mixed up in the Game. They got killed because of it."

God—why had she blurted it out like that? Cat could feel herself turning red.

Flora regarded her gravely. "Then I am sorry, too."

She gave a small, bleak smile, which Cat returned. For the moment, it was enough.

Toby was the first to return, zigzagging breathlessly past the boulders, and brandishing the hip flask above his head.

"Hey, guys! Look what I've got! Jeez, it was a total *nightmare* climbing over the rocks—until we got to this really cool grotto with a naked goddess statue and everything. I think the water made my insect bites better. Or maybe not. How's your ankle, Flora? I wanted to try the spring water on it, as a test, but Blaine said we should save it for the iceman."

An unwelcome thought had occurred to Cat. "Wait— what about the no-intervention rule? If the other knight drowned this one to win, we don't want to mess things up by getting him out again."

"This move's finished," said Blaine impatiently. "Knight Number One's already taken his water to the threshold. He'll be safely home by now."

He was standing at the ice's edge. The figure within, stuck in his moment of terror like a fly in amber, was all the more grotesque for being surrounded by the beauty of the valley and its diamond-bright sky. It was hard to imagine the ace's act of violence in such a peaceful place. Yet it had turned a quiet pool into a tidal surge, liquid into solid, life into death.

"I'd like to do it," Flora said, holding her hand out for the flask. Toby looked disappointed but he passed it over. Steadying herself on Cat's shoulder, Flora unscrewed the cap and leaned over the ice so that the water fell in a sparkling arc.

It was as if she had poured a flask of acid. The ice hissed on contact and there was a burning, sulfurous smell as the water ate through its glassy surface, dissolving it into slush. The prisoner twitched, then began to flail about, choking and thrashing—and very much alive.

Blaine waded into the pool to pull him out. The man's skin was mottled white and blue, and he couldn't speak for shaking. But once they settled him on dry ground, the shudders subsided and the color returned to his face with remarkable speed. In fact, Flora had only just begun to wrap her coat around his shoulders when he shook her off roughly and leaped to his feet.

"Where is he?" he shouted. "What have you done with him?"

"It's fine," Toby said soothingly. "You're safe: the other knight's long gone."

The Knight of Swords' face contorted with rage. "All the triumphs in all the Game won't be any help once I've caught up with him. Dirty snake!" He grasped Cat by the shoulder. "Where did he go, girl? Back to the threshold?"

"I'm not sure. . . ."

But the man was already sprinting away, still dripping, with savagery in his eyes. A pearly white mist had begun to wind through the valley, and his figure was soon obscured from view.

"You're welcome!" Toby called after him. "Huh. What an ungrateful sod."

"That's all the thanks we need," said Flora, pointing. "Our Root of Water."

For the pool was evaporating before their eyes, until there was nothing left but a shard of ice in a grassy hollow. When Flora picked it up, it was cold and wet, but it didn't melt in the warmth of her hand. It had drowned a man in eternal winter, yet the closer they looked, the more its depths shimmered with rainbows, and light.

KNIGHT OF PENTACLES

Chapter Seventeen

THE SKY ON THE OTHER SIDE of their next threshold was low and gray. Shabby buildings loomed around a threadbare patch of grass and shrubs enclosed by a fence. A trash can on the pavement overflowed abundantly, as if to compensate for the barrenness everywhere else. They were back in the garden at Mercury Square.

For Cat, it was doubly familiar. The exhausted-looking apple tree in the center of the garden was encircled by a ring of scorched earth. A crushed beer can lay underneath a bench where, until recently, a tramp had snored. Looking toward Temple House, she half expected to see herself doubled over by the railings, retching with shock.

Blaine was watching her. "Seems just like yesterday, doesn't it?" he said.

It was the first time he'd acknowledged how they'd met. Cat still didn't know if, like her, he had wandered into the move by accident, thanks to Temple House's overlap with the Arcanum, or if his visit was a deliberate part of searching for his stepfather. She was momentarily dizzy with the remembrance of it all: the helplessness, and the horror.

This time, however, there was no visible blurring between the two of sides of the threshold. The move in play here might not have required any fantastical shifts in scene, but was unmistakably part of the Arcanum landscape in the way that aspects of the familiar world seemed exaggerated, others less defined. It was shrouded in silence.

The quiet didn't last. A rustling by the railings made them draw together, faces tense, as a figure edged out furtively from behind a shrub. Cat immediately thought of the guys with the hooded sweatshirts and truncheons. However, whoever it was seemed even more nervous than they were. A boy of eighteen or nineteen, with a sharp bony face and close-cropped hair.

"You," he said, half accusing, half panicky. "You just come from nowhere. I seen you do it."

"Er, yeah. There's a threshold over there," Toby replied.

The new arrival stared. "What's he talking about?" Then, plaintively, "It's not right. Nothing's right. Why's it so quiet? Where's everybody gone? They must've been and closed off all the streets for miles around. Here"—his face creased in alarm—"you don't reckon we're in one of them terrorist alerts, do you?"

"He's a chancer," said Flora wonderingly.

"But he can't be," said Cat. "There are only four of us in the Game. The Hanged Man said—"

"That comes later. The Magician's die is taking us back into the *time* as well as place where the aces were last played, remember? And this is the move where you and Blaine first met, isn't it?" Cat nodded: she had told Flora about their encounter when she'd agreed to try to find the fourth chancer. "Well then. This boy might have been one of us last Saturday, but"—she lowered her voice—"anything could have happened to him afterward. . . ."

"Hey—I'm not 'this boy.' I'm Liam." He looked from one to the other, gnawing his lip. "Who are you people?"

"We're like you," Blaine said shortly. "Tell us what happened. About what happened to you this afternoon."

"I dunno!" he replied, exasperated. "I dunno *nothing*. All I did, right, was follow some bloke into one of them houses. Over there." He pointed toward Temple House. "Because he left the door open, see, and it was all very nice inside, a class act, you know? So I thought I'd best go in and warn him about the security risk. Opportunistic theft. After all, you can't be too careful in this neighborhood." He sniggered a little. "And then—then—all this weird stuff kicks off. There's crazies waving cards and droning about Fate and Forces and suchlike, and I thought, stone me, it's them doomsday-cult nut jobs. So I exited sharpish and when I come out, things was different. Different like this."

"But how did—" Blaine was beginning, when his eye was drawn by movement at the end of the square. The light was fading fast, but they could just make out hooded figures gathering in the shadows of one of the streets leading off the north corner. The Knaves of Wands had returned.

243

"Quick. We have to get out of here," said Cat urgently, hurrying to the garden gate and casting around for an escape route or hiding place.

"This way," said the new chancer. He darted ahead and up to one of the windows of a shut-up house. One of the boards was loose, and he was able to pry it open without difficulty. "Got no idea what's going on, but I knows trouble when I see it. Pretty good at getting out of it, too." And he grinned, flashing a mouthful of yellow teeth.

One by one, they squeezed through, clambering down from the sill into the disarray of an abandoned office. It looked as if it had lain undisturbed for years. The tops of the filing cabinets and desks were furry with dust.

Cat put her eye to the gap in the boards and watched as the four knaves swaggered into the dusky garden. One squatted down to inspect the scorched earth around the apple tree, while the others muttered in a huddle.

There was a yelp from behind her. Liam was sucking a finger and scowling at the birdcage, which Cat had set on top of an ancient photocopier. "I didn't know birds bit! Usually travel with your budgie, do you?"

"It's our team mascot," said Cat distractedly, still peering at the knaves.

Flora came to join her. "I think we're OK; they're here for the knight, not a few stray chancers." She turned to Liam. "Did you see anyone else before we arrived?"

"Nobody but some old wino. That's how I knew to come in here—I seen him scramble through the window."

"So the knight must still be in the building!" Toby exclaimed. "I wonder if our ace is in here, too."

"Now then," said Liam. "I can see how you're anxious to avoid the gang out there. But there's no harm in us having a poke around the place, right?" He appeared to have got over his earlier fears. In fact, he looked almost cheerful. "You never know what the movers might've overlooked— could be some good gear lying about."

He was already moving toward the dilapidated reception area. But after picking their way past mounds of moldering folders and broken computer equipment, they found that the main stairs were blocked by a fallen bookcase. It looked as if their explorations were confined to the lower levels of the building.

"Here, Cat," Blaine said quietly in her ear. "About our first time in this move: how many knaves did you see?"

"Uh . . . four, I think. Plus you at the other end of the garden—though when you came up to me later, I figured you were, you know, ordinary. From the home side."

"But I was never in the garden. I was staying well clear, behind that Dumpster."

"Oh." She thought back to the boy who'd been throwing pebbles at the cat, and had stared at her with such intensity. A vague shape in a baggy sweater, too far away to distinguish his features properly. She had just assumed that he and Blaine were one and the same. "OK then: there were five of them. That makes sense. Five of Wands, like the card."

"Yeah. So why're only four out there now?"

"Shhh!" Flora hissed from ahead, as they shuffled past stacks of storage crates and yet more filing cabinets. Light glimmered from a door just a little way down the passage, behind which a slurred voice was raised in song.

"'Luck—hic—be a laaady toniiiiight . . .'"

Liam turned to look at the other four huddled behind him, his face pallid in the gleam of Toby's flashlight. He put a finger to his lips and winked conspiratorially, before turning the handle on the door.

It opened into a small bare room lit by a single bulb. A man was slumped on the floor in a heap of ragged clothes and wild gray hair. His hands and feet were bound with an old electrical cord. "Wha—wha?" he mumbled, blinking up at them with bloodshot eyes.

"Brought you some company, old man," said Liam. He grinned. Then, in one swift shocking movement, he drew out a knife and held it to Cat's throat.

"You three: against the wall behind Pentacles," he rapped out. "And don't think of trying any tricks."

The blade stung coldly against Cat's neck. She swallowed and felt the metal prick into her skin. The warmth and weight and smell of Liam's body were pressed against her in horrible intimacy.

"Time to lose Tweetie Pie. Set it on the floor—nice and slow now."

Cat bent her knees, holding the cage with one unsteady hand, and Liam bent down alongside her without loosening his grip. She set the cage a little distance from her feet; when she stood up, the bird beat its wings in agitation against the bars as if to echo the leaping of her heart.

Meanwhile, Flora, Blaine and Toby had lined up along the wall behind the knight. His song over, he appeared to have passed out, and was filling the air with rich bubbling snores.

"You've already got your man," Blaine said tightly, "so fetch your mates and finish the move. We've got nothing to do with this, and nothing to do with you."

Liam sneered. "Typical gutless chancers. You're an even bigger waste of space than Pentacles here. The boozing idiot gets his hands on an ace, one of the powerfullest cards in the deck, and practically throws it away—didn't even have the sense to use it to seal off the threshold and make his escape." He spat on the floor.

"Three hours I kept watch on his little bonfire. Three hours! Soon as it started to die away I could've gone for backup. But no, I knew better'n that. I waited. And I watched, just like I'd watched this one"—he leaned in to Cat, so his breath tickled sourly against her cheek—"go all weak-kneed at the threshold. I got a feeling in my gut that her business here weren't finished, and in this Game, it's gut instinct what gives you the edge. Course, a whole gang of yous turning up was an unexpected surprise."

"So what do you want from us?" Flora asked coldly.

"Easy. I want one of you fine ladies and gents to deliver this here Knight of Pentacles to the Knaves of Wands."

"But—but he's already your prisoner."

"Ah, but I wants something more. The main chance. Or in this case—chancer. A chancer what'll bring the power of Wands down on Pentacles, and win this move for my court. *And* for me. Get it?"

Nobody answered.

"A knave what catches a chancer meddling gets set free from his forfeit: that's the rule." Liam sniggered at his own cunning. "Thanks to the intervention you'll be so kind to make, I goes back to being a knight, while one of you gets to be the King of Wands' shiny new knave. Bonus points all round."

"Wait," Toby tried. "You don't need to do this. The four of us are on a quest. We're going to overthrow the—"

"Shut it."

"But—"

"I said, *shut it.* Chat, chat, chat, hoping to distract me . . . I weren't born yesterday. No, I'm the one what's doing the talking, 'cause I'm the one in charge." His eyes glinted dangerously. "I want a volunteer in the next thirty seconds. Else your friend's losing streak is gonna turn fatal."

At this, he pressed the knife tighter so that Cat felt warm blood trickle on clammy skin. She stared out at the concrete cell with unseeing eyes. Was this how her mum and her dad had felt, waiting helplessly as the stranger raised the gun? It wasn't just her life that was at stake, either. To save her, one of the other three would have to give up their freedom for enslavement to the Court of Wands.

"P'raps," Liam mused as he drew the blade—lightly, teasingly—toward her ear, "you're thinking I'm the type for idle threats. P'raps I should start off with a little nibble of the knife, just to show how easy—"

"I'll do it," said Flora. She looked at the others' stricken faces and waved her hand dismissively. "It's fine: I'm bored of being on the sidelines as it is. Who knows, I might even get a career break like Liam here. And a knave's one up from a fool, wouldn't you say?" Then she pushed herself off the wall and stepped over the drooling body of the knight, giving him a contemptuous kick on the way.

Liam tensed and pressed the blade against Cat's throat again, but Flora barely glanced at them. Instead, she bent down and picked up the birdcage. "I'll have one advantage, at least," she said briskly. "There are few knaves who have a real live ace up their sleeve."

"Ace?" said Liam, frowning. "That card's been played. And put that thing down, I don't—"

Too late. Flora flicked open the gilded door, swung the cage through the air and flung the bird at his face.

It might have been a creature of the Arcanum, conjured by a magician, and forged from the raw element of air. But it was also just a bird. A frightened bird, in a squawking, scrabbling fluster of beating wings and beak and claws.

Instinctively, the knave put up one of his arms to protect his face. He didn't release Cat, but his grip slackened. Even so, he would have recovered from the distraction in seconds if it wasn't for the knight, who suddenly swung his bound legs up and across the floor, jackknifing into the backs of Liam's knees.

The next minute or so was all confusion as Cat scrambled

out of the way and the knight and knave flailed about on the floor. The knight had somehow managed to work his hands free, but his legs were still tied, and Liam had the knife. However, the knight was neither as old nor as drunk as he had first appeared: there was bulk beneath his tattered layers of clothes and a ruthless gleam in his eyes. Before the others quite knew what had happened, Liam's head had hit the concrete ground with a crack and his body collapsed limply.

"Little bastard," said the knight with satisfaction. He took the knife to cut the remainder of his cords, which he used to truss up his former captor. "Still breathing, more's the pity." He then produced a battered version of Toby's hip flask from within his layers and took a hefty swig.

"You all right, Cat?" Blaine asked quietly.

Cat nodded. She had backed into a corner of the room and was holding one hand around her throat.

"Let me see." He reached to take her hand away, then touched, very gently, the scratch made by Liam's knife. "There," he said, as if his touch could rub out the mark, lightly and easily, like an eraser on a pencil. Their eyes met, as they had that first time in Mercury Square. It already felt like a lifetime ago. The bird swooped down from its perch on a hook in the wall and settled on her shoulder, cooing contentedly.

Toby was still gawping. Flora looked similarly stunned.

"Here you go, princess," said the knight, holding out his hip flask. "This'll put some color in your cheeks. Pass it round, if you like."

Flora managed a weak smile. "Not for me, thank you. Though you're very kind."

"D'you think Wands could make the case that Fl . . . our involvement has won this move for you?" Blaine asked the knight, leaving Cat's side to rummage through Liam's pockets.

"Hmm." The man rubbed his bristly chin. "I'm not home and dry yet. Got to get back to the threshold first. As for this little weasel . . . well, all knaves are cheats and losers. I reckon I could've taken him down on my own, but I can't swear to it. It's a close call." He took another swig from the hip flask and belched loudly.

"Too close for comfort," Toby fretted. "At this stage of the Game, the kings and queens will use any excuse to take one of us out of play."

"So it's just as well Liam was carrying this, then." Blaine held up the thin black lighter that the Magician had conjured from the Ace of Wands.

The other three chancers heaved shaky sighs of relief. "Thank God," Flora whispered.

"Y'know," mused the knight, "I never come across one chancer before, let alone four. I never saw a bird like that one, neither. A quest, you said . . ." He squinted round at them with shrewd wet-rimmed eyes, then gave a hoarse chuckle. "I know: don't ask, don't tell. Gotta keep my mind on the job at hand, anyhow, if I'm to get to that threshold with all my bones intact."

He went to the door of the room and looked up and down the corridor. "Still, this particular gang can't be the cream of Wands' crop, not if they left our rat-faced friend here in charge of surveillance. I reckon I've a decent enough chance of pulling through."

"We should get moving, too," said Blaine. "We've got what we came for—and Temple House is only three buildings to the right of this one."

"Off to HQ, eh? Then you'll just need to keep going through the rat run; as far as I can make out, the basements are all joined up on this side of the threshold."

Taking a final gulp from his flask, the knight tucked it away, stretched enormously and rubbed his hands through his dirty hair. "Time to be up and at 'em. Cheerio, chancers."

Striking a match from a box in his pocket, he turned left and sauntered into the darkness, singing under his breath. " 'Luck be a lady tonight . . .' "

"Come on." Flora wearily turned in the opposite direction.

"What about him?" said Cat, prodding Liam with her foot. The knave stirred slightly and let out a faint groan.

"Leave him for his crew to find," Blaine replied. "We've got other priorities."

They nodded, grim-faced. They were so close. But they didn't dare hope. Not yet.

The knight was right about it being a rat run. Their corridor soon diverged into a jumble of nooks, crannies and crooked passageways; after a while the office clutter changed to household junk but the dust and dilapidation were the same. Some stretches had bulbs that flickered into sallow life; in others, Toby's flashlight was the only light they had to guide them. The Ace of Wands remained in Blaine's pocket.

Cat dropped behind to talk to Flora, shifting the birdcage awkwardly in her arms. "Thank you. For what you did back there, and the risk you took."

"Obviously, none of us would have stood by and watched you get your throat cut. I happened to move first, that's all," Flora said calmly. "I'd seen that knight had got his hands loose, so it seemed worth a shot." She bit her lip. "I'll just have to hope we get to the Hanged Man before the forfeits get to me."

"We won't let that happen—to you or anyone. We're in this together."

"We're in this for ourselves," the other girl replied. "Don't get me wrong—I don't want anything bad to happen to you or Toby or Blaine. Of course I don't. But at the end of the day, the four of us have to look out for each other because that's our best chance of survival, and our only chance of success."

Cat knew Flora was right. She only had to let her guard slip for a moment and she would be flooded with a terrible hunger for the memories awakened by the Six of Cups, and all-consuming grief for what came after. But expert as she was at suppressing her own hopes and fears, Cat was beginning to find that blocking out other people's was a different matter.

Toby's voice broke into her thoughts. "This is it, team. Go through there, and we'll be right under Temple House."

The next dividing wall had a gate in the middle—a gate with the design of a wheel worked into its rusting bars. An empty cellar lay beyond, its walls plastered in peeling whitewash.

"You say the Hanged Man is imprisoned under this building?" said Blaine.

Toby nodded solemnly. "Far below. But the stairs are hidden behind the ballroom door. You got the key, Flora?"

"All present and correct." Flora flourished the little silver key that she had carried ever since the Triumph of the Moon.

"And I've got the die," said Cat.

Smiling with relief, she stepped forward to make its final throw. A few seconds later the scars on their palms matched the wheel in the gate, and the die itself had crumbled away into dust. Its task was done, for the last threshold it had created would take them out of this move and back into their own time.

Everyone's spirits lifted. They had captured the aces and won their round. And once Toby raised the threshold coin, and spun them out of the Five of Wands, they knew they were right where they needed to be: just a few floors below the mirrored doorway that would take them to their prize.

QUEEN OF CUPS

CHAPTER EIGHTEEN

WHEN THE FOUR CHANCERS emerged from the basement and into the entrance hall of Temple House, it was to find that the dust sheets and junk mail of their last visit had disappeared. Luster gleamed from every surface; a drowsy richness warmed the air. The checkered hall was deserted and the golden curtain pulled closed.

Even so, there was something unsettling about the stillness. As they began to climb the stairs to the ballroom, it felt as if the whole house was drawing its breath.

"This place is equal to all players, remember," Flora said, as if to reassure herself. "We can do what we like."

"Oh, my dear," said the Queen of Pentacles, "that's where you're wrong."

Lucrezia had emerged from behind the black-and-gold doors at the head of the stairs. Her expression was amused, and a little indulgent: an adult surveying fractious children.

She was dressed in another of her voluptuous evening gowns, and its emerald skirts rustled like paper as she moved. "For as long as the courts hold sway, every one of us must obey the rules. One of which is that all play is suspended while a Lottery takes place." She smiled dazzlingly. "And since a Lottery is in progress this evening, I'm afraid you'll have to wait."

Her three companions were close behind. Alastor, looking sleepy and rumple-haired, was the last to emerge. As he did so, he took a blank card from within his coat and passed his hand over its face. When he held it up, they saw a leering thief-figure. "Seven of Swords," he said with his customary nonchalance. "Or, if you prefer, the Reign of Futility."

Behind him, the doors to the ballroom quivered, then melted into a solid wall. They took the only route to the Hanged Man's tomb with them.

"You—you can't do that!" gasped Toby in outrage.

Ahab regarded them dispassionately. "It appears we just did."

Blaine moved as if to challenge him, but Flora put a restraining hand on his arm. "It's fine," she said, tight-lipped. "We'll just wait until the Lottery's over. They can't delay us for much longer."

None of the kings and queens looked in the least concerned. Alastor swung ahead, whistling under his breath. They continued down to the hall and through the curtain without so much as a backward glance at the four chancers.

The square outside was thronged with people, and the Game Masters' arrival was greeted with a ripple of applause.

The table and wheel from the ballroom had been set on the center of the lawn; the apple tree behind was a cloud of white blossom in a rose-flushed sky. As the kings and queens took their seats, the voice of the doorkeeper raised itself above the murmur of the crowd. "Ladies and gentlemen, princes and vagabonds, players all . . ."

The four chancers slumped on the front doorstep. They had no choice but to sit it out.

And in the drowsy atmosphere of Temple House, energy and urgency alike began to ebb. As the bird preened its feathers, and the audience laughed, clapped or sighed as events required, Cat could feel a gentle lull stealing over her. On the far side of the square, just past the lace of spring leaves and twinkling lights, the rosy sky had darkened to black. Flakes of snow were spiraling onto the pavement. A lone pedestrian, muffled up against the cold, didn't give the interior of the garden a second glance. Their own world: so near and yet so far.

"Maybe we should hit the GMs with our aces," Toby suggested at last. "They should be super-powerful."

"Not in the form they're in now," Flora replied, rousing herself a little. "What can we do—set fire to the King of Wands' hair with the lighter? Stick an ice cube down the Queen of Cups' neck? No, our only hope is to get the aces to the Hanged Man's tree, like the Magician said."

"Then what?" Blaine grunted.

"Then . . . then we're supposed to plant them in some way," Cat said sleepily. "Isn't that right? I s'pose we can ask the—"

The doorkeeper was standing before them, staring with pale clouded eyes. His face was stern.

"The courts require your presence," he announced. "Come."

The four chancers unsteadily got to their feet. Cat's birdcage felt unusually heavy, and dragged at her arm. As the crowd parted to let them through, the line of faces was like one long pale snake filled with eyes. It seemed to take an inordinate amount of time to cross the lawn to where the Game Masters were waiting.

Ahab was the first to speak. "It appears," he said ponderously, "that the courts are due recompense. An unlawful intervention has been made."

The audience seethed with scandal and delight.

Cat was wide awake now. "No," she said, her voice sounding childishly high and thin. "No, you're wrong. That knight would've got free of Li—of the Knave of Wands without any of us having to do anything. You can't know if our being there made a difference as to whether he won his move or not."

"I entirely agree," Lucrezia purred. "The whole business is *far* too complicated to bother disentangling. Both Wands and Pentacles have agreed to put the issue aside."

"The case in question here," Odile said in her light, precise voice, "is a petition brought by the Court of Cups."

The doorkeeper stepped forward. "Let the Knight of Cups bear witness."

A plump, anxious-looking young man came out from the crowd. It was the first knight from the Triumph of the Star.

He pointed at the four chancers with a trembling hand. *"You,"* he quavered. "You four released Swords from the ice. He caught me, and attacked me, and the urn broke. Its water spilled before either of us could reach the threshold. You ruined *everything.*"

There was a stunned pause.

"But you had ages to leave that move!" Toby exploded. "What the hell were you hanging around for?"

"The threshold was far down the valley," the knight said aggrievedly. "The mist rose, and I lost my way. Besides, I thought I was safe, that I'd *won.* And I had, too, until you intervened and—"

"The situation is clear," Alastor interrupted, looking up from swirling the ice in his glass. "These four cost Cups—or possibly Swords—the success of his move. All are liable for forfeit."

"Indeed. And since the intervention in the case of Wands versus Pentacles is unresolved, I would like to propose the allocation of one knave to each court," said Ahab. "They will remain by our side, doing our bidding, until such a time as we see fit."

"Agreed," said Odile. "Lucrezia?"

"Oh, absolutely."

"But you cheated us," Flora was saying furiously. "We were about to go to the Hanged Man and you blocked our way. *You* intervened. You—"

"The courts respect the rules of the Game," Alastor's voice cut in, cold as steel. All his indolent charm was gone. "Here and now you had the opportunity to complete your venture. Yet you failed to act. *Fortunae te regendum dedisti, dominae moribus oportet obtemperes.*"

The doorkeeper stepped up to the wheel, set it spinning and pronounced, "The courts have ruled. Fortuna's Wheel turns. These fools are forfeit. . . ."

Time slowed. Cat saw the others frozen in disbelief: white-faced and staring-eyed. When the Wheel stopped spinning, they would be bound to the courts. No longer fools, but slaves.

Elsewhere, the audience buzzed with anticipation while the Game Masters lounged and yawned. Above them, the apple blossom ruffled, as if moving to a wind that only it could feel. A man at the front of the crowd tipped his hat at Cat, mockingly. . . .

Ta-da!

Round and round whirled the wheel, faster and faster, building to the moment of reversal. . . .

As above, so below . . .

The shadow of a greater tree . . .

Return to Yggdrasil, and plant each root . . .

What if the King of Swords was right? What if they *had* been given the opportunity to complete their task after all? What if—

It was like the other time at Mercury Square: her voice had rusted and her gestures dragged clumsily, as if she was moving underwater. "The tree," she croaked, fumbling with the catch on the birdcage. "As above—the tree—*it's the same one*—as below—"

Toby was the first to understand, and the first to act.

As the wheel spun into a blur of speed, and the world around them seemed to revolve, too, he took the clay disc from his pocket and crushed it in his fist. Lurching past the table, he hurled his handful of dust beneath the tree.

At once, the ground began to shake. A mound of earth buckled, sending the wheel crashing down. As the crowd, tumbling into disorder, cried out in fear, the tree groaned and swayed, its roots exposed by the heaving of earth. The tremors subsided. It was crippled, but its slender trunk stood firm.

The kings and queens were standing also, although their table had been toppled with the wheel. Their faces blazed but they did not move or even cry out in protest. Alastor had spoken the truth when he said that the courts obeyed the rules.

Cat could feel a roaring in her ears. A fierce delight surged through her; the blood sang in her veins. She flung her head back and laughed as Flora stepped forward, grasping her shard of ice over the twisted roots so that the water dripped from her hands. As the roots shriveled, the blossoms turned dirty brown and the bark oozed with the stench of decay.

Blaine flicked open the lighter and touched it to a branch. For a moment, every twig, every petal bloomed rosy-gold before the tree burst into a crackling, spitting inferno that burned and burned but did not die.

Only one thing remained.

Cat had opened the door of the cage. For the last time, she held the Root of Air, warm and soft within her hands, before she launched it into the sky.

261

The bird flew straight into the heart of the blaze, where it came to rest and opened its throat in song. As if in answer, a great wind came and roared through the tree of flame, blowing its sparks everywhere and nowhere, until they were nothing but ash; soft white ash, thick as blossoms, as snow, that drifted all around.

A man emerged from the blizzard of whiteness. His face was both old and young, his eyes shone innocent blue. "*Ave Fortuna*. Behold, my deliverance has come!"

The spiraling flakes were as hot as embers, but in a very little while their sting became the coldness of snow. The wind had scoured away the spring leaves and rosy light, leaving winter and darkness in its wake. And an ordinary apple tree. But Mercury Square still flickered between the two sides of the threshold as the players thronged around. They were in far greater numbers than before, although now their presence was as quiet and shadowy as ghosts. Among them, Cat thought she glimpsed faces that she knew: the costumed revelers from Hecate's, a muscular athlete, a ragged tramp. . . .

The man advanced toward the chancers. "My four wise fools! What marvels you have worked! And so together we embark on the final play."

They looked back at him, uncomprehending, past the power of speech, movement, thought . . . anything.

"Now is the round of new turns and reversals, as the Lady of Fortune sports with the Lord of Misrule." He turned, exultant, to where the kings and queens were standing. "You have had a fine run, but the Wheel has turned and your hand is played out. Will you renounce your mastery?"

The Queen of Pentacles answered through bloodless lips, "We abide by the rules of the Game—as always." All four were already curiously diminished: bleached of color, their faces showed new lines and hollows. Their shoulders shivered in the dark.

Meanwhile, the man's dark clothes were flooded with all the color and glitter of the triumph deck. His smile had triumph in it, too. "Well, there are new rules now. New fates for you. You were common players once, and in exile you will be again. I return you to the past moves of your knighthoods. This time, though, you will taste defeat, not victory."

Somewhere in the rush and roar of the wind, the wheel had righted itself so that it stood in its former position beneath the apple tree. *"Sum sine regno,"* said the King of Swords, with a ghost of his old smile as, of its own accord, the wheel began to spin. *I am without reign . . .* There was a great sighing from the crowd; in one revolution the kings and queens had vanished.

Their vanquisher raised his hands. "Let every card be free to turn, every die to roll and every move to be completed. My friends, it is time to play freely and fairly. Pick your card and make your move. Claim your prize if you are able."

Cat looked down at the crumpled card in her hand. The card she had carried out of the Hanged Man's tomb, with its promise of justice. The card that was still blank.

"I—I have one," she faltered.

"Of course you do!" He laughed delightedly. "It is yours for the playing. The right card for the right venture, as I promised you all beneath Yggdrasil's shade. Behold!"

At this, four metal objects came rolling across the grass toward their feet: a die each, this time with a silver wheel on every side, ready to create a threshold for their next moves.

"But remember, a card has two faces, a die four or six. A man, even more . . . And each has its place in the Game."

As if on cue, the audience broke into applause, the rippling thunder of a thousand thousand clapping hands. The sound seemed to come from very far away. And suddenly Cat's card was flooded with shape and color, until she was once more looking at the stern-faced woman with her sword and scales.

The Game's new Master fixed her in his shining gaze. "Justice! A noble goal. Play well, and your parents will be avenged."

He turned to Blaine. "The player you brought into the Game remains within the Arcanum. The Knight of Wands card will take you to him; do with him what you will."

The man gave Flora a benevolent smile. "Your sister awaits you in the Eight of Swords. The move is open for you to find her."

Finally, he turned to Toby. "And you, my young champion! Yours is the card that rewards all risks, and makes all games worth playing. The Chariot is the hero's prize. I know you will be worthy of it."

Flora, Cat, Toby and Blaine looked at each other and

smiled. Cat felt Blaine's arm brush against hers, and was flooded with warmth. Her heart trembled. After such a dark and perilous journey, this moment of victory shone as radiant as a dream. She was half afraid she might blink and find her triumph was just another illusion. And so, although she wanted to shout and sing and laugh until she had no voice left, Cat held still. She held completely still, hardly breathing, and clutching Justice in her hand. Around the four one-time chancers, the shadow of the Arcanum began to whirl . . . then fade. . . .

"At last," said the Lord of Misrule, as his smile slanted and his eyes burned with blue fire. "At last, the true Game of Triumphs may begin."

ȂUTHOR'S ȃOTE

Playing cards are believed to have arrived in Europe from the East at some point in the fourteenth century. There are many theories about the relationship between our modern deck and Tarot cards, and I have touched upon some of the most colorful in my story. One of my inspirations for the Game came from reading about the trick-taking game of Tarot, where using the Fool card ("the excuse") exempts one from the rules of play.

The Rider-Waite Tarot deck is probably the best known of the classic Tarot designs. Its illustrations of the Major (Greater) Arcana are based on early Renaissance playing cards, which themselves drew on mythological, religious and heraldic themes; the scenes on the Minor (Lesser) Arcana derive from traditional divinatory and occult symbols. This is the deck that most closely resembles the cards dealt in the Game of Triumphs.

I Trionfi, a poem by the fourteenth-century Italian scholar and poet Petrarch, describes the triumphs of Love, Chastity, Death, Fame, Time and Eternity in similar terms to the Allegory of the Triumphs in Temple House. Scholars still debate the connection between Petrarch's poem and the early Tarot decks.

Fortune and her Wheel are an enduring motif throughout history. The Latin epigrams quoted by the Magician and the King of Swords, and inscribed in the Triumph of Time, are taken from speeches given to Fortune in a sixth-century work by Boethius, *De Consolatine Philosophiae* (The Consolation of Philosophy). The verse at the beginning of this book is from the Burana Codex, also known as *Carmina Burana,* a thirteenth-century collection of poems and songs that was set to music by Carl Orff in 1937. Among the literary and mythological sources I have used, the Hanged Man's account of the origin of the Game owes a particular debt to a short story by Jorge Luis Borges, "The Lottery in Babylon" (1941).

The writer Italo Calvino described the Tarot as "a machine for telling stories"; when all speculation and superstition is put aside, this is, of course, their true magic.

Acknowledgments

Contrary to popular belief, books aren't written in isolation. These are the people I would like to thank for helping me make this one.

My agent, Sarah Molloy, for her unflagging good humor, patience and enthusiasm.

My editors, and Band of Triumphs: Kirsty Skidmore and Sarah Lilly at Orchard Books; Nancy Siscoe, Cecile Goyette, Katherine Harrison, Marianne Cohen and Janet Frick at Knopf.

All the people—you know who you are—who endured my ramblings about the Wondrous World of Tarot and listened politely.

My sister, Lucy, who read the first few chapters and said, "More, please."

My parents, for everything.